ELLE GRAY
BLAKE WILDER
FBI MYSTERY THRILLER

DOUBLE
CROSS

CHAPTER ONE

Road Prophets Clubhouse; Scottsdale, AZ

F AR OUT IN THE DESOLATE BROWN AND RUST-RED DESERT landscape, far away from the lights of the city, the world around them was bathed in the silvery monochromatic light of the half-moon hanging in the sky above them. And if not for the muffled sound of the hard driving guitars, frenetic drumbeats, and harsh growl of James Hetfield's voice, the silence would be absolute. Alpha leaned out from behind the large, rough pile of rock and eyeballed the structure fifty yards away.

"Equipment check," Alpha said quietly. "We set?"

Echo and Delta checked their vests and weapons, then nodded. Alpha pulled the balaclava down and then the tinted goggles, covering their face entirely, and surveyed the small campus in front of them. It was surrounded by a high wall topped with concertina wire, but Alpha had studied the blueprints and satellite photos of the campus and knew it forward and backward.

The main clubhouse was a one-story, ranch-style structure with a flat roof made primarily of wood and adobe that they were sure was reinforced with steel rebar. There was a garage to the right of the main structure where the club worked on their bikes and stored the vans they used to make their runs. The windows were set deep, and earlier recon showed they were thick, double-paned plexiglass, making ingress through them impossible. They were all but bulletproof.

To get into the clubhouse, assuming they made it through the main gates, they would have to enter either through the front door, which was not ideal given the virtual army of road-hardened, heavily armed, former-military-turned bikers likely to be in the front room. The back door would probably be less heavily guarded but was more likely to have some sort of surprise waiting for them. What that was, Alpha wasn't sure. It could be merely a camera that alerted the men inside when they crossed into its range, or it could be wired to blow. But it seemed to be the point of least resistance, so that would be their entry point.

Alpha keyed open their mic. "Gamma, what do you have?"

"Stand by," came the voice through Alpha's earpiece. "Okay, thermal imaging shows twelve bogeys in the front room. Rear of the house is clear. You're good to go."

"Copy that. Keep watching."

"Eyes open."

Alpha turned to Echo and Delta, giving them a nod. Moving low and swiftly, they came around the rock structure they'd been sheltering behind and made the fifty-yard dash across the open scrubland to the wall that surrounded the clubhouse.

"Echo, camera," Alpha said.

"On it."

The black-clad figure pulled a small box from their pack and flipped a couple of switches, turning the device on. A green light appeared, and Echo pushed the button. A moment later, the small red light on the camera stopped blinking.

"They're blind," Alpha said. "Delta. Door."

Pulling a small leather kit from their pocket, Delta kneeled before the door and quickly picked it. Sliding the kit back into their pocket, Delta stood and brought the M4 in their hands to the ready. Echo counted down from three on their fingers, then opened the door. Delta was through first, Echo followed, and Alpha brought up the rear. Moving across the back area of the campus beneath the bright, silvery light of the moon, Alpha felt absolutely exposed.

Alpha gritted their teeth, waiting for the chatter of gunfire as the trio crossed the grounds. They made it to the rear door without being cut down, though, and Alpha let out a soft breath. The music was louder now—even outside, it was like being in the front row at a concert—which was a blessing since it would mask any noise they made.

"Camera," Echo said. Pulling the device from their bag again, they quickly disabled it and gave Alpha a nod, quickly tucking it away and bringing their weapon to bear. "Clear."

Delta was already kneeling before the door, using a device they'd pulled from their bag. The seconds ticked by as they waited, and with every grain of sand that fell through the proverbial hourglass, Alpha's shoulders grew tighter. Time was not their friend. They needed to get in, get what they came for, and get out before the rest of the Prophets arrived. Twelve was manageable. Just barely. But if reinforcements arrived, they were screwed.

"Door looks clear," Delta said. "No traces of explosives or electronics attached to it are detectable."

"Good. Open it."

Delta put their device away and pulled out their lock-picking kit again. As they worked, Alpha's earpiece crackled.

"Trouble inbound," Gamma reported.

Alpha clenched their jaw, silently cursing as if merely thinking about them had somehow summoned more of the motorcycle club.

3

"What do you have?" Alpha whispered into their mic.

"Twenty at least," Gamma replied. "Ten minutes out. Maybe fifteen if you're lucky."

Alpha swallowed down the string of curses. Echo cast them a worried glance, but Delta worked the lock faster. A moment later, Alpha heard the click of the lock disengaging. Bringing their weapon up, they turned the knob and pushed the door inward. Moving single-file, the three figures in black stepped into the back room and hunkered down to get their bearings.

"Prophets are still inbound. Getting closer," Gamma's voice came through.

Alpha pointed at the door to the right. They knew from recon that was their count and store room. The Prophets' product and cash would all be inside.

"Delta, bag everything as quickly as you can," Alpha said. "Echo and I are on crowd control. More Prophets are inbound, so work fast."

"Copy that."

Alpha turned to Echo. "You ready?"

"Ready."

"Keep your head on a swivel. Do not take your eyes off any of them."

Echo nodded. Delta stepped over to the door and quickly disappeared inside. Alpha waited a moment, body taut, waiting for shouting or gunfire from inside, but heard nothing. Delta was clear. They turned back to Echo.

"All right. Let's go," Alpha said.

Moving swiftly around the boxes and crates that filled the back room, Alpha led Echo to the door that opened to the main room. The music was deafening but, amazingly, the voices of the men were somehow even louder. They sounded drunk, which Alpha counted as a positive.

"On three," Alpha said.

Echo nodded as Alpha counted down on their fingers. When they hit one, Echo burst through the door first with Alpha right on their heels. Echo fired a burst into the ceiling then a second burst into the stereo, plunging the room into a sudden and blessed silence. The men in the room turned as one, faces tight with anger.

A few of them reached for weapons, but Alpha and Echo leveled their own at the men's faces.

"Don't do it," Alpha growled.

One of the men sneered and continued reaching for the weapon in his waistband, as if daring them to act. Echo stepped forward and slammed the butt of their weapon in the man's face. As he staggered backward, blood pouring from his nose, Echo smoothly extracted the Glock from his waistband and took a few steps backward. The man fell on his backside with a loud grunt, then cupped his face with his hands, glaring at Echo as the blood squeezed between his fingers.

"I'm gonna kill you," he hissed.

"No, you're not," Echo sneered in return.

Alpha swung toward another man who started to move, training the barrel of their weapon on his face. He stopped and raised his hands chest-high, glowering darkly at Alpha.

"Move one more inch and I'll put a hole in you big enough to drive your Harley through," Alpha said, their voice hard.

He did as he was told, but his expression made it more than clear he wasn't happy about it. Echo and Alpha swept the barrels of their weapons back and forth, keeping their eyes on everybody in the room.

"All right, weapons on the floor," Alpha called. "Move slow and easy, boys."

The men hesitated, but a man with long white hair, a matching Fu-Manchu-style mustache, and a patch on his black leather kutte that read "Vice President" nodded, telling them to do it. The men complied, and a host of handguns and knives hit the wooden floor with a loud clatter. It was so loud and went on so long, it sounded like it had started to rain weapons. When everybody was disarmed, the VP turned to Alpha.

"Happy?" he sneered.

"Almost," Alpha replied. "Everybody against the back wall. Now."

The VP's expression soured further, but he nodded and motioned for his men to step back and line up against the back wall. With Echo covering Alpha, they stepped forward and started kicking weapons out of the men's reach.

"You've got five minutes. Max. You guys better wrap things up in there," Gamma's voice came through the earpiece.

Echo glanced at Alpha, feeling the seconds passing by every bit as keenly. They were quickly running out of time. As if on cue, Delta stepped into the room, their own weapon up and ready.

"Good to go."

"Grab the weapons," Alpha ordered.

As Echo and Delta collected the arsenal on the floor and threw them into their bags, the VP took a step forward, staring down the barrel of Alpha's weapon but with his arms half-raised, palms toward them. He stared at them for a long moment, his jaw clenching and unclenching.

"Y'all do know who it is you're stealin' from, yeah?" he asked, his voice deep and gruff.

"We're aware."

He nodded. "All right. Just didn't want there to be any misunderstandin' when your bodies are hangin' from a freeway overpass and your families get your heads in a FedEx box."

"There won't be any misunderstandings."

He shrugged and chuckled ruefully. "Your funeral, friend."

"We're good, let's roll," Delta said.

Walking backward, weapon still up and ready, Alpha followed the others through the door and into the back of the clubhouse. Slamming the door, Alpha scooped up the bag of contraband and ran for the back door. As expected, the bikers stormed into the back room, not willing to let them get away with their cash, product, and weapons.

"Beta, we're going to need a ride," Alpha called into the mic.

"Ready and waiting," came the reply.

As Echo and Delta disappeared through the back door and plunged into the darkness beyond, Alpha dropped the bag, then pulled a pair of canisters off the bandolier around their chest. As the shouts of the men drew near, Alpha pulled the pins and tossed the flash-bangs into the room. Turning again, Alpha scooped up the bag and sprinted out the back door, following Echo and Delta at a full sprint. The muffled thuds of the flash-bangs going off behind Alpha were quickly followed by the screams of the bikers caught in the blast. Alpha laughed.

Bursting through the back door, Alpha found the truck already there with Beta behind the wheel. Delta and Echo were in the bed of the truck along with their bags, weapons up in case they were being followed. Alpha grunted, tossing the bag into the bed of the truck, then clambered over the side and pounded on the cab's window.

"Go, go, go!" Alpha shouted.

The engine roared, and the tires spun on the hard-packed earth for just a moment before the truck shot off into the night. Behind them, Alpha saw the Prophets bursting through the gate and a few muzzle flashes from the weapons they hadn't managed to confiscate. The truck sped through the desert, bounding through uneven ground for several minutes before they got to the highway. They weren't quite in the clear just yet, but they were close.

Knowing the Prophets would be on their tails quickly, the truck raced down the highway, cresting a small rise and descending into a small valley where the eighteen-wheeler waited. Beta pulled onto the shoulder and smoothly drove up the ramp and into the trailer. A couple of minutes later, the doors were closed, and the semi was on the road, looking for all the world like any other semi that ruled the roads in the desert.

The lights in the trailer snapped on, and Alpha slumped back against the cab, finally able to breathe a sigh of relief.

"We did it," Echo said with a giggle.

Alpha pulled off her balaclava and grinned. "Nice work, ladies. Very nice work."

Astra and Paige stared back at Blake, their faces flushed, relieved laughter bursting from their mouths. Blake opened the window in the cab of the truck. Mo turned around and blew out a long breath, shaking her head.

"Can't believe that worked," she said.

"You doubted my plan?"

"I don't now," she replied with a chuckle.

"Where's Rick?" I ask.

"Got his drone packed up, and he's already en route back to the war room."

"Copy that."

Astra kicked the bag at her feet. "I didn't have time to count it all, but we got a nice haul of their dope and money. This one's going to hurt."

"Excellent," Blake said. "It's all starting to come together."

Wrung out, Blake leaned her head back against the cab of the truck and closed her eyes, taking a little time to relax as the semi rocketed them home.

CHAPTER
TWO

ATF Operational Center, Southwest Division; Phoenix, AZ

"FIFTEEN BRICKS OF HEROIN, EIGHT THOUSAND PILLS I'm sure will turn out to be fentanyl once we get them tested, and seventy-five thousand in cash," Sonny says with that syrupy Texas drawl of his. "That's quite an impressive haul."

"This should put a pretty big dent in the Road Prophets' day-to-day ops," I say.

"And that's not going to make Santiago and Diego very happy."

"That's the plan."

I sit slumped in a chair at the end of the table watching the DEA's evidence collection team on the other side of the operational center, which is really just a repurposed industrial warehouse, parsing through our haul, cataloging and boxing up everything we ripped from the Prophet's clubhouse last night. It's the third op we've run with Sonny's team and other DEA elements in the last two weeks, and despite having more bodies in the field than I'm used to having to coordinate with, things have gone surprisingly smoothly.

Sonny perches on the edge of the table beside me, his icy blue eyes boring into mine. He rakes his fingers through his wavy, sandy-blond locks and frowns, and I can tell he's doing his best to keep his emotions in check. We've been seeing each other on the condition that we leave it all at the door when we clock in. We can't afford to have our emotions clouding our judgment while we're on the job. Any personal relationships have no place in the field.

"Where's the rest of your team?" he asks.

"Out getting something to eat. They should be back soon."

He nods. "Heard you all had a close brush out there last night."

His voice is soft but filled with concern, as are his eyes. It irritates me for reasons I can't fathom. It's unreasonable, but his concern makes me bristle. It makes me feel like he doesn't think we're capable of taking care of ourselves. It's not what he means, I'm sure. But it bothers me all the same.

I shrug. "Not really. We got out clean."

He pulls a face. "I read the after-action reports. Twelve inside the clubhouse and twenty more of them bearing down on you? Seems like a close brush."

"We had eyes on them the whole time and were gone before they got there," I say with a shake of my head. "It wasn't as close as the reports make it out to be."

"Knowing you like I do, I'm sure it was probably closer," he says with a wry twist of his lips.

"We all got out unscathed and with everything we came for. It's a win," I snap. "There's no sense in dwelling on almosts and what-ifs since it all went well and nothing bad happened to any of us. So, just drop it, all right?"

He clenches his jaw, his frown deepening. I tell myself again that his worry is rooted in concern for me and my reaction is stupid. It's sweet, and I appreciate him looking out for me, but it has no place here. We agreed when we started to see each other that we wouldn't mix that with the job. It just won't work if we can't keep our worlds separated.

"All right. I apologize," he says quietly.

And now I feel bad, which is one of the many problems of dating somebody you work with. Granted, given that we work for different agencies, our paths don't cross often. But right now, our paths are not only crossing; they're completely intertwined. My team is only here in Arizona because we're working his case. It's an important case, and we need to dismantle this cartel, but there's a part of me that's starting to regret working shoulder to shoulder with a man I'm dating. Or maybe that part of me is just regretting dating him in the first place.

"I appreciate that you're concerned about me, but I'm not some porcelain doll that needs to be protected. I'm not fragile. And believe it or not, I know what I'm doing," I tell him. "I've been doing this job for a long time now, and I'm damn good at it."

A pensive expression on his face, Sonny glances around the room as if to make sure nobody is listening in to our conversation. They're not. Frankly, I don't think our interpersonal dynamics are worth eavesdropping on, but I suppose people love the drama and gossip, and Sonny is just trying to keep from giving them fodder, which is something I can appreciate.

"I know that. I know you don't need somebody to protect you," he says. "But I care about you, Blake... so of course, I'm going to worry about you when you're out in the field. Especially when you're taking on somebody like the Arias brothers. These guys do not mess around."

"I don't either," I tell him. "And anyway, it's not like I'm in this alone. I've got my team and your team covering my butt. If anything goes sideways, you're all there to pull me out of the fire."

"Not everything can be accounted for. This plan of yours... it's a really great plan, but you're taking a really big risk."

"This is the job, Sonny. Taking risks is part of it," I tell him. "This is who I was before you met me. This is who I'm always going to be. And if you can't accept that then—"

He puts his hands up chest high, his palms facing me, showing me that he surrenders. "I'm not asking you to change. I'd never ask you to change. The way you attack the job is one of the things I admire most about you. But again, you're putting yourself right in the line of fire, so of course, I'm going to worry. That's all I'm saying. I didn't mean anything else by it."

It's possible I'm in a constant state of defensiveness. Being with somebody in a romantic sense is so foreign to me that it makes me feel off balance. So, I suppose it's possible that I'm seeing slights or criticisms or even doubts about my ability to do my job that don't exist anywhere but in my own mind. Suffice it to say, I'm not very good at this dating thing. I've got more baggage than an airport carousel and am a bit of a mess. Honestly, I'm baffled that Sonny would even want to see me. If I were him, I sure as hell wouldn't date me.

As if listening to my inner dialogue, Sonny gives me a cocky smirk. "Are you ever going to stop thinking I'm trying to change you or run you down just because we're dating?"

I glance down at my hands which are sitting in my lap. "We can hope."

"Good thing I'm a patient man."

"I'd understand if you ran out of patience and—"

"Hey," he cuts me off. "Look at me."

I reluctantly raise my head and stare into his icy blue eyes. He offers me a smile that sends a rush of warmth through my veins and makes my heart flutter. It's a feeling that's been uncommon in my life, and although it's not unpleasant, I'm still trying to get used to it.

"I won't run out of patience, and I'm not going anywhere," he says. "We've all got baggage. We've all got things we need to overcome. I like spending time with you, Blake. I'm not going to throw in the towel just because you've got some things you're dealing with. Let's just keep enjoying the time we have together and not let things get so heavy."

"I can do that."

"Good girl."

"Hey, Boss."

We both turn to see Gloria Cooke—Glory to everybody—Sonny's second-in-command, stepping over to us. Five-six with coal-black hair that falls to her shoulders and eyes to match, Gloria is a former Marine. She's fit, athletic, and could probably kill a man with her bare hands without breaking a sweat. She's tough, smart, and doesn't take any crap from Sonny or anybody else. I liked her from the moment Sonny introduced us.

"Hey, Blake," she says. "Nice haul last night. Wish I could have been there with you guys."

"I wish you had been too. We could've used another body."

Sonny and Glory had another assignment they'd had to deal with last night and couldn't be part of our op. But they'd left us in good hands with the rest of their team.

"What's up, Glory?" Sonny asked.

"SAC Muñoz wants to see us at the FO," she replies.

Sonny sighs. "Did he say what he wants?"

She shrugs. "Above my paygrade. You know he doesn't talk to peons like me unless he's handing out orders."

"You're hardly a peon," Sonny says.

"Tell him that," she replies. "But I've got a feeling that until I'm a Supervisory Special Agent like you, I'm never going to be anything but a glorified gopher."

"Don't let him get you down," I tell her. "You guys are the backbone of your agency. Guys like Muñoz are just the pimples on its backside."

"Your lips to God's ear," she says with a laugh.

Sonny gets to his feet with a sour expression on his face. "Guess we better not keep boss man waiting."

"That's probably wise," Glory says.

He turns to me. "Let's have dinner tonight and go over the next phase of your plan."

I snap him a salute. "Aye, aye, Captain."

He silently chuckles. "All right, I'll see you later then."

I offer him a smile. "See you later."

He and Glory walk out of the op center, and I slump back in my chair, blowing out a long, frustrated breath as a myriad of thoughts and emotions churn inside me. Why do dating and relationships have to be so freaking messy and complicated?

CHAPTER
THREE

Ibarra Family Cantina, Encanto District; Phoenix, AZ

"SO? WHAT DO YOU THINK?" HE ASKS.
I nod as I finish chewing what's in my mouth. "This is, honestly, some of the best Mexican food I've ever had in my life."

One of the fifteen urban villages that make up Phoenix, the Encanto District encompasses the midtown and uptown portions of the city's borders. It's got a vibrant energy and a burgeoning hub of nightlife and upscale eateries. But it still has plenty of less flashy mom-and-pop establishments that have been around for years. Decades in some cases.

"The Ibarra family immigrated to Phoenix back in the eighties and opened this place. Been running it ever since," he says. "Brought some of their family's best recipes with them."

"It's incredible."

Ibarra Family Cantina—or Ibarra's, as the locals call it—is a small place with less than two-dozen booths and tables. The place is clean, and the lighting is dim, but the colors in the place are vibrant. The walls are lined with photos of the Ibarra family through the years, many of them of an older woman Sonny says is the matriarch of the family and the woman responsible for most of the recipes the restaurant was built on. Everything about the place is authentic and doesn't seem like the artifice most of the large chain restaurants put on to simulate the soul of places like this.

Personally, I've always loved the smaller hole-in-the-wall places. I've found them to have the best, most authentic food— far better than some of the upscale chains that, to me, have always been more style over substance. Knowing my penchant for those kinds of places, Sonny brought me to Ibarra's for dinner and margaritas, ostensibly to talk about the case over a meal. But I have a feeling he just wanted an excuse to get away from the office for a little while, just the two of us. And honestly, even though I was resistant at first, I can't say I totally hate the idea. Getting away from the office, decompressing, and unplugging for a bit feels nice.

"Thank you for this," I say.

"For dinner?"

I nod. "When I'm working a case, I tend to get so consumed by it that I shut everything else out and fixate on the work."

"You don't say. I hadn't noticed," he teases.

"Shut up," I reply with a smile. "All I'm saying is that I appreciate you forcing me to take a step back and shut that part of my brain down for a little while."

"Oh, I forced you, huh?"

"Pretty much, yeah."

"I don't recall putting a gun to your head."

A smirk crinkles the corner of my mouth. "You invited me here under the pretense of talking about the case, which just feeds my addiction. So, yeah, it's pretty much like you putting a gun to my head. And I think you know that."

He laughs. "Oh, I fully intend to talk about the case," he says. "But I thought mixing it in with some tasty food, a few margaritas, and a little fun conversation might be a good thing."

"Calling yourself a good conversationalist is pretty presumptuous."

He claps his hands to his chest. "Madame, you wound me so."

"You're such a clown," I say with a laugh.

"Yeah, but you like that about me."

"You're lucky I do."

"Trust me, I know that," he replies.

His tone is serious, and the way he's holding my gaze makes the meaning behind his words all the more obvious. I've known from the start that he's been more invested in this—whatever this is—than I am. According to my therapist, Dr. Azar, I'm straddling the line and have one foot out the door. She thinks the fact that I tend to hold people at arm's length and expect the worst going in—that I'm usually just waiting for the other shoe to drop and for the relationship to fail—reinforces my belief that they're temporary. She says it's a self-fulfilling prophecy.

Dr. Azar thinks this all stems from the death of my parents, which is probably a fair assessment but nothing I've really considered all that much. I've always been pretty self-contained and haven't ever needed another person to feel whole. The one thing she's said that's stood out and continues to bother me like a splinter just below the skin is her belief that I throw myself into the job as much as I do to compensate for my inability to maintain a healthy relationship. She thinks I'm using my work to avoid letting myself get attached to another person.

I haven't decided what I think about all that just yet. I'm still trying to process it all, but I can't deny her words ring with some truth. And that bothers me for reasons I don't quite understand yet either. All I can say is she's given me a lot to think about. But I'll have to do that thinking later when I'm not on a case and there aren't lives on the line.

"You know the way I feel about you, don't you?" he asks.

My heart drops into my stomach, and I quickly avert my gaze. This isn't the sort of conversation I want to be having right now. But more than that, it seems way too early in—in whatever this thing between us is—to be analyzing our feelings, let alone talking about them or putting a label on it. It doesn't help that I'm just no good at these kinds of things. That's part of the reason I've always avoided romantic entanglements altogether.

The dismay in my heart must be showing on my face, because Sonny laughs softly. He reaches across the table and takes my hand, gently tracing my knuckles with his thumb, the expression on his face softening.

"Relax. I'm not trying to freak you out, darlin'," he said in that thick Texas drawl.

"No? You just have that effect on a girl naturally, huh?"

"I suppose so," he says. "But it wasn't my intent."

"Then what was your intent?"

He took a sip of his drink and seemed to be choosing his next words carefully. He seemed like a man who was standing on the edge of a precipice and knew one small misstep could send him tumbling into a bottomless chasm… or send me running.

"I understand you're dealing with a lot—that you've got a lot of baggage from your past on your back—and because of that, you don't normally do the relationship thing," he said. "You've made that abundantly clear."

"I just want to make sure you understand how lucky you are," I reply with a sly grin.

"Oh, trust me, I hear you," he says, tipping me a wink. "I understand you're scared, or maybe just uncertain, about this thing between us… and all I meant to say is, I care about you, Blake. And I've got your back. I'm not going anywhere. So, do what you need to do to work through everything you're working through, and just get it through your head that you aren't going to scare me off."

"No?"

He shakes his head. "Nah."

"I'm not easy to deal with."

"You're complicated, no question about it," he says. "But I grew up hunting with my daddy, so I learned to be a patient man."

It's strange. I never intended to have this sort of conversation with him. I've been actively avoiding this sort of conversation with him, to be honest. Relationships are complicated, and when two people actually start discussing their emotions, things tend to get thornier. Things start to get real. And when things get real, people start getting hurt.

But sitting here and talking with him doesn't feel as strained or awkward as I'd feared it would. A little bit, perhaps. But that's probably because I'm just awkward when it comes to emotional things anyway. There's an openness and honesty to our conversation that's refreshing. That feels… nice. I actually don't feel like he's trying to back me into a corner or that he's trying to extract something from me. As strange as it sounds, it seems as if he's simply trying to have an honest, adult conversation. It's not something I'm used to.

"Just understand I'm not askin' anything of you, Blake. I'm not tryin' to pressure you to declare your emotions for me," he says. "I just wanted to tell you where I'm at right now… and that I'm happy to wait for you to catch up."

"I'm going to be honest. You could be waiting a while."

"I already figured that," he replies with a nod. "I just felt like I needed to tell you where I'm at after that scene in the op center earlier today because I didn't like how that all played out. I don't want you to think I'm asking you to change or do anything differently. Like I told you, I admire that you put everything of yourself into the job. But it's because I care about you that I worry when you put yourself into the middle of an op like this. The Arias brothers are savages. They're animals. The things I've seen them do…"

His voice trails off, and he glances down at the table, a haunted look in his eyes. I've seen the photos of their handiwork, but photos can't compare to seeing their atrocities up close and in person. Pictures can't compare to the sight and smell of the blood. He's right to be worried about me. Hell, I'm worried about me.

But it's not just that. One of their victims was Agent Sara Beller—Sonny's former fiancée. This case is personal for him in ways even I can't fathom, and I can't blame him one bit for the terror and worry that comes with opening your heart once again, only to find yourself facing down the same monsters that took away the woman you loved. It's an experience I can sort of relate to, given my history with Mark Walton. The situations aren't the same at all, but as I look at the warmth and tenderness in Sonny's eyes, I realize that he's had to do just as much healing as me.

"Anyway, I just wanted to get that out and hopefully clear the air between us," he says. "What I said to you earlier in the op center was coming from a good place."

"I know it was. And I appreciate you looking out for me. And I'm sorry I snapped. Like I said, I'm a lot to deal with, and I wouldn't blame you for packing it in and heading for the hills now."

That charming grin finally returns. "Trust me. It takes a lot more than that to scare me off, darlin'," he says. "And now that I've said all that, just so you don't think I lured you here under false pretenses, let's talk about the op."

"You know what? Let's not," I say with a flirtatious glimmer in my eye. "Not tonight."

CHAPTER FOUR

Frost, Downtown District; Phoenix, AZ

"LOOK AT THEM ALL," I SAY.

"Remember when we had that kind of energy?" Astra asks with a chuckle.

I brush a strand of hair out of my face. "I don't recall ever having that kind of energy."

The crowd is heavy and hyped up for a Tuesday night. I stand at the smoked glass windows looking down at the writhing, frenzied crowd on the dance floor. Most of them are likely on one drug or another, but I'm sure there are a few who just get high on the crazed atmosphere of the club itself. For some folks, dancing it out is a form of therapy. I guess I can understand that. Sometimes when I'm stressed out, I like to go to the range and shoot things.

The thick windows muffle the worst of the hard thumping techno music that fills the club but doesn't eliminate it completely. I hate the music. It's an assault on my senses. It's like pouring acid straight into my ears. This would not have been my first choice of places to run the op out of. It seems too cliché and too derivative of bad cop movies where the big, bad drug dealer runs their empire out of a nightclub. But here we are anyway.

Sonny's team had set this place up a while back to use it for their own covert ops—nothing like what we're planning right now, but they've run their investigations through here and had some great successes. Although I argued for setting up a place of our own, preferably a jazz club, Frost is already a known quantity in the community with a dedicated clientele of mostly college students who come in from UA or ASU to cut loose on the dance floor. Sonny argued it was best to run our op out of this place.

This op is most likely going to burn this place. It'll be useless as a front for any future ops they want to run. But he thinks it's a fair trade if it helps us nail the Arias brothers.

"How are you feeling? You ready for this?" Astra asks.

"I'm good. I'm ready."

"You seem tense."

"Do I?"

"Little bit."

I turn away from the window and walk to the mirror on the far side of the office, scrutinizing my reflection. The wig falls just below my shoulders, is blacker than midnight, and has straight bangs. It's actually kind of cute. I touch it gingerly, half-afraid I'm going to knock it loose, which would be an unmitigated disaster.

"You're fine. Gorgeous even," Astra says. "Stop messing with your fit."

"I'm not messing with anything. I'm just checking."

"Uh-huh."

"You all right?" I ask, turning the spotlight on her. "You ready for this?"

"You know me. I live for this kind of stuff."

It's true. Astra is a bit of an adrenaline junkie. But I'm not sure she's ever played with the stakes this high. Either way, she definitely lives for the danger.

"You sure my nose doesn't seem... crooked?" I ask.

She steps over and gives me a thorough once over. To run this op, Sonny brought in a Hollywood-caliber makeup team to give us our look while we put together our cover stories, which Rick and Nina have backstopped online. The disguises are mostly for our safety. Astra and I have both been on the news before, so to prevent anybody from recognizing and then targeting us or our loved ones, we are both wearing prosthetics to change the shape of our faces, contacts to change the colors of our eyes, and lifts in our shoes to change our heights.

Dressed in black from head to toe, wearing a feminine-cut three-piece suit with two-inch lifts in her boots, Astra cuts an imposing figure. I opted for white. White slacks, shirt, and jacket with a blood red pocket square for a touch of color. I frown at my reflection. I'm not nearly as imposing as Astra, but I guess the all-white image is perhaps a bit more regal, which seems more fitting for my position. It's critical I project the right image.

"Your nose looks fine," she said. "Those makeup techs know what they're doing."

My nose has a more aquiline shape than normal, and the contacts I'm wearing make my eyes a light, icy blue instead of my normal shade of green. Astra has a platinum white wig cut in a short bob, a nose appliance similar to mine, and makeup shading that gives her the appearance of higher cheekbones than are usual for her. The effect somehow makes her seem more elegant and even more like a runway model than she normally does. Not even a team of Hollywood makeup artists could manage to do that for me.

My cellphone buzzes with an incoming text. Walking back to my desk, I snatch up the phone and quickly scan the message.

"Get your game face on. They're on their way up," I say.

Astra grins. "It's showtime."

After our last rip at the Prophets' stash house, we figured the MC was going to be getting desperate for product. In the meantime, we've been using Sonny's street-level contacts to put out the word that I'm the new player in town and that I've got the best—and only—product in town. We rolled the dice that Rico Nagy, leader of the Road Prophets and key distributor of the Arias cartel, would turn up here at some point to either threaten us for taking their product, try to cut a deal to get more, or perhaps both. So far, so good.

The op is simple. We plan on using Rico and his motorcycle club to climb the ladder that will eventually get us to the Ariases themselves. Ultimately, we need to make the Arias brothers feel enough pain that they'll come to the States themselves—something they haven't done in fifteen years at least—to sort their whole distro mess out themselves. And once they're here, we are going to scoop them up and put them away for the rest of their miserable lives.

It's taken some time and patience, but our gamble seems to be paying off. We got the call this morning from one of Sonny's informants that Nagy has been sniffing around, looking for product and the identity of who ripped off the Prophets, and they turned him on to us.

I sit down behind the large, ornately carved desk while Astra, who is serving as my bodyguard, takes her position just off my right shoulder. There is a knock at the office door.

"Come in," I call.

The door opens. Mo and Paige have both undergone similar transitions with the makeup team, and like Astra, are decked out in all black. They step into the office, their faces appropriately grim.

"Rico Nagy and his associate, Crank," Mo announces as she takes a position near the door and Paige posts up on the other. "They've both been disarmed and patted down. They're clean."

A tall man, six-two or six-three, steps inside and takes a quick look around the office before his gaze settles on me. His salt-and-pepper colored hair is tied back into a tail that falls to the middle of his back, and his dark eyes are hard and flinty. He's got a chiseled face, strong jawline, and a goatee that matches his hair. He's wearing blue jeans, black boots, and a black long-sleeved

T-shirt beneath a black kutte with a patch that reads, "President" over the right breast.

The man who comes in after him is like a mountain on legs. Six-six or six-seven at least, and as wide as he is tall with biceps as big around as my thighs. He's bald with blue eyes, has a dark, thick mustache, and sports a nasty, jagged scar down the right side of his face, only adding to his terrifying visage. The man looks like he can tear a Volkswagen apart with his bare hands just for fun. The patch on his kutte identifies Crank as the club's sergeant at arms.

Rico smirks then walks over to the sideboard and inspects the bottles sitting on the tray. He picks up a bottle of expensive scotch and pours himself a glass. Crank stations himself at the back of the office, hands at his sides, and glares at Astra. She returns his glare with a cocky half smirk on her face, silently daring the big man to make a move. She's like half his size, but if I were putting money on the fight, I'd put it all on her.

"Help yourself," I say, dusting my words with a well-practiced Ukrainian accent.

"I do appreciate a fine scotch, and this here," he says, holding up the glass and admiring the amber liquid, "this is a very fine scotch."

Nagy is crude and has no manners, but at least he has good taste. That really is a fine scotch. He drops into the chair that sits in front of my desk and takes a sip, eyeballing me over the rim of the glass. Rico Nagy is a former major in the Army, a combat veteran who did tours in Afghanistan and Iraq before he got caught up in a scandal that involved the theft of ancient artifacts as well as some of the pallets of money being spread around over there.

The military wasn't able to definitively prove his involvement, so they couldn't prosecute him, but they had enough to strip him of command and muster him out. After his discharge, he came home to Arizona, founded the Road Prophets, and has been running drugs, guns, and women while being a general dirtbag ever since. There are half a dozen bodies on him from more than a decade ago, but nobody has been able to make a case stick, and he's somehow been able to avoid serious trouble.

Not content to play in the minors, though, he took advantage of the fall of a rival MC—perhaps one he helped engineer—and positioned himself to be the Arias cartel's main supplier in the southwestern corridor. Nagy is intelligent. Crafty. Street smart. Ambitious. He's also ruthless. Cunning. He lacks empathy and is a borderline sociopath.

"So, you're the new girl in town, huh?" he asks.

"Nadia Petrenko," I say, giving my cover ID.

He waves me off. "Doesn't matter. You're not going to be around long enough for me to even care about learning your name."

My lips twitch with a faint smile. "Is that so?"

"It is," he says. "But let me get to the reason we're here."

"Please do."

"You have something that belongs to me."

"Oh? I do? And what might that be?"

His face darkens. "Don't play with me, lady. It was you who hit our places. Don't think you're that slick. You and your bimbo squad here ripped off our product and cash," he says, then grins. "And let me just say… I'm impressed you had the stones to pull the rips yourself. It was a stupid move, but hey, kudos."

"Where I come from, we believe if you cannot do the work yourself, the work is not worth doing," I say. "But with regard to your product and cash, I have no idea what you're talking about."

"Lady, you don't want to play with me. And you sure as hell don't want to play with my business partners."

I give him a half shrug. "I do not know what to tell you. I am a simple businesswoman."

He takes another sip, his eyes narrowed and his jaw clenched. "I came here as a courtesy. To give you one chance to make this right," he says. "Return what you took, get out of town, and all will be forgiven. If you don't… well… you really don't want to go down that road with me."

"While I appreciate the offer, as I said, I have no idea what you are talking about," I tell him. "I am here to conduct my own business."

"That brings me to the second problem we have. You don't have permission to do business here," he says. "This territory belongs to me and the Arias brothers."

"I do not recall seeing a sign."

He chuckles. "You've got stones, lady. Big, shiny stones."

"Let me make you a counteroffer," I say.

There's a twinkle of amusement in his eyes, and he gestures to me. "Let's hear it."

"Well, I understand that you may be short on product," I tell him. "I just so happen to be flush at the moment, and if you are looking to buy, I might be willing to cut you a deal."

His grin turns feral, and his face clouds over with anger once more. "Lady, you don't even understand the size of the pile you're stepping in right now."

I lean forward and hold his gaze. "There is something you need to get used to, Mr. Nagy."

"And what's that?"

"I am the new power in this area," I say coldly. "All business starts and ends with me. Everything will go through me from here on out. Everything. Am I making myself clear?"

His grin lacks any sort of warmth or mirth. "You declaring war?"

"I am just telling you how things are. You are cash poor and out of product. People do not care about your petty politics. They will purchase from whomever has the goods to sell them. That would be me," I tell him. "Now, if your bosses want to sit down with me and discuss the matter, I might be willing to come to an arrangement. If not, then I am fully capable of defending what is mine. If you doubt that, then step up and let us see what happens."

He seems unfazed as he drains the last of his drink. Nagy gets to his feet and sets the glass down on my desk, then leans forward, holding my gaze.

"This is the only warning you're gonna get," he says.

"Yes, you have said that a few times already."

He smirks and nods for Crank to follow him. "Thanks for the drink."

"My pleasure."

"I'll see you around."

"Yes. I suppose you will."

CHAPTER FIVE

Sun Devil Warehouse Park, Industrial District; Tempe, AZ

"WHAT DO YOU THINK THIS IS ABOUT?" ASTRA asks.

"I haven't the foggiest," I reply. "Tempe isn't on our ops plan, so I'm wondering if something's gone off the rails."

"Sounds about right for one of our cases."

"Right?"

Best known as the home of Arizona State University, Tempe is a thriving city with a vibrant arts, music, and culinary scene along with a growing population. It's a beautiful city with a lot of culture and history. But the beauty and vibrancy of the city doesn't extend to this section of town. This corner of Tempe is dominated by industrial warehouses, many of which are abandoned and collapsing in on themselves.

Just up ahead, I see a pair of black SUVs in the parking lot of one such dilapidated structure, so I pull in and drive over to them and park. I see Sonny, Glory, and a couple others I haven't met yet milling around what looks like it might be a body on the ground.

"This doesn't look like a promising start," I say.

"Again, sounds about right."

"Let's go."

We climb out of the Yukon and make our way over to the crowd gathered around what is indeed a body on the ground. Early-twenties male, thin with suntanned skin, long, brown hair, and brown eyes wide open and fixed on some point in the next world. He's wearing dirty blue jeans, tennis shoes with holes in them, and a white long-sleeved T-shirt with a band's decal that's so faded and cracked I can't make out what it is. He's got the pale, drawn look of a habitual drug user.

The man is riddled with bullet holes, making the cause of death pretty easy to determine, but I have no idea who this guy is. He's not on our target list, isn't one of the Road Prophets, and isn't a member of the cartel. My brow furrowed, Astra turns to me, the confused expression on her face no doubt matching my own.

Sonny is standing a bit apart from the rest of us, hands on his hips, staring off into the distance. I walk over and stand next to him, searching his face for any clue what this is about.

"Sonny, who is this?" I ask. "What are we doing here?"

When I turn to him, I can see that his face is pinched and clouded over. His jaw is clenched, his eyes narrowed, and he seems to be fighting to keep himself from tearing up. He runs a hand over his face and clears his throat. Sonny is such a big, Texas-tough kind of man that seeing him battling his emotions makes it clear that this—whatever this happens to be—is personal and is hitting him incredibly hard.

"This is Dustin Kemper," he says, his voice thick. "He was my CI."

"I'm sorry."

My heart goes out to him. Regardless of the letters of our agency, we're all taught to keep a professional distance from our human assets. Some are in the grips of addiction, and some are just bad people looking to get out from under a charge. The bottom line is they can't be trusted with our deepest, darkest secrets. But every once in a while, one of them gets into our hearts. Once in a while, despite our training and our efforts to maintain that professional distance, we sometimes get attached to our confidential informants. It's not hard to see that's the case for Sonny here. He was clearly very attached to the dead man on the ground behind us.

"Dustin was a good kid," Sonny said, still staring into the distance. "He was really doing his best to get his life turned around. He wanted to be better for his baby girl."

Knowing he had a child puts a stitch in my own heart. "That's awful."

He nods. "Yeah."

I glance back at Astra who gives me a half shrug, asking me with her eyes the same question that's rattling around in my own brain: What are we doing here? It's then that I realize what this scene is missing—local cops. Why are Astra and I standing over a body with a group of DEA agents rather than the local LEOs?

"Listen, I'm really sorry about your CI. It's difficult to lose somebody you've grown close to," I tell him. "But isn't this a matter for Tempe PD to handle?"

He turns to me. "This isn't a case for the locals, Blake. This is the cartel's doing."

"Did you use Dustin against the Ariases?"

His brow furrows as he lowers his gaze. "Well, no. He wasn't working the Ariases. But they know I've been working their case. And these guys do their homework, so I'm sure they know Dustin is my guy. They took him out to send me a message."

"I hear you, but we're going to have to call in the locals," I tell him. "You know that."

"I do. I just … I wanted you to get a look at the crime scene and the body before they get here and start trampling over everything."

"Sure, I can do that. But to what end? Once the locals get here—"

"The locals have their uses. Dealing with a cartel hit isn't one of them."

"Sonny, how can you be sure this is a cartel hit?"

"Because Dustin was my CI. Who else would have wanted him dead?"

"He was caught up in the drug life—"

"He was trying to get out of it."

"Trying to get out of it," I say. "But not fully out of it yet."

Sonny frowns, and his face darkens. "What are you saying?"

"I'm saying that he still had a foot in that world, right?" I ask. "It's entirely possible somebody from that world did this."

"I don't think so, Blake. It doesn't make sense. He was really getting his act together."

I kick at a small rock near the toe of my boot. "Sonny, we're right in the middle of an op—"

"Between your team and my team, we've got more than enough personnel to run this case and our op concurrently," he says.

"So, you're asking that we split our resources while we're taking on the Prophets and the Arias brothers?" I ask, flabbergasted.

"We've got all the resources we need," he argues. "We'll focus on our op, of course. But we can work on this one at the same time."

"Sonny—"

"Come on, we've both worked simultaneous cases before."

I turn and stare into the distance. It's hard to accept when somebody we care about is killed, and of course, we look for somebody to blame. We need a bad guy. And we usually reach for the easiest suspect whether it makes sense or not. And in this case, the cartel going after a street-level informant with a nasty habit doesn't make a lot of sense. But the look on Sonny's face tells me he can't see it… that he won't see it.

"Why aren't you saying anything?" he asks.

"Because I really think we should let local PD handle this," I tell him. "We don't have jurisdiction and haven't been invited in."

"Since when have you ever let somethin' like jurisdiction get in your way, darlin'?"

"Believe it or not, I do have respect for the rules."

"So long as it suits you."

I give him a half shrug and a crooked grin. "Shut it."

"Listen, I'm tight with the local cops around here. I can get them to ask you in and clear the path for you. That's not going to be a problem."

Sometimes the only way to get somebody to see the truth of a matter is to show it to them. God knows I've learned that lesson myself a time or twelve.

"I know this is a big ask, Blake."

"I can see this is important to you—"

"It is. And my team isn't trained for this kind of investigation. That's not how we're wired. Yours is. I mean, this is what y'all do," he says. "I can't trust that the Arias brothers don't have their fingers into the local PD. You're the only person I can trust with this."

This is going to get messy and will probably create some tension between us. He's too personally and emotionally invested in the outcome of this case, and he's already determined who's responsible. What he really wants me to do, even if it's not a conscious thought on his part, is find the evidence that will back up his theory. And that's not going to work for me.

"Please, Blake. I don't want anybody else working Dustin's case."

I turn and fix him with a firm gaze. "If I do this, you're not going to be involved—"

"Blake—"

I shake my head, cutting him off. "You're too close to this. Your judgment is compromised. If we want to find out who killed him, we have to go in clear-eyed and levelheaded. I don't think you're in that space right now, so you're not getting anywhere near this, and you will not interfere with my investigation whether you like where it's going or not."

"You can't really expect me to sit on my hands and do nothing."

"That's exactly what I expect," I tell him. "Those are my terms. If you can't abide by them, then turn the case over to the locals."

Muttering darkly under his breath, he turns away. Planting his hands on his hips, he takes a few steps away, considering my terms. Sonny turns around with a loud sigh and nods.

"All right. We'll do this your way," he says.

"I mean it, Sonny. Zero collaboration or interference."

"I understand. And I won't get in your way. I swear it," he says. "I just want to find the person responsible for killing Dustin."

My gaze falls to the ground as I try to drown out the chorus of voices in my head telling me what a mistake I'm making. Being pulled in two different directions when we're running an op as delicate as the one we're here for is foolish. Reckless. But I can't pretend I don't see how bad this has shaken up Sonny. I can't pretend I don't see how bad he's hurting. And I can't see it and not do something about it. It's possible I'm the one who's too invested in this.

"Do I have your word? No interference?" I ask. "You'll stay one hundred percent on the Arias op and let me do my thing with this case?"

"You have my word."

"All right. Let me get my kit out of the truck," I say. "You call the locals, clear the path for us, and get them to send a forensics team and the coroner's bus."

His lips quirk in a grin. "Thank you, darlin'. I appreciate this."

As I turn and walk toward our car, all I can hope is that I don't end up regretting this.

CHAPTER SIX

ATF Operational Center, Southwest Division; Phoenix, AZ

"SOMEBODY'S BEEN LOOKING INTO YOU," RICK SAYS.
I walk into the conference room and close the door behind me. The long, rectangular room is a fishbowl in the center of the ops center with walls made of glass. Sonny is on the other side of the op center doing his best to appear like he's not watching us when I keep catching him sneaking glances our way. The feeling of being watched is unsettling.

"This is going to be awkward," Astra says as she takes her seat.

"I can help with that," Nina says.

She gets up and walks over to a small box on the wall, then presses a button. A high-pitched whirring sound fills the room, and I try to keep from laughing as I see Sonny's disapproving frown as he watches the privacy shades being automatically lowered, shutting out all the prying eyes. A moment later, the shades are all down, and the fishbowl has been turned into a windowless room that feels a bit claustrophobic but gives us the privacy we'd been lacking just two minutes ago.

"Kind of feels like we're all in a cave now," Rick says.

"Something I think you'd be used to," Mo teases.

"Bite me, Mo," Rick replies with a chuckle.

"Honestly, I'd rather sit in a cave than have all those eyeballs on us," Paige chimes in. "Being stared at like a zoo exhibit is creepy."

"Agreed," I add.

"So… why do we need all the privacy in the first place?" Rick asks.

"We'll get to that," I respond. "You said somebody's been sniffing around. Tell me."

"Somebody tripped the wires I set up around your Nadia Petrenko ID in the immigration database," he replies. "I was able to follow their trail and see what they were looking at. They were thorough and did a deep dive on you."

"Do we have any idea who's doing the digging?" Astra asks.

"Not specifically, but the search is being done from a computer at a known Prophets stash house," Nina replies.

"Did my cover hold up?"

Rick pulls a face and scoffs. "Do you think I do shoddy work? Of course, it held up."

"We backstopped everything and put it all in the appropriate databases. Unless they've got a mole in the DEA who tipped them off to your cover, whoever's in there poking around isn't going to find a thing to blow your cover," Nina says.

The good thing is that the details of this op are restricted to Sonny's team, and the granular details—like my cover identity— are restricted even further. There are fewer than a dozen people familiar with the Nadia Petrenko name, which is by design since we know the Arias brothers have a long reach. It's sad to say, but even federal law enforcement officers can be bought.

My cover, Nadia Petrenko, was born in Ukraine and immigrated to the US when she was thirteen years old, after her parents, leaders of a criminal organization in Odessa, were killed. They planted stories online to buttress that piece of her history. Nadia came to the US to live with an aunt, received US citizenship when she was eighteen, and went on to attend the University of Washington where she obtained a degree in chemical engineering.

After that, her story gets sketchy with plenty of insinuations that she used her knowledge of chemicals to build her own illicit empire running drugs and guns, starting in the Pacific Northwest and slowly expanding southward. Rick and Nina sprinkled in plenty of fake FBI and DEA investigations that ultimately didn't amount to anything, adding to her mystique. Nadia has a reputation for ruthlessness with the suggestion that there are dozens of bodies on her, although nobody has ever been able to make a case against her stick.

It's this person we've put out there for the Prophets and the Arias brothers to get to know… and worry about. And I'm glad to see that our first meeting with Rico Nagy piqued his curiosity enough that he's having his guys look into Nadia.

"Now that we know who's running your cover ID, we've got a line into their computer," Nina says. "We'll scan their emails and give you a heads up if there's anything worrisome going out."

"It'd be better if we could get up on their phones," Astra says.

I nod. "It would be. But we work with what we have."

"So, all that to say while there's some movement, we don't have a lot," Nina says. "And certainly nothing earthshaking to report."

"Hopefully we'll get something good. Just stay on top of it," I say.

"So? Where were you and Astra this morning?" Rick asked. "And why is everybody staring at you like you've both grown second heads?"

"Sonny called us out to a crime scene this morning," I say. "One of his CIs was murdered last night. Shot multiple times."

"And what does this have to do with our op?" Mo asks.

I spread my hands. "No idea. Could be nothing."

"So, why are we looking into this?" Nina asks.

Astra toyed with a lock of her onyx-colored hair. "Because Sonny is convinced it was the Arias brothers, perhaps by way of the Road Prophets, that murdered him."

"He doesn't trust the locals to run the case because he's afraid the Arias brothers have their fingers in that pie," I tell him. "He only trusts us to look into this."

"Why doesn't he have his team do it?" Rick asks.

"Because they're DEA. They're not really equipped to run a murder case, and this is pretty much in our wheelhouse," I answer. "He was tight with his CI, so this is really personal to him, and he just wants to make sure it's done right and the right person goes down for it."

"I don't want to sound insensitive or anything, but given that we're working on a pretty serious op, do we have the bandwidth to take on a murder case too?" Paige asks.

My lips are a tight slash across my face. "As Sonny was kind enough to point out, we've worked multiple cases at the same time, and we've got all his resources at our disposal," I say. "But the Arias op is our priority. We work this case when nothing else is going on."

The op will have periods of inactivity and require a lot of patience. Essentially, we're waiting for the Prophets to take up the bait we've been laying out which, we hope, will lead to the bigger fish up the line—the Arias brothers themselves—needing to take action. Santiago and Diego Arias, to the best of our knowledge, haven't been in the US in a very long time. As their cartel has grown, so has the heat on them, so to stay ahead of the law, they work through intermediaries they send across the border.

Our plan is to put the clamps on the Prophets, choking off product and cash to such a degree as I position myself as the new player in the area, that the Ariases will have no choice but to come here to deal with me in person. And when they do, if all goes according to plan, we'll snatch them up and dismantle the cartel altogether.

But this op is like fishing. It will require a lot of patience and won't happen on our time. When things happen, I have a feeling it's all going to happen at once. But when it all happens is anybody's guess at this point. Which means, we'll probably have time to work the murder of Sonny's CI, against my better judgment.

"All right, so where do we start?" Nina asks.

"Nina, I want you to dig up anything and everything on Sonny's CI," I say. "His name is Dustin Kemper. Give me whatever you can dig up on him."

She gives me a thumbs up, then goes to work. Her fingers fly over the keyboard as I sit back in my chair, tap my pen against my lips, and think about our next steps.

"Rick, see if you can get into the Tempe PD database," I tell him. "I want to know about any of the street-level players. My guess is that one of the local dealers actually popped Dustin. Could have been over an unpaid debt or something. I want to find an alternative because my gut tells me this kid wasn't tied in with the cartel. He's just too low level."

"On it, Boss," he says.

Nina looks up. "Okay, Dustin Kemper was born and raised here in Tempe. Dropped out of high school, has worked a number of low-paying, menial jobs, but never seems able to hold on to them for long," she says. "He's got a pretty lengthy list of arrests, most of them drug-related, but a few petty theft collars, and he was arrested twice for breaking and entering. He's never done any serious time."

"Sonny mentioned he has a daughter?"

"Uhh… one second," she says, then nods. "Yep. Amelia. Two years old. Her mother's name is Daisy Pierce, twenty-one years old. She's clean. No sheet. Looks like she works as a hairdresser and is taking classes at the local community college. Seems to be a straight arrow."

"So, how'd she get mixed with a burnout like Dustin?" Astra said.

"That's a question we'll have to ask her," I say. "So, there's no other movement with the Prophets right now?"

Rick shakes his head. "They're digging into Nadia pretty hard. Looks like they're just in the fact-finding phase at the moment."

"Okay, good," I say. "Mo, Paige, post up down at Frost just in case anybody comes by unexpectedly and has questions."

"Copy that."

"Astra and I are going to pay Daisy a visit, but call me if anything pops off," I say, then turn to Astra. "All right, let's roll."

CHAPTER SEVEN

Pierce Residence, Holdeman District; Tempe, AZ

I PULL THE YUKON TO THE CURB IN FRONT OF A MODEST, single-story, Spanish-style home in a working-class neighborhood. Most of the homes look roughly the same. They're all made of either beige, white, or yellow stucco and have red terracotta tile roofs; they have rounded windows and doorways and decorative wrought iron typical of Spanish-style architecture. The landscaping in the front yard of the Pierce residence is minimal but well-kept, and the home itself is tidy.

A late model, black Audi is parked behind a ten-year-old red Corolla in the driveway, and as we walk up the flower-lined path to the front door, the sound of a woman's agonized wail echoes out of the house. I swallow hard and glance at Astra who grimaces.

"Sounds like she's talked to Sonny already," I say.

"Sounds like it."

We step onto the low porch, and I knock on the screen door. A moment later, a woman steps into the doorway and stares at us for a moment. Five-six with a thin, petite build, she has ash blonde hair and light hazel eyes. She's wearing dark blue scrubs with a pink long-sleeved thermal beneath the top and white rubber-soled tennis shoes. She looks like she's either about to go on shift or just came off.

"Yes?" she asks.

"Unit Chief Wilder, SSA Russo, FBI. We'd like to speak to Daisy," I say as we badge her.

"FBI? Is this about Dustin?"

"Can we speak inside, ma'am?" I ask.

"Just call me Shirley, please," she replies as she opens the door for us.

"Thank you," I say. "I'm Blake. This is Astra."

We follow Shirley into the kitchen where a distraught young woman who I assume to be Daisy is sitting. She's at a small, round table clutching a crumpled tissue in her hand. Daisy is about the same height as her mother, with the same blonde hair. Her eyes are a darker brown, but she's got the same fair, smooth complexion, slightly upturned nose, and delicate features as her mother.

"Honey," Shirley says gently. "These are FBI agents. They want to talk to you."

Her face is splotchy, her eyes are red, and her cheeks are stained with tears. She raises the tissue in a hand that trembles wildly and wipes her eyes. She remains sitting in profile, refusing to meet my gaze. Shirley turns, her lips a tight slash across her face, and gestures to the other chairs at the table as she reclaims the seat she'd pulled over beside her daughter. Astra and I walk around to the other side of the table and sit down.

Daisy buries her face in her hands, her shoulders shaking hard as she sobs quietly. Shirley offers me an expression of apology and clears her throat.

"Obviously, we heard about Dustin," Shirley offers. "Agent Garland called a little while ago to tell us. Do you have any idea what happened?"

"We're still in the early stages of our investigation," I tell her.

"So, what is it you think we can do for you? And why is the FBI looking into this rather than Tempe PD?" Shirley asks.

"We're just lending a hand," I tell her. "So, you've known Dustin for a while?"

She nods. "He and Daisy have been friends since junior high school. They obviously got a lot closer over the years. I've tried to tell my daughter that he's trouble. During high school, he started running with a rough crowd, got mixed up with drugs—"

Daisy finally raises her head. "He's a good guy, Mom. He's just… he's got demons. We've all got demons, don't we?"

"Not all our demons are as destructive as his, baby. You know that."

Wiping her eyes with the tissue again, Daisy turns to us. "He's not a bad guy, Agents. He just had a hard time growing up. His home life was less than ideal, and the drugs were his escape."

Shirley snorts and turns away, her face etched with disgust. Her view of the young man is obviously different from her daughter's. Their differing views seem to be, at least to me, the difference between young love and a mother's love.

"Agent Garland said he was getting his life turned around," I say.

Daisy nods. "He's been clean for six months now. He's looking for work and seemed really determined to provide for me and Amelia. He swore—"

"He's made the same promises time and time again. And yet, we somehow always find ourselves back to square one," Shirley cuts her off.

"It's not easy to get off drugs, Mom."

"It's even harder when you don't really try."

"He's trying!"

Daisy covers her face and starts to cry again. Shirley rolls her eyes but tries to reel it back in and adopt a more sympathetic expression and puts her hand on her daughter's shoulder. This isn't getting us anywhere. Given that Daisy just lost somebody she obviously loves, I don't want to be callous or overbearing, but I need her to pull it together long enough to give us some answers.

"Daisy, since you knew him best, I need to ask you some questions," I say.

She raises her tissue again but seems to realize it's used up and tosses it onto the table, then snatches another one from the box. Daisy sits up and wipes the tears from her eyes. Shirley strokes her daughter's hair, then turns to us. I can see the mama bear starting to come out.

"Agents, I don't think this is the right time—"

"I'm sorry, Ms. Pierce, but gathering information in the immediate aftermath is critical," I tell her. "If we can just have a few minutes, I would appreciate it."

Daisy shakes her head. "I'm not sure what I can tell you, Agents. Like I said, he was really working hard to turn everything around."

"Well, we understand that he's been clean for six months, but is it possible he still owes money to somebody?"

"Not that I'm aware of. But he didn't really discuss his finances with me."

"That's because he doesn't have any finances to speak of. He sponges off you."

"Ms. Pierce, please," I say. "Daisy, was there anybody he'd had a fight with? Any sort of altercation, no matter how slight it might have seemed at the time?"

She lowered her gaze and seemed to think about it. "Not that I can think of, no."

"So, there isn't anybody you can think of that Dustin had a problem with?" Astra presses. "Or anybody who had a problem with him?"

The sound of a child crying echoes from the back of the house, making Shirley leap to her feet. She glances down at us then at Daisy, conflict on her face.

"It's okay, Mom," Daisy says gently. "I'll be fine."

Her lips tight, she nods then turns to us. "I'm just going to go check on Amelia. I'll be back in just a second," she says, almost like a warning.

When her mother disappears through the rounded doorway, Daisy turns back to us, her expression apologetic.

"I'm sorry. I know she can be a little intense," she says. "It doesn't help that she's never really liked Dustin. Not even when we were just kids."

"It's hard to fault her though," I say. "It sounds like he was into some bad stuff; she just wants to protect you. It's a mother's job."

Daisy raises her shoulders in a half shrug. "I guess."

Astra leans forward. "Daisy, is there anything you want to tell us now that your mom is out of the room? Anything at all?"

"Anybody you know of who Dustin had a beef with that you didn't want to mention in front of her?" I ask.

She shakes her head. "No, not that I know of. He never mentioned having any problems with anybody. Not to me."

"All right," I say. "And how was your relationship with him?"

"I mean, we had our problems, of course. It's not easy being with an addict," she says with a frown. "But we loved each other. He was trying to get himself right, and we were trying to make it work. He really wanted to get better for Amelia."

She chokes back another sob and wipes away a fresh tear. She looks like she's about to lose it again but manages to pull it together as she lets out a long, shuddering breath.

"I loved him, Agents," she said. "He really was the love of my life."

"And can you tell us where you were last night?" Astra asks.

Her face pales as she turns to Astra, and an expression of horror dawns on her face. "You can't believe I had something to do with this."

"It's just a routine question," Astra says. "It's important in helping us establish a timeline. So, can you tell us where you were last night?"

She shook her head, anger spreading across her features. "I had a client and was at the salon until around eight. I came home to my daughter after that."

"And when was the last time you spoke with Dustin?" I ask.

She sniffs. "It's been a couple of days."

Astra's eyebrow arches. "A couple of days?"

"We had a fight," she says.

"May we ask what about?" Astra presses.

"It was nothing. Just... he lost his job... again. We argued about him getting a new one," she responds. "I'm trying to keep from leaning on my mom for everything, and I need his help to provide for Amelia. I was just frustrated. I just..."

Her words trailed off in another wave of tears that she quickly wiped away.

"You just what?" I prompt.

"I just can't believe I'm not going to get a chance to apologize," she finishes.

"I think that's enough for now," Shirley says as she steps into the kitchen. "My daughter is grieving. Please, give her some peace."

"Just one more question," I say.

Shirley stomps her foot and folds her arms over her chest, glaring at us icily. As much as I want to remind her that we're in the middle of a murder investigation, I understand she's simply looking out for her daughter and swallow down the attitude.

"Daisy, do you have a gun?" I ask.

"What kind of question is that?" Shirley explodes. "That is enough!"

"I'm sorry, Ms. Pierce. It's just a routine question," I say.

"It's an asinine question," Shirley huffs. "I do not allow guns in my home."

Daisy shakes her head and ignores her mother. "No. I don't like guns," she tells me. "I'm not comfortable around them."

"That's enough, Agents. It's time for you to go," Shirley demands.

"Of course. Thank you for your time," I say as Astra and I get to our feet. "We're likely going to have some follow-up questions, but we'll circle back to you later."

As we head for the front door, Daisy stops us.

"Agents, I'm not sure if it's important, but I just remembered that Dustin had a fight with a guy named Gary Colston. It was a couple of years ago, so I can't say if it's relevant. But a couple of weeks ago, I just remembered that Dustin said he'd called him. I have no idea what it was about or anything, but Dustin mentioned in passing. I didn't think anything of it until just now."

"Gary Colston," I say.

She nods. "Yeah."

"Please leave, Agents," Shirley hisses.

"Okay, great. That's really helpful, Daisy," I say. "Thank you. And I'm really sorry for your loss."

Astra and I give her a nod and head out of the house. It may not be much, but at least it gets the ball rolling and gives us a direction to run in.

CHAPTER EIGHT

Desert Vista Apartments, South Mountain District; Phoenix, AZ

Located at the southernmost end of Phoenix, clinging to the city like it's trying to keep itself from being consumed by the vast desert on the other side, is South Mountain. On the one hand, it's a great spot for those who love the outdoors: the scenery is breathtaking, and there are plenty of hiking trails to enjoy since it sits on the edge of the South Mountain Park and Preserve. On the other hand, it's a relatively low-income section of the city with low wages (for those lucky enough to find a job), high unemployment, and a soaring crime rate.

It's here that Nina was able to track down Gary Colston. Thirty-five years old with a jacket as long as my arm, Colston is an Arizona native. He's a high school dropout turned street-level dealer, primarily of heroin and meth, though he's apparently dabbled in fentanyl as well. He's not a major player and has no known cartel ties, so not surprisingly, most of his offenses are drug-related with a few thefts and assaults sprinkled in for a little flavor. He's somehow managed to avoid anything too heavy, which surprises me since his jacket reads like a guy who likes to partake of his own supply then make even more terrible decisions.

Run down and dingy, the Desert Vista apartments have a refurbished motel feel to them that has me looking around for the sign that declares they offer free HBO, air-conditioning, and hourly rates. It's about where I'd expect to find somebody with Colston's pedigree. We walk up the uneven, pitted walk, stepping on or around all the weeds that are sprouting up through the cracks, and find our way to Colston's apartment. Sublime's hit song "What I Got" is muffled but still perfectly clear coming through the door.

"Smell that?" Astra asks.

"Kind of hard not to."

"If my drug test comes back dirty, this is why. You make sure that's noted."

I chuckle. "Noted."

I bang on the door with the side of my fist and step back, my hand near the butt of my Glock. Colston doesn't have any offenses involving a weapon, but I don't like to take chances. Astra leans against the wall to the right of the door, her body taut, hand on her weapon as well. A minute goes by with no response, so I bang on it again but harder. This time, the music inside is lowered, and I hear heavy steps coming toward the door. A moment later, it opens.

"What the fu—"

As his gaze falls to our weapons, the man's eyes widen, and he blanches. His mouth falls open as he turns his palms to face us.

"Hey, I'm clean. I ain't got no weapon or nothin'."

"Gary Colston?" I ask.

"Yeah?"

I pull my hand away from my Glock and pull out my badge. "Unit Chief Wilder, this is SSA Astra Russo, FBI."

"Umm… okay?"

"Mind if we come in?"

He glances nervously behind him. "Umm… kind of."

"We can smell the weed out here, Gary," Astra says. "We don't care."

"It's been legal in this state for four years now," I tell him.

"Right. I knew that," he says, clearing his throat. "Umm… sure, come on in then, I guess."

He steps aside, and we walk into the small front room of the apartment. Colston closes the door, then quickly turns off the stereo and waves his hands in the air, futilely trying to dispel the cloud of pot smoke that clings to the ceiling like the layer of smog that hugs the LA skyline. Seeing his efforts are fruitless, he walks over and opens the window in the dining nook, thankfully letting in some fresh air.

Colston is a few inches taller than my five-nine frame and has a lean, wiry build. His skin has a waxy, pale pallor, and his blue eyes are dull, watery, and rimmed red. His sandy-blond hair hangs to his shoulders limply, and his sharp, angular face looks like it hasn't seen a razor in a week. He's barefoot, isn't wearing a shirt, and is wearing blue jeans that are as dingy as the building itself and hang loosely on his hips. He grabs a black tank top off the back of the ratty, beat-up sofa and quickly pulls it over his head.

"So, what's this about?" he asks.

Astra points to the coffee table where a tall bong sits next to an open bag of weed. "Looks like more than an ounce there, Gary."

"Weed's legal. You said so," he says, his voice tight.

"You can have up to an ounce for personal use," Astra says.

"Oh, come on, man," he complains.

"We're willing to overlook that if you answer our questions," I tell him.

He sighs and rakes his fingers through his hair. "Fine. Whatever. What do you want?"

"Dustin Kemper," I say.

"What about him?"

"When's the last time you saw him?" Astra asks.

He raises his shoulders, giving us a listless half shrug. "I don't know. Been a while."

"Yeah? And when's the last time you spoke with him?"

"I tried calling him a couple weeks ago. Why? What's this about?"

"We heard you two had beef," Astra says.

"We had beef because he's a dirtbag who doesn't pay his bills," he tells us. "He's a cool guy otherwise. But he needs to learn to pay his debts."

"And how much does he owe you?" I ask.

"About a grand," he answers. "Now, what's this about?"

"You said you tried calling him a few weeks back. Why? What did you need to talk to him about?" Astra asks.

"I'm trying to collect what he owes me, man. I got bills to pay," he tells her. "Now that I'm out of the game, it ain't easy to make a living. I'm working some crappy part-time job down at the Mexican food joint on the corner, and I need to call in all the debts I'm owed. It sucks, man."

I frown. "You're out of the game?"

"Yeah."

"You're not dealing anymore?" Astra asks, gesturing to the coffee table.

"I smoke and maybe sell a bit on the side. But that's it," he replies. "I got out of everything else I was dealin' before."

"Why is that?" she asks.

"Wasn't worth it anymore. Got tired of gettin' hassled by the cops," he tells us pointedly. "But more than that, it's just gettin' too dangerous out there anymore."

"What do you mean?"

He looks at us like we're stupid. "People gettin' smoked left and right for dealing out on the streets. Three dudes I was tight with got themselves dead in the last couple of months."

"Yeah? How'd that happen?" I ask, though I have a pretty good idea already.

"Come on," he says incredulously. "You're the freakin' FBI. Like you don't know what's goin' on down here."

"Pretend we don't," Astra says.

"The cartels, man. They're movin' in and wipin' out anybody who's dealin' on the streets," he says. "They've got some biker gang—the Street Preachers or somethin' like that—runnin' distro and bein' the muscle. They're who killed my friends."

"The Road Prophets," I correct him. "That's the MC."

"Right. Them. See? You feds know what's up out here," he replies. "Anyway, the cartels who are pullin' all the strings are makin' it so us small-business guys can't make a livin'. Not without catchin' a bullet and gettin' our heads lopped off. And I ain't tryin' to go out like that."

"Yeah, it's kind of like when Starbucks moves in and drives out all the small, family-owned coffee houses. The big box takeover of small business America is tragic," Astra says.

"Exactly," he says, completely missing her sarcasm. "Anyway, I had two choices. I could either get out of the game and go straight or get my head cut off. Call me a coward or whatever, but I chose to keep my head."

"I don't think you're a coward," I tell him. "I think you did the smart thing."

"Yeah, well, bein' smart sucks. I'm barely gettin' by."

Colston shuffles his feet and lowers his gaze for a moment, as if admitting that he's trying to do the right thing and live as a productive member of society is a shameful thing or something. He clears his throat, then turns to me.

"So? I've answered your questions," he says. "What's this all about now?"

"Dustin Kemper is dead," I state.

His face pales even more, and his mouth falls open again as he absorbs what I said. But then just as quickly, his eyes narrow and his gaze flits back and forth between us, his body tensing as a wariness creeps onto his face.

"I hope you don't think I had anything to do with that," he says. "Is that why you're here? Because you think I did him?"

"Did you?" Astra asks.

"Hell no!" he shouts. "I just told you I liked the guy. Why would I kill him?"

"Money is a pretty good motivation to kill," Astra says.

"And what sense would it make for me to kill him when he owes me money? I kill him, I never get it. Are you dumb?" he snaps.

"Maybe you were frustrated he wasn't paying you. You two argue about it, things went sideways, and you snapped," Astra offers.

"Didn't go down like that. I ain't seen him face-to-face in a while," he responds. "I called him a few weeks ago and asked him to get me the money he owes me. He said he was working on it and asked me to give him more time. I did. Because, like I said, if he's dead I don't get paid, and right now, I need every damn nickel just to survive."

It's plausible. It even makes sense. More than that, though, I hear the ring of truth in the man's words. He may be a dope-slinging scumbag, but I'm not getting the sense that he's a killer— or at least, that he didn't kill Sonny's informant anyway. But I need to find some proof he wasn't involved before I'll feel comfortable crossing him off the list.

"Can you tell us where you were last night?" I ask.

"Work. I was there until after midnight," he responds.

"And after that?" Astra asks.

"I came home, smoked a bowl, and went to bed."

"And I suppose there's nobody who can corroborate that?" I press.

His cheeks flush, and he lowers his gaze as he shuffles his feet uncomfortably. It's not hard to see there's something he's not telling us.

"Gary, this is a murder investigation, and right now, you're on the suspect list," I tell him. "If there's somebody who can confirm your story about being here last night, now would be the time to tell us everything."

He scrubs his face with his hands and shakes his head but says nothing.

"This is serious, Gary," Astra says. "Unless you want to go down for Dustin's murder—"

"Fine," he snaps. "I was online last night. Until about three this morning."

"Online?" I ask. "You were what, gaming?"

He sighs as his face reddened. He won't meet our eyes and looks like he's going to throw up.

"I was on with a camgirl, okay? Her name is Ruby, and she's on a site called Handmaids, all right?" he grumbles. "Happy now?"

As I realize what he's talking about, it's my turn to look nauseous. Astra hides her mouth behind her hand, doing her best to keep from laughing. Gary hangs his head and seems to draw in on himself, absolutely mortified. I clear my throat and nudge Astra in the ribs with my elbow, silently telling her to straighten up and be professional. Her lips continue to twitch, but she stands up a bit straighter and tries to adopt a professional demeanor.

"Okay, that shouldn't be too difficult for us to check," I say.

"Yeah, great," he mutters.

"Last question. Do you have a gun?"

"Of course, I do. I got a nine."

"If you're out of the game, why do you still have a gun?" Astra asks.

He finally raises his head. "Just because I'm done with the game don't mean the game is done with me. I keep it to protect myself."

"Right. Well, we're going to have to take that gun," I tell him. "We need to compare it to the weapon that was used to kill Dustin."

"You really going to leave me naked out here?"

Astra frowns. "Is the gun registered to you, Gary?"

He rolls his eyes and blows out a breath of exasperation. But he doesn't say another word as he turns and disappears through the doorway. A moment later, he comes out holding the weapon by the end of the barrel, his fingers well away from the trigger, and hands it to me. Astra drops it into a plastic evidence bag and seals it.

"I didn't kill Dustin," he says.

"All right," I respond.

"Am I going to get that back?" he asks.

It's not registered and shouldn't exist. Tempe PD will probably want to melt it down with other seized weapons once they're done processing it. But I can see how scared Gary is to be without some sort of protection. With outlaw MCs and cartels running around Phoenix like it's the Wild West, I suppose I can't blame him.

I offer him a small smile. "I'll see what I can do."

"Which means no," he grumbles.

"It means I'll see what I can do," I tell him. "You're not even supposed to have this gun, and I think you know that."

He pulls a face and shrugs. "Yeah, whatever."

"Gary, one more thing," I say. "Can you think of anybody else Dustin owed money to? Anybody else he might have had beef with?"

"I don't know about anybody he owed money to… it ain't like we all discussed that or nothin'," he says. "But I know a few guys were talkin' tough about him. Bad dudes. I thought that's why Dustin went MIA, because he was afraid of 'em."

"And who are these bad dudes?" Astra asks.

"Poke, Bullet, and Razor. Those guys are tight, and I know Dustin did somethin' to piss them all off. And those are the wrong dudes to piss off," he says.

I stare at him for a moment waiting for him to give us their real names. He doesn't.

"Do you have their real names?" I ask.

"Nah. I only know 'em by their street names."

I nod. It's better than nothing. "Okay. Thanks for your help, Gary."

"Please," he says. "Do what you can to get me that gun back? I don't like bein' exposed like this, and I ain't got the money for a new one."

It's hard not to feel sorry for him, but I can't promise anything. Putting an unregistered gun into the hands of a known criminal and back on the street probably isn't the smartest thing I can do. But it really does seem to me like he's trying to get out of that life—like he's trying to turn himself around. And for whatever reason he's doing it, that's something I can at least respect.

"Like I said, I'll do what I can," I respond.

CHAPTER NINE

"**Y**OUR BOY COLSTON WAS TELLING THE TRUTH," Nina tells us. "He clocked out of his shift at the restaurant at twelve-ten, and he's on their internal security cameras."

"Yeah, but he still conceivably could have clocked out and killed Dustin after that."

"That would be true if the other end of his alibi didn't hold up. I got into his computer, and he was indeed chatting with a lovely camgirl named Ruby on Handmaids-dot-com." Nina says with a sickly grimace. "He recorded the session, and I really don't think you want to know what I saw. Let's just say the website's name is grossly accurate."

"I'm going to pass on that," I reply.

"I hate you for exposing me to that," she says. "But Colston was chatting and whatever with Ruby until a little after three."

"Huh. What do you know? He was being honest. I'm shocked. Maybe he really is trying to get his life turned around," Astra says.

"Looks like it. I still want to get that gun tested though," I say. "You never know what's going to come back on it."

"True enough."

"Okay, moving on then. Rick, what do you have for us?"

"Thought you'd never ask," he says. "Okay, according to the Tempe gang and organized crime databases, Poke is the street name for Drew Graves, Bullet is Raymund Orazco, and Razor is Hector Aliva. And let me just say, whoever is in charge of giving these clowns their nicknames needs to be fired because those all suck. I mean, I've seen grade school kids give each other better nicknames. It's embarrassing. I'm embarrassed for them."

"We'll be sure to pass on your thoughts on the whole nickname situation when we talk to them," Astra says.

"I'd appreciate that," he replies.

"Okay, give me what you can on these three clowns," I say. "Nina, do you have the reports from PD on the crime scene?"

"I do. Give me just one second," she replies and glances down at her laptop screen. "Okay, Dustin Kemper was shot seven times in total with a nine-millimeter, and the estimated time of death is somewhere between eleven that night and three that morning."

"Which, since Colston was handling his business until three, should be enough to take him off the suspect list," Astra says.

"I'd say so," I say. "Do you have the crime scene photos?"

"Coming right up."

Sonny had brought a large flatscreen monitor on wheels into the room for our use. As Nina works her keyboard, it lights up, and a moment after that, the photos of the scene start popping up on the screen. Taken from a variety of angles, I can see the seven bullet holes in his body—two in the abdomen, two in the chest, one in the neck, one through the left cheek, and one in the shoulder.

"Whoever killed this guy wanted to make sure he was dead," Mo says.

"Right?" Paige agrees.

"Those all look like they were done at close range," I note. "Almost like they were standing over Dustin when they pulled the trigger. I'm going to guess they got him on the ground somehow then put seven in him."

"Any defensive wounds noted on the body?" Astra asks.

"Nothing noted," Nina replies. "Wait… it's not defensive, but there is a wound to the back of his head. It looks like blunt force trauma. Like he was hit from behind."

"And that's how he ended up on the ground," Astra notes.

"Do we have the autopsy report to confirm any of this?" I ask.

"Not yet," Nina says. "Still pending."

"This also isn't where Dustin was killed," I say. "He was dumped here."

"Are you sure?" Paige asks.

Getting to my feet, I walk over to the monitor and circle the body with my finger. "There's no blood underneath him. If he'd been killed in that lot, there would be a pool underneath him."

"Great. So, we don't have a crime scene," Astra says. "That isn't going to make it more difficult for us or anything."

"Quick question," Mo chimes in. "How does this link up with our op? Is there anything definitively connecting this guy's death to the cartel? I've heard chatter around this place, and Sonny seems to think this is a cartel hit."

"I know that's what he thinks. But he's wrong," I say. "This isn't a cartel hit."

"What makes you say that?" Paige asks.

"It's something Gary Colston said to us… a couple of times, actually," I say.

Astra nods. "The line about having his head chopped off?"

"That's the one," I say. "Cartels display the bodies very loudly and very publicly. They hang bodies from freeway overpasses or leave a pile of heads in a town square. They make a spectacle of their victims because they want to instill fear… send a message."

"But Dustin's body was left in an out-of-the-way place and was completely intact. There was no spectacle to it. There doesn't seem to be any message," Astra continues. "I agree with Blake. I don't think this is a cartel job either."

Paige tucks a strand of her golden-blond hair behind her ear. "Sonny really strongly believes there's a cartel link."

"I'm positive he's wrong, but we're not closing the door on anything completely," I say. "The evidence is going to guide us. And right now, I'm not seeing anything that indicates we're looking at a cartel job. But we'll keep an open mind."

"Okay, that's fair," Mo says. "So, we're thinking maybe Dustin ran afoul of one of these street dealers then? One of these clowns with the terrible nicknames?"

"Thank you," Rick says.

"That's kind of what I'm thinking," I respond. "But until we have something concrete, this stays between us. I don't even want Sonny getting a whiff of what we're looking into."

Paige turns to me. "I thought he was cool with you having free rein and letting the facts and evidence dictate the course of the investigation?"

"That's what he says, yeah," I tell her. "But this one is personal to him. And we all know what it's like when something hits too close to home for us. We see things that aren't there—try to make connections that don't exist. Because he's been investigating them for so long and has locked up some of their people, he believes the cartel is sending him a personal message. I would rather not have to swim against that tide. So, until we know anything, one way or the other, we keep a lid on it all. Understood?"

"Understood," the team agrees in unison.

"Good. Excellent," I say. "Now, Rick, what can you tell me about our local bozos?"

"All right, let's start off with Drew Graves, aka Poke," Rick starts with a roll of his eyes. "Forty-five years old, is unaffiliated, and has a lengthy criminal history, including an assault with a deadly charge. He apparently used an ice pick on some guy in a bar, which is disturbing, and I guess is where he got his nickname—"

"Well, look at that," Astra says. "The nickname actually does fit."

"It still sucks," Rick replies.

"Why is he carrying an ice pick into a bar?" Paige asks.

Rick grimaces. "I guess that's his thing. Anyway, he's been picked up multiple times for dealing meth and fentanyl. Not a very good guy."

The man's booking photo comes up on the screen and shows a man who's lived a hard life. His eyes are a deep brown but are flat and emotionless. He's got sunbaked tan skin, black hair, and a long, angular face with deep acne scars dotting his cheeks. The booking information lists him at six-one, and he has a lean, wiry build. He looks like a guy well used to scrapping.

"Yeah, he looks exactly like the kind of guy I'd expect to use an ice pick to shank somebody," Astra says.

"Right?" Paige asks.

"He's got dead eyes," Mo offers.

"Bachelor number two is Raymund Orazco, otherwise known as Bullet—"

"Let me guess, he's got weapons charges," Astra says.

"Really? How'd you guess?" he cracks. "Thirty-seven years old, and in addition to the aforementioned weapons charges, he, too, has been arrested numerous times on drug charges. He's avoided getting popped with any real weight, so he's avoided serious time. But he's been in and out of the system since he was thirteen, so you could say he may be a bit radicalized. He's also got a loose affiliation with the West Side Kings, a local street gang."

"Do the Kings have any ties to the cartel?" Astra asks.

He shakes his head. "Unclear, but it doesn't appear so."

Orazco is my height, has slicked back black hair and matching eyes that, even in a booking photo, glimmer with rage. He's a scary man who definitely seems like he's been radicalized by jail.

"And our final contestant is Razor, otherwise known as Hector Aliva," Rick goes on. "Mr. Aliva is thirty-three years old and a product of the Arizona Department of Children's Services. His bona fides include weapons, drugs, and assault charges. Of our three bachelors, he's got the most violent crimes on his sheet. The man is apparently willing to fight anybody, anywhere, anytime."

Aliva has a thin scar along the left side of his jawline, running from chin to ear, a white line that cuts through his black goatee and across his tawny skin. He's got hard, flat eyes as dark as his hair, and in the booking photo on the screen, his lips are parted slightly, revealing two golden front teeth. Three teardrop tattoos dot the right side of his face, and his neck is covered in them as well.

"Gang affiliations?" I ask.

"Yep. He was a hardcore member of the Disciples, which appears to be the mortal enemy of the West Side Kings," Rick tells us.

Astra turns to me. "Didn't Colston tell us these three guys were friends? Or at least, were running together these days?"

"He did," I respond.

"And yet, despite their gangs being mortal enemies, they're running together," she says.

"For whatever it's worth, Tempe PDs gang database lists them both as inactive members," Rick tells us. "It looks like they both got out."

"I didn't think you could get out of a gang," Mo says.

"I didn't either," I say. "But what do I know?"

"What if they got out and formed their own little syndicate?" Astra asks. "That would explain how these guys are running around together. I mean, they're all in the drug game, so what if they joined forces just to make money?"

"That would make sense. Love of money tends to bring people together."

"If they did, Tempe PD has nothing on it," Rick tells us.

It makes sense though. If these three pooled their resources and set up their own little drug syndicate, and Dustin ran afoul of them, maybe got into a hole and couldn't get out of it, I can see that they'd put a few bullets into him to settle his debts once and for all.

"Do we have an address on these guys?" I ask.

"One moment, please," Rick says as he starts working his keyboard.

"What are you thinking?" Astra asks.

"I'm thinking we're going to go have a chat with them."

"Should we get a tac team together?"

I shake my head. "I don't want to go in heavy just yet. I want to get a feel for what these guys are up to first."

"Could be dangerous."

"You scared? You getting soft on me?"

Astra laughs and gives me the finger. Before she can say anything more, though, Sonny bursts through the door. Thankfully, Rick is on the ball and shuts off the monitors, preventing him from seeing what we're looking at. He apparently didn't need to worry about it, though, because Sonny didn't even glance at them. His eyes are fixed on me.

"We have some movement," he says.

CHAPTER TEN

ATF Operational Center, Southwest Division; Phoenix, AZ

"M**OVEMENT?**" I ASK. "WHAT'S GOING ON?"

Sonny plants his hands on the table, bracing himself, an excited gleam in his eyes. "Seems that the Prophets contacted their bosses and let them know they're getting ripped off. We got intel that a new shipment to resupply them is coming up from Mexico in the next couple of days."

"Earlier than normal," I say.

He nods. "Earlier than normal."

I sit back in my chair, tapping the tip of my pen against the pad of paper in front of me. That's good news for us. If they're having to call for an early resupply, that means we're putting a dent in their operations. And it gives us a shot to blow an even bigger hole in them.

"What do you think?" he asks.

"I'm not sure yet."

The cartel's operation typically works on a set schedule that rarely, if ever, deviates. Once a month, a truck comes up from Sonora, just across the border, and into Arizona. It's like clockwork. The trick is figuring out when and where those trucks are coming across. They're clever about how they move their poison across the border, and finding it before it lands is always the challenge.

"If we can hit this shipment, it might be enough to draw the Ariases across the border either to deal with the Prophets' inability to safeguard their product, or if we're really lucky, to cut a deal with Nadia," Sonny says.

"It's possible," I respond. "How reliable is the intel?"

"Reliable."

"How reliable?"

"One hundred percent," he replies. "This informant has never done me wrong. Why are you so skeptical about my intel?"

"Because you know how tight-lipped the cartel is. Intel about their shipments is almost impossible to come by. It just seems convenient to me that we suddenly get the time and place of one of their shipments."

He frowns and glances around the table as he considers my words, which he knows to be true. In his excitement and zeal to make the case, he didn't stop to think it through.

"What did your CI give you?" I ask.

"Said there's a truck coming up from Sonora the day after tomorrow. The driver will be leaving it in the parking lot at the Desert Sky Mall, and one of the Prophets will be picking it up and taking it the rest of the way. All standard stuff," he says.

"And how did your CI come by this intel?"

"Said his girl is friends with one of the Prophet's old ladies," he responds.

"It doesn't strike you as odd that one of their old ladies has all this sensitive intel?"

He shakes his head. "Not really. I don't credit some of those clowns with a lot of smarts. Plus, the Prophets aren't quite as tight and controlled as the Ariases. Also, girls talk."

Astra gives me a half shrug, seemingly as unsure of the intel as I am. It's not unheard of. People talk, and like I always say, criminals are stupid. Whereas a group like the Arias cartel is likely to be run like a strict military organization with severe punishments for breaking ranks, a gang of outlaw bikers like the Prophets are going to be a lot looser and less organized. If there's a leak, it's more likely to be on that end.

"Why do you seem so unsure?" he asks.

"Because I don't like it when things seem too convenient."

"It's true," Astra says. "She always likes to have to work for the answers."

A wan smile touches Sonny's lips. "Oh, trust me, I'm well aware of Blake's penchant for taking the road less traveled."

"That is an impressively diplomatic way to put it," Paige says. "We usually just say she likes making things harder than they need to be."

"She's not wrong," Mo adds.

That touches off a round of laughter and even snarkier comments about my way of doing things and my stubborn nature from everybody.

"All right, all right," I chime in. "Shut it. All of you."

The laughter and the commentary on my character eventually taper off, leaving me to shake my head and chuckle to myself. Bunch of clowns.

"Anyway," Sonny says, still grinning like a fool. "To answer your question, the intel is solid. I think we're going to get a real shot at their truck."

I know I'm being a bit paranoid. Maybe even a bit overly cautious because of it. But given that we're working against an organization whose calling card is leaving headless corpses everywhere they go, I don't think I can really be blamed. These are some very bad men, and I'm worried about slipping up or walking into a trap and putting my team at risk. If anything happened to any one of them because I didn't take the appropriate precautions or take the threat the cartel poses seriously enough, I would never forgive myself.

"We can do this, Blake. We might be able to take another step closer to taking down Santiago and Diego Arias and dismantling their entire cartel," Sonny presses.

"Okay, if they're going to be here the day after tomorrow, then the clock is ticking. Let's game this out and get a plan together," I say.

Sonny claps his hands together, his excitement growing. "Now you're talkin', darlin.'"

It's just after eleven and I'm sitting alone on the balcony of my hotel room staring out at the endless vista of the desert. The darkness in the desert is different from the darkness at home. It's deeper. More absolute. The stars above glitter like chips of diamond, cold and distant, and the landscape is bathed in the silvery, monochromatic light of the moon. It's stark but beautiful.

The sound of Grover Washington Jr.'s smooth, soulful saxophone plays in the room behind me, and I've got a nice glass of Glenfiddich Original 12—a gift from Sonny to thank me for bringing my team down—in my hand. I turn my face up to the sky and close my eyes, letting the music and the scotch work their magic and soothe my soul as I wind down for the night.

After a long day in the ops center putting together a game plan for the truck that's coming in, I'm spent. I'm tired, and I'd love to be able to get a little sleep tonight so I can get back to it tomorrow refreshed and energized. There's a lot riding on this op, and we need to be sharp. We need to be on top of our game. One mistake could bring the larger op crashing down around us in a fiery heap. Or worse. If things really go off the rails, somebody could get killed out there. The cartel does not play around.

I think our plan is solid. If it works, it'll put a major kink in the Ariases' supply chain and a big, fat dent in their operations as a whole. The intel, if it can be believed, is supposed to be a major resupply, and if we can get our hands on it, we're going to create havoc for both the Arias brothers and for the Prophets. It will also position me, posing as Nadia Petrenko, as the only game in town. That is either going to force the Arias brothers to deal with me directly or, if things go sideways on us, it could touch off a war.

Being that war is expensive, is bad for business, and is guaranteed to draw unwanted heat on people who prefer to work in the shadows, we're banking on the idea that the Arias brothers will want to avoid all that and have a sit-down with me. It's a calculated risk, especially when you're dealing with psychopaths like Santiago and Diego Arias. But if we want to shut them down once and for all, we have no choice but to roll the dice.

As I take another sip of my drink, I close my eyes and roll it around on my tongue, savoring the rich flavor. I feel the stress of the day starting to fall away, and my body begins to relax. My cell phone rings, shattering the stillness of the night around me, and my shoulders immediately tighten back up.

"Dammit," I mutter.

Setting the glass down on the table beside my chair, I get up and go inside. My phone is sitting on the bed, so I snatch it up and see that the call is coming from an unknown number. Not an unusual occurrence, so I connect the call and press the phone to my ear.

"Wilder."

"You're in danger."

The call's voice is low and modulated, the tinny, almost robotic sound keeping me from being able to tell whether it's a man or a woman on the other end of the line.

"Who is this?" I ask.

"You are being set up," they reply.

"Can you be a little more specific?"

"The truck that's coming into the Desert Sky Mall, plate number MNW-2984, is a decoy. It's a trap," the caller says. "A team of heavily armed sicarios will be waiting for you if you show up."

Adrenaline surges through my veins, and my entire body tightens up. I take a deep, steadying breath and let it out slowly.

"How do you know this?" I ask.

"There is a resupply truck coming, plate number ZKE-9212. It will be driven to the Arizona Mills Shopping Center," the caller says. "The Road Prophets will be picking up the truck from there."

"Who is this?" I ask. "And how do you have this information?"

"I am somebody in a position to know."

"Why are you telling me this?"

"It doesn't matter. All that matters is I'm telling you."

I strain my ears, listening to the background, listening for any distinctive sounds—anything that might tell me who this person is or where they're calling from. But there's nothing behind the caller. The silence is absolute, almost like they're in a sound dampening room or something.

"How can I trust you?" I ask.

"Trust me or don't. I'm going out on a limb to give you this information," they say. "What you choose to do with it is up to you. But just know, if you show up at the Desert Sky Mall, you will find a truck with no drugs and end up in a shootout with Arias sicarios. The truck you want is going to be at the Arizona Mills Center."

The phone pressed to my ear, I pace back and forth, my mind spinning, entirely unsure what to make of this. Of any of this.

"I need to know who you are," I say.

"Who I am doesn't matter. Just know that I know who you are, Blake Wilder," the caller says. "I know who you also are… Nadia Petrenko."

My heart falls into my stomach, and a lump forms in my throat. I swallow hard, trying to work some moisture into my mouth as I blot my hands on my pants. How could this be? My cover is solid. Who in the hell could possibly know? This makes no sense at all. Not unless there's a leak in Sonny's office.

"I need to know who you are and how you know who I am," I say.

"Arizona Mills Center," they reply. "That is where you will find what you're looking for."

There's an audible click on the other end of the line, and then it goes dead. If I thought it would do any good, I would call Rick and ask him to scrub my phone to get the number of the person who called me. But I have a feeling whoever was on the other end of the line is a professional, which means by now, the phone is already in a hundred pieces.

My hands on my head, I walk around my room, suddenly wide awake and restless. I'm so wired, I know sleep is not going to come easy to me tonight, if it comes at all. Not only am I stressing about my mystery caller and how they know not just my real identity but my cover ID as well. On top of that, I'm worried about whether I'll be walking my team into a trap by sending them into the Desert Sky Mall… or if the real trap is at the Arizona Mills Center.

"Bloody hell," I mutter. "What a mess. What an absolute, freaking mess."

CHAPTER ELEVEN

Marylee's Kitchen, Downtown District; Phoenix, AZ

❝ IT'S EARLY," ASTRA SAYS. "DO YOU KNOW HOW EARLY IT is?"

"I do. It's six-fourteen," I reply.

"The sun isn't even up yet."

"It'll be up in an hour," I tell her. "Have some more coffee."

"I'm not sure there's enough coffee in this entire diner."

I arch an eyebrow at her. "You wake up and run at five-thirty every morning. This isn't early for you. Stop whining."

She grins. "Somebody's testy this morning."

"I didn't sleep much last night."

After spending most of the rest of the night after my mystery call staring at the ceiling in my room, I grabbed a scalding hot shower before the sun was up, then sent Astra a text telling her to meet me here for breakfast. Marylee's is a small, quaint little place that's only open for breakfast. There is seating at a long counter and a couple dozen tables are situated on the main floor. The walls are all beige and lined with photographs of desert landscapes. Everything is clean, and the air is redolent with the mouth-watering aroma of the food that's being cooked on the large griddles behind the counter.

Our waitress, a middle-aged woman named Margaret, ambles over to our table and offers us a wide smile. Her ash-blond hair is in a tight bun atop her head, and her cornflower blue eyes are framed by thin, purple-framed glasses. The diner is almost full as people come in to fuel up on food and coffee for the coming day.

"Mornin' ladies," she says. "What can I get for you?"

"Coffee. Lots of coffee," I say. "I'll also have the Denver omelet, wheat toast, and bacon, extra crispy. Please."

"Sounds good. And you, Miss?"

"Umm… I'll take the chilaquiles with flour tortillas please. And a tall orange juice."

"You got it."

As she walks away, a busboy drops off a carafe of coffee, a pair of mugs, and a small pitcher of creamer. I pour us both a cup of coffee and start to dress mine with sugar and cream. Astra raises her cup and takes a swallow of the strong, dark brew.

"So? What's this about?" Astra asks.

I take a sip of my own coffee, giving myself a minute to let the caffeine hit my veins. Once it does and I feel something closer to human, I tell her about the phone call I received last night. At some point while I'm relating the conversation, Margaret drops off our meals, and I keep talking as we pick at our food. When I'm done, Astra takes a bite of her food and chews slowly as she silently mulls over what I've said, then washes her food down with a swallow of orange juice.

"Okay, that's a problem," is all she says.

"You think?"

"And you have no idea who the caller was? No clues and nothing you picked up on?"

"Nada."

She whistles low. "It sounds like we're compromised."

"It sounds like it," I say, then grimace.

"Maybe we should pull the plug on the op. It's a pretty big risk—"

I shake my head. "We can't. It is definitely a big risk, but if we pull the plug, we might not get another shot at these animals. And we've put in too much time and effort to flush it all."

"We might not have a shot at them now. This could be an ambush."

I pause and think about it for a minute. "It could be," I agree slowly. "But it also sounds like maybe we've got an ally."

"Blake—"

"I didn't get the sense that we were being set up. I'm not saying we can necessarily trust whoever called me, but it feels to me like they're working their own agenda—"

"Yeah, they absolutely are working their own agenda."

"And part of their agenda is taking out the Arias brothers. They need us to do that."

"I recall just yesterday, you saying that you don't trust information that comes to us too easily," she says. "I don't think it gets any easier than this, Blake."

"So, you don't think we can trust it."

"Do you?"

"I'm not sure what to think, to be honest," I reply. "But if there's any chance that it's true, I do not want to send the team to that mall with the possibility that they're going to be running into a bunch of sicarios. The last thing we need is a public shoot-out because those animals don't care whether they shoot up a bunch of innocent people or not."

"That's true. But that's a mighty big *if* in that sentence," she says.

"Okay, even if you don't believe what they said about the trucks, there's the bigger issue that they know who I am," I say and look around to make sure we're not being overheard. "And they knew my cover ID."

"I agree that's a big problem. What are your thoughts on that?"

I shake my head. "The only people who know are our team and Sonny's team."

"You don't really think Sonny sold you out, do you?"

"Like I said, I don't know what to think right now."

"No way. There is absolutely no way he gave you up."

"Let's not pretend it would be the first time I got involved with somebody who turned out to be a bad guy—a bad guy who tried to kill me, by the way."

"Okay, historically speaking, you haven't always picked the best guys to get involved with," she says with a chuckle. "But I don't get that vibe off Sonny—or anybody else on his team for that matter."

"Maybe they're good at covering it."

She frowns. "I don't see it. And to what end, anyway? Let's say you're right—let's say Sonny gave you up to the cartel. Why would he then call you to warn you? If he'd given you up, there would have been a team of assassins at your door, not on the phone."

I sit back and take a sip of my coffee, mulling it over for a minute. She's right. If Sonny or somebody on his team had sold me out to the cartel, I would have gotten a bullet, not a phone call... which makes this all make even less sense.

"What in the hell is going on?" I mutter.

"That's what we need to figure out," Astra replies. "But given what you told me, I have to wonder if maybe this warning you got is legit. What if the truck at the Desert Sky Mall really is a setup? And what if the real supply truck is at this other place?"

"I'm missing something here. Something just isn't making sense."

"There's a lot that's not making sense," Astra agrees. "I think you need to fill everybody in on what's going on. We need to put our heads together and come up with a plan."

"Right."

"I don't like this, Blake. Not one bit."

"I don't like it either. But this is where we're at," I say. "So, let's get to work."

"Copy you," Astra replies reluctantly.

"Jesus," Sonny groans. "And you have no idea—"

"None," I say. "They used a voice distortion tool, and there was nothing distinguishable in the background. It was like they were in a sound-dampening room. Whoever it was, they know what they're doing."

"And you can't even hazard a guess as to who it was?" Glory asks.

"I've got no idea."

Despite everything that Astra and I talked about, I find myself still side-eyeing Sonny and even Glory as we stand in the conference room. The shades are all down, giving us privacy for obvious reasons, and I'm standing against the back wall, arms folded over my chest. Astra is right. It doesn't make sense that Sonny or any of his people would give me up to the cartel only to call and warn me that we might be walking into a trap. If I had truly been compromised, I'd likely be just as dead as Sonny's CI. And yet, despite the logical arguments against any of them being involved, I can't help but worry about it all the same.

Sonny sits back in his chair and rakes his fingers through his sandy-blond locks. His face is pinched, his shoulders bunched. If I'm being honest, he seems as disturbed by this development as I am. He chews it over for a minute, then sits forward and lays his palms flat on the table in front of him as he blows out a loud breath.

"All right, this is a problem," he says. "But I think I'm with Astra on this one. Going through all the trouble of setting you up doesn't seem to track with how the Ariases operate. If you've been compromised, they would have sent a hitter rather than a warning."

"I tend to agree. But the bigger problem here is that somebody out there knows my cover ID," I say. "And the only people with that piece of information are here in this room."

Glory's face hardens as the implication of my words sinks in. She turns to Sonny who, as if intuiting her thoughts, holds his hands up to prevent the stream of angry words that seem to be sitting on the tip of her tongue. He turns to me, his expression sober.

"You don't really believe my team leaked your ID, do you?" he asks.

"I don't know what to think right now," I respond. "All I know is that somebody has my cover ID, and the only person who could possibly know that is somebody with access."

"My team doesn't leak," Sonny says coldly.

"Mine doesn't either," I respond. "And yet, here we are."

Tension fills the air in the conference room, and everybody sitting around the table cuts glances at one another, their faces tight but awkward, feeling like children caught between arguing parents. I understand Sonny taking up for his people, but there is no other way my cover ID could have leaked if not for one of them.

"I need a list of everybody who has access to this op," I say.

Glory showed her teeth. "Who in the hell—"

"Glory. Enough," Sonny's tone was sharp, his face hard as he turned to me. "While I understand where you're coming from, I don't appreciate your accusation."

"And I understand that," I tell him, my tone just as cold. "But I'm still going to need a list of everybody with access to the details of our op."

We engage in a tense stare down, the silence in the room heightening the apprehension that's crackling in the air. Sonny finally lowers his gaze and nods.

"Glory, get her the list—"

"You can't be serious—"

"Get the list. Now," he said.

Glory shoots me a dirty look before turning and storming out of the room. Sonny waits a moment, then turns back to me.

"You're wrong about this. My people don't leak," he says.

"I hope I'm wrong. I really do."

He rubs his jaw, the stubble on his face making a dry, scratchy sound. "We need to put this crapshow aside for the moment. We still have work to do. What are your thoughts?"

"I think we should hedge our bets," I say. "Split our resources. Half our team goes to Desert Sky, the other half to Arizona Mills. If there is a truckload of sicarios out there, we need to round them up and prevent a firefight. We also need to get our hands on that resupply. We need a new plan, and we don't have a lot of time to put it together."

He strokes his chin and ponders everything for a moment. "Agreed. Let's figure it out."

CHAPTER TWELVE

Arizona Mills Shopping Center, Downtown District; Tempe, AZ

"WE'RE IN POSITION," ASTRA SAYS. "ALL QUIET over here so far. How are things over there?"

"Frosty," I reply.

"Understandable. I mean, you did accuse the guy of being a cartel double agent."

Pressing my hand to my forehead, I pace back and forth behind our cover van. Sitting inside with Sonny for the last few hours has been awkward, to say the least. He refuses to look at or speak to me outside of what is necessary to do the job. Part of me understands. I'd be pissed if somebody accused my team of leaking sensitive information too.

The other part of me is pissed that he refuses to see things from my point of view. It's *my* life on the line, and somehow, somebody got ahold of information that can be used to end it. And with such a small circle of people who have said information, the leak could only have come from one of those inside that circle. That he can't or won't see that is infuriating. That he seems more concerned with his team's reputation than my well-being is even more disappointing.

I grimace. "Not exactly. Not him specifically. And let's not forget that somebody did in fact leak that information."

"I know. I'm just saying there might have been a more delicate way to approach it."

"And when have you ever known me to be delicate?"

"True. You tend to be a bull in a China shop," she says. "But it's not often the person you're accusing of going Benedict Arnold on you is somebody you're involved with."

"I don't know. Maybe he's not the person I thought he was," I say. "I mean, he's either the leak … or he's protecting somebody who is."

"That's a pretty binary way of thinking."

"Is there a third option?"

"What if somebody hacked into our systems? What if they got the information that way?" she asks. "I mean, we know the Prophets were doing a deep dive on your cover ID. What if one of them stumbled onto the truth?"

I open my mouth to respond but close it again without speaking. It's an angle I haven't considered. I don't think it's likely, but I'm not tech-savvy enough to say for sure one way or the other. It's something we'll have to consider.

"It's a possibility, you have to admit," she says.

"Yeah. That's true, and we'll look into it," I reply. "But it's like we've been saying: if one of the bad guys figured out my cover ID, I'd be dead right now. No, I don't think that's it. This … this feels like something different."

"Well, just keep an open mind," she says. "I have to bolt. Our truck was spotted heading our way. We need to get set up."

"Be careful," I tell her. "If you get shot, I'm going to kick your butt."

"Ditto that. Stay safe out there."

I disconnect the call and drop the phone into my pocket as I pace back and forth behind the van, my mind spinning. Is it possible the leak didn't come from Sonny's team? Anything's possible, I suppose. I've got Rick and Nina running backgrounds and really drilling down on everybody who has access to our investigative files, so I guess we'll see soon enough.

If I end up being wrong, I have no idea how I'm going to apologize to Sonny. I have no idea if he'll be willing to even hear my apology. Have I found a new and unique way to tank yet another relationship? Sabotaging and destroying my relationships is like my superpower. It's something I'll probably want to talk to Dr. Azar about at some point.

The van's back door opens, and Sonny sticks his head out. "Our truck is inbound."

I plug my earpiece back in and give him a nod, then climb back into the van and sit down in front of the bank of monitors to watch the camera feeds. We were granted remote access to the mall's security system, so we've got full coverage of the entire parking lot that surrounds the mall. We watch as a small, do-it-yourself moving truck enters the lot from the western side. A quick check of the plate confirms it's the one our mystery helper flagged as the truck carrying the product.

I key open my mic. "All positions, we're live. Truck is inbound. Stay sharp."

We watch the truck roll into the parking lot and find a space far away from the front doors of the mall. The driver gets out and subtly leaves the keys on top of the tire before walking away. He crosses the lot and heads into the mall, disappearing from view. We'd already agreed to let him go. Scooping him up would have looked suspicious and ruined the rest of our plan. The driver is a little fish and is ultimately irrelevant.

"Black panel van entering from the eastern entrance," Paige's voice comes through my earpiece. "Looks like the Prophets have landed."

"Copy that," I say.

We find the black van on camera and track its movements as it approaches the truck. My stomach tightens as I watch it slow down then stop. A man in a Prophets kutte jumps out of the passenger side. He closes the door and looks around for a moment before slapping the side of the van. It drives off, and the biker walks over to the truck, swipes the keys off the tire, and climbs behind the wheel.

"All positions, we're green," I say. "Repeat, op is green. Get set."

Sonny and I climb out of the van and dash to the black Suburban parked nearby. He gets behind the wheel, and I get in on the passenger side. I key open my mic.

"Position three, what's your status?" I ask.

"Drone is up, and eyes are in the sky," Rick replies. "I've got the truck exiting the parking lot and turning southbound. He appears to be sticking to surface streets."

Sonny gets the Suburban on the road, driving quickly until we get the truck in sight. He stays a discreet distance behind it, just far enough that the driver likely won't make us as a tail, but not far enough that we can't keep an eye on it. A moment later, I see our other teams pass us by, driving quickly to pass the truck and get set up when we get a location.

"Copy that," I reply. "Can you spot a decent place to spring the trap?"

"Stand by."

"All units, get on the road. Pass the target truck and wait for instructions."

The other teams check in with their confirmation. I cut a glance at Sonny, but his eyes are fixed on the road ahead, his jaw clenched, his expression tight. He refuses to even look at me. Yeah, I'm kind of thinking I've dropped a grenade on this burgeoning relationship between us. Surprisingly, the thought that I've ruined it sends a needle of pain through my heart. I try to temper it by reminding myself that it's still very possible Sonny, or one of his people, leaked my identity. But it doesn't work. The hurt I feel in my heart lingers.

I clear my throat and turn to stare through the windshield, doing my best to get my mind right and focused on the task at hand. There will be plenty of time for apologies and recriminations later—depending on how it all shakes out. For the moment, I need to get my head in the game. The situation we're in is every bit as dangerous as the one Astra and her team are in, and one lapse in attention could prove fatal.

"All right," Rick's voice comes through my earpiece. "We've got a long stretch of empty road coming up about five miles from your current position. No traffic in either direction. Situation looks to be optimal."

"Copy you," I say. "Units two and three, do you copy?"

"We copy. Moving into position now," Paige replies. "We'll be ready."

"Maintain visual," I tell Rick. "Let us know if the situation changes."

"Will do," he replies. "You all be safe out there."

"Copy."

I turn to Sonny. "Time to party."

He grunts but doesn't say anything. Instead, he pulls on his black balaclava, situating it so only his eyes can be seen. That done, he puts on a pair of generic sunglasses. Frowning, I turn and pull my balaclava on, then cover my eyes with a pair of sunglasses as well.

"One mile," Sonny says into his mic. "Units two and three, are you ready?"

"In position and ready," Glory replies.

"Target truck will be on units two and three in ten seconds," Rick reports.

Sonny pilots the Suburban, moving closer to the back end of the truck as I count down to ten in my head. Up ahead, I see the other two Suburbans shoot out of their hiding spots, forming a barrier across the road. The taillights on the truck flare as it stops short. Sonny jams on the brakes, and I'm already throwing the door open as it comes to a screeching halt.

Jumping out of the SUV with my M4 in hand, I dash around to the side of the truck, shouting at the driver who looks back at me through the driver's side window. Glory, Paige, and their team stand in a line in front of their Suburbans, M4s raised, slowly approaching the truck. The man behind the wheel puts his hands up and glares at me, hatred in his eyes.

"Open the door and get out," I shout.

He gives me the finger and mouths a certain four-letter word I recognize all too well. Pointing the barrel of my weapon up, I squeeze off a burst, then lower it again, taking aim at his face.

"Get out of the truck," I repeat firmly.

The door flies open, and he jumps out, cutting his eyes from me to the firing line in the middle of the road. His hand hovers near the butt of what looks like a .45 in the waistband of his jeans, and he seems to be trying to decide whether to pull or not.

"Don't do it," I say. "You don't need to die today."

"You're makin' a big mistake, lady."

"Get on the ground. Now!"

He glares at me and sneaks a peek at the other gunmen, uncertainty painted on his face. Seeming to realize he has no shot at coming out of this alive if he draws, the man gets down on his knees. Paige dashes forward and slips a pair of plastic cuffs around his wrists, securing them behind his back. Glory then steps to the man and sinks a needle into the side of his neck, quickly pushing the plunger down and giving the man a big dose of a fast-acting sedative.

He winces at the sharp prick of pain but keeps his eyes fixed on me until he slumps to the ground, out cold. Glory nudges him with the toe of her boot, then leans down and twists his ear good and hard but gets no reaction from him. She looks up.

"He's out," she reports.

"All right. Babysit him. Everyone else to the back," I say as the team sidles up alongside me. We approach the rear door in a tight formation, our guns drawn.

This is the most delicate part of the operation. For all we know, there could be an armed gunman or two in the back as one final fail-safe. They wouldn't know why we stopped, but they'd be ready to open fire the second we open it up.

Sonny reaches forward and unlatches the lock, gives us a silent count to three, and then lifts the door quickly as we raise our weapons...

And fortunately, there's nobody there.

I pull the balaclava off my head and shake my hair out. "Good work everybody. That was smooth. Really nice job."

Sonny whistles low. Glory pokes her head around the corner and gives me a glare, but I ignore it while we climb up into truck and begin rifling through the boxes stored inside.

"There have to be at least a hundred bricks of cocaine in here. Another fifty of what looks like heroin," I say and nudge one of the boxes on the floor with my foot. "And these are filled with fentanyl pills. Thousands of them."

"This is quite the haul," he says.

"This one is going to hurt."

"Yes, it is," he replies with a toothy smile—the first I've seen all day.

"Boss, what are we doing with this clown?" Glory asks, motioning to the biker.

"Load him up and get him out of here," he says. "He'll wake up in one of our black sites. We'll sit on him until this op is over. As far as he'll know, he'll be sitting in a Ukrainian prison."

"You got it," Glory says.

She and Paige manage to drag the unconscious man back to one of the SUVs and get him into the cargo bay.

"Can we hold him without a lawyer?" I ask.

Sonny shrugs. "We'll designate him as part of an ongoing terroristic threat."

"Terroristic?"

"We have intel that the Arias brothers are using the proceeds from their drug sales to buy weapons which they then sell to elements of known terrorist groups. It'll stick."

"Is that intel real?"

"It's real enough," he replies. "This is a whole new world, Blake Wilder. Working with terrorist groups gives us a lot of leeway. Don't worry, it'll be fine."

"All right then," I say. "Let's get this truck back to the ops center for processing. The balls are all now in play, and we just have to wait to see how it all shakes out."

"I've got a good feeling about it."

He starts to climb out, but I grab him by the wrist, turning him back to me. My mind continues warring with itself as I gaze into his eyes, struggling to get the words out. Seeming to intuit my thoughts, his face softens as he grabs my hand and gives it a squeeze.

"It's all right, darlin.' We're going to figure it out and get some answers," he says, letting me off the hook for reasons unknown to me.

"Thanks, Sonny," I reply softly.

CHAPTER THIRTEEN

ATF Operational Center, Southwest Division; Phoenix, AZ

A S IT TURNS OUT, RICK AND NINA DRILLED DEEP INTO everybody on the team and didn't find a thing. No strange phone calls. No unexplained bank deposits. Nobody living beyond their means, nobody with a new and expensive car, luxury home... nothing. They didn't find a single thing that might indicate somebody has been compromised. Nothing that indicates somebody working on the team gave me up.

"Well, damn," I say.

Sonny walks over and hands me his handkerchief. Almost like a reflex, I take it from him, then cock my head as I pull a face.

"What's this for?" I ask.

"I thought you might need something to wipe that egg off your face, darlin.'"

Everybody around the table giggles like middle school children, and all I can do is shake my head as a wry expression crosses my face.

"Yeah, yeah, okay," I say. "I deserve it."

"Maybe a little. But it's understandable," Sonny says, suddenly serious. "We really do need to find out who compromised your cover ID. That's not a laughing matter."

"No, it's not," I say. "Is there anything on the streets about it?"

He shakes his head. "Nope. Not a word that I've picked up. As near as I can tell, your cover is still intact. And I have to believe if they knew the new big player in town was actually a Fed, that'd be all over the streets."

"I'm also pretty sure there would be bullets flying all over the place. Somebody would have taken a run at you by now," Glory adds.

"Agreed," Sonny says.

"Well, I want to apologize to you guys for accusing you," I say. "Sonny, Glory… I was wrong. I'm sorry."

"Don't sweat it. In your place, I would've been pissed too," Glory says.

"Appreciate your understanding," I respond.

"All right, if our touchy-feely, emotional bonding session is over, can we get back to the task at hand?" Sonny says with a toothy grin.

"Please," I say.

The feeling of a thousand-pound weight that has been lifted off my shoulders hits me hard. It's unexpected. I don't think I quite realized just how hard I was taking the possibility of this thing between Sonny and me being snuffed out until just this moment. I mean, I knew it didn't feel good. But knowing that we're okay and that we're still in a good place, despite my accusations, has taken a dark shadow off my heart.

"All right, where do we start?" Glory asks.

"The first thing we need to do is get eyes and ears on the streets," Sonny says. "We need to keep listening to make sure Blake's name and cover ID aren't floating around out there. Just because we haven't heard anything yet doesn't mean somebody isn't going to start talking."

"I'll start talking to my CIs on the down-low," Glory says.

"Good. Do that, and I'll do the same," Sonny tells her. "If you hear anything at all, let me know because we're going to need to pull Blake out."

"Copy you," Glory says.

"And now that we hit their shipment, I suspect the streets are going to be buzzing," I say as I sit forward. "I'm not sure what the Prophets are going to do just yet, so let's get more security over at Frost. Just in case they come strapped for war, I want to have more guns than they do."

"On it," Sonny says.

Before I can say anything more, Astra and Mo walk into the conference room, drawing a breath of relief from me. Astra smiles and raises her arms.

"How'd it go out there?" I ask.

"Smooth and easy," Mo says as she drops into her chair.

"There were half a dozen sicarios in the back of the truck. They were strapped and ready for war, but your plan worked out," Astra says. "We had local PD backing us up when we hit the truck. We had more guns, so they gave up without a fight—which was surprising, but welcomed. Anyway, we had Tempe PD make the arrests, so it all looked legit."

"Excellent. That is good news," I say. "I'm very relieved this all went off without a hitch."

By having Tempe PD make the arrest, it should keep the Arias brothers from suspecting it was a DEA operation that took his men out. It looks like a local, rather than a federal response. That should also help deflect suspicion about who hit their resupply truck. It should look like two separate events, and hopefully, the truck heist will make them think that—like the Prophets' stash houses—was carried out by Nadia Petrenko and her people.

That will hopefully have a cascading effect. The Ariases were clever about getting their product into town and—I have no doubt—kept the circle of people who knew the plan small and tight. The fact that it got hit anyway will hopefully make them start asking questions like who leaked the information in the first place. I've got a feeling our actual source was clever enough to cover their tracks. That's going to leave them scrambling to figure out who the leak is, and unless our mole set up a patsy to take the fall, should lead to discord and chaos within their ranks… which will only work in our favor.

That's the hope. What happens over the next few days is going to tell whether that hope comes to fruition or not. It's either going to be war on the streets of Phoenix, or Nadia is going to get a request for a sit-down with the Arias brothers. Obviously, we are hoping for the latter.

"We also need to know if the Prophets or any of the Ariases' other proxies are gearing up for a fight. We need to know it's coming before it pops off," I say.

"Understood," Glory says. "I'll have my people keeping a close eye out."

"What's our next move?" Sonny asks.

"We wait," I answer.

"I hate waiting."

"Same. But we need to know what the Prophets and what the Ariases are planning to do before we know what our next move is going to be."

"Yeah, that makes sense," he grumbles.

"In the meantime, Rick and Nina, have either of you been able to get a line on whether our investigative files were hacked?" I ask.

"Not yet, Chief," Nina says. "We're scanning the servers and trying to figure out if they've been breached, but so far, there's nothing concrete."

"I'd be shocked if somebody was able to hack into the servers," Sonny says. "We've got a dedicated server room and cutting-edge security."

"I can't think of another way somebody got my cover ID. If you have any other suggestions, I'm all ears," I say.

He purses his lips. "Yeah, I really have no idea."

"We'll keep searching," Rick says. "If somebody was able to breach the servers, we'll find it. It's just going to take us some time."

"Understood," I say. "And yes, please. Keep searching. We need to know who has my cover ID and what they intend to do with it."

"Copy that, Chief," Nina says.

"Given that things are about to get really tense in the city and there's still a possibility that your ID is compromised, I don't think it'd be a bad idea for you to have somebody watching your back," Sonny says. "I'd offer to do it, but I'm pretty sure I'd be recognized on sight, and I worry that if the wrong person sees you hanging around with a known fed and makes the connection—"

"No need to worry. I've got Astra watching my back," I say. "I appreciate that you're concerned about me though."

"Barf," Astra teases.

"Get a room already," Paige adds.

"Keep it up and see what happens," I reply lightly.

Sonny chuckles. "While we're out there pounding the bricks, what are you going to do?"

"We're going to try to figure out who killed your CI."

A shadow crosses over his face, and his good humor fades a bit. But he clears his throat and pulls himself together.

"Any leads yet?"

"We're running down a couple of different avenues."

"Care to share?"

"Nope. I don't," I respond. "You don't get to be part of this process. We agreed on that."

He holds his hand up. "I know, I know. I told you I wouldn't interfere, and I won't. I just want to know one thing. Can you answer one question for me?"

"Depends on the question."

"Is it looking like this is cartel-related?" he asks. "Is this the Arias brothers' doing?"

I know why he's asking, and honestly, it kind of breaks my heart. He's asking because he thinks if the Arias brothers are behind it, then it's his fault Dustin Kemper is dead. That's because he's been taking shots at the Ariases for a long time, and he suspects they're retaliating and trying to hurt him by taking somebody out who's close to him. I know he's been punishing himself for the mere possibility that Dustin's death has anything to do with his work.

"It's not looking like it to me, Sonny," I tell him. "From what we've uncovered so far, this doesn't look like it has anything to do with you."

His shoulders sag as the weight he's been carrying on his back lifts slightly. He's still affected by the death of somebody he'd sort of taken under his wing—somebody he was close to—but he looks relieved at having the burden of responsibility taken off his shoulders.

"Thanks, Blake," he says.

"Of course," I respond. "I'll fill you in when I have something concrete to tell you."

His eyes linger on mine for a moment before he gives me a nod, then turns and heads out of the conference room. He's still hurting, but I'm glad that we could at least ease some of his pain. It's not much, but it's something.

CHAPTER
FOURTEEN

The Wagon Wheel Lounge, South Mountain District; Phoenix, AZ

"CUTE PLACE," PAIGE SAYS.

"I bet they have a fantastic happy hour," Astra adds dryly.

The Wagon Wheel Lounge is nothing to look at. It's a squat, beige stucco building with a red tile roof. A pair of rectangular windows flank the front door, and wooden pillars that are chipped, cracked, and scarred with graffiti hold up an awning made of wooden planks that are warped and sagging. Wagon wheels lean against the wall beneath the windows, and cigarette butts surround the wooden bench on the far-right side of the concrete porch.

The place has a worn, dingy look. The stucco is faded, the windows are caked with dust, and even out here, it smells heavily of cigarette smoke. It's definitely a dive bar and the sort of place you'd expect to find guys named Poke, Razor, and Bullet. According to the meager bit of intel we were able to dig up with the help of Tempe PD's gang task force, this is where they tend to hang out. I assume they're running their wannabe drug empire out of this place.

I open the door and step into the dimly-lit, gloomy little bar. It's as dingy inside as it is outside. There's a long bar to our left, the surface nicked and scarred, the brass railings all smudged and smeared. There's a wagon wheel painted on a mirror behind the bar, which, like the brass fixtures, is equally smudged, and cracks mar the lower right-hand corner. Half a dozen tables line the middle of the floor, and to our right is a row of booths along the wall. Country music issues from the speakers hung in the corners, the hard twang setting my teeth on edge.

The interior is the same dingy beige as the stucco outside, and other than the Arizona state flag hanging in the back, the walls are devoid of any other pictures or decorations. A row of cone lights hangs down the center of the bar, leaving most of the interior in murky shadows, and the air is thick with the stench of cigarette smoke and stale beer. It's a place for people to come drown their sorrows, not socialize—as evidenced by the four men sitting at the bar, heads down, gazes fixed on their glasses, not talking to anybody.

"Back there," Astra says quietly.

Sitting in the booth at the back of the place, furthest from the bar, are Poke, Bullet, and Razor. They're eyeballing us and making quiet remarks to one another that get them laughing. The bartender gives us a scowl. None of the other men hunched over the bar even bother to look up, so consumed with their own problems they perhaps don't even know we're there. I give the bartender a polite nod as we head for the back of the room.

The three men are snickering as they watch us approach. Their murmured conversation stops, but they continue to grin as they stare at us, seemingly amused by our presence.

"Look, fellas, it's the estrogen squad," Poke says.

"Are you here to arrest us for having too much testosterone, Officers?" Razor remarks, and the three of them burst into laughter once more.

"I'm impressed you even know the word testosterone," Astra says. "I'll give you a bonus point if you can spell it."

Razor gives her a suggestive wink, the tip of his tongue circling his full lips as he reaches for Astra's hand. Part of me wants to warn him not to, but the other part thinks he deserves what he's about to get. He takes her hand.

"Instead of spelling it, why don't I show you just how much testosterone I got, baby?"

A feral smirk flickers across Astra's lips, and I grimace, knowing what's coming. In one deft movement, she pulls her hand from his and bends his wrist back awkwardly, drawing a sharp squeal of pain from the man.

"Lemme go! Lemme go! Let go of my wrist—you're gonna break it!" he cries.

Astra holds it for another couple of seconds before letting go of Razor. He shrinks back in the booth, cupping his injured wrist with his other hand and glares at her hatefully. Astra stares back at him, grinning darkly.

"You need to learn to keep your hands to yourself, Hector," she snarls.

Razor sneers. "Screw yourself, bi—"

"Enough," Poke, aka Drew Graves, snaps.

Razor falls silent, telling me who the top dog in this little outfit is. Poke seems to be the brains while Razor and Bullet, if I had to guess, serve as the muscle. He turns back to us, his lips slightly upturned, amusement still glittering in his eyes.

"What can we do for you, Officers?" he asks pleasantly.

"Agents, actually," I correct him. "Wilder, Russo, and Boyle, FBI."

He nods, feigning being impressed. "Wow. And what makes us so special that the feds are coming to talk to us?"

"Don't flatter yourself. You're not special," Paige answers.

His expression darkens slightly, but he catches himself and manages to keep his demeanor light and pleasant.

"All right. What can we do for you, Agents?" he asks.

"We're here about Dustin Kemper," I say.

"Yeah? What about him?"

"He's dead."

"Yeah, we heard," he responds. "People talk."

"If you think we had somethin' to do with that fool gettin' capped, you're wrong," Bullet says hotly. "Agents."

"Are we though?" I ask.

"You are. Very wrong," Poke replies.

"And can you tell us where you were the night he was killed?"

"Probably here," he says. "We're always here."

"Any way you can prove that?" Astra asks.

"Talk to Tony," Razor says. "He's behind the bar."

I glance at the bartender to find him watching us with interest. "Anybody else who can confirm your alibi?"

"We didn't do it, Agents," Poke says testily.

"I heard you had issues with him."

Bullet scoffs. "Dude had *issues* with everybody. Deadbeat junkies tend to be like that. Takin' product and not payin' your bills has that effect and is a sure way to catch a beatdown."

"He caught a little more than a beatdown," Paige says.

"Wasn't us," Poke tells us. "Wouldn't do us any good to kill the dude. He owed us money, and dead dudes don't pay."

"He wasn't paying anyway," Astra says. "Maybe you got tired of waiting for something that didn't look like it was coming."

Poke pulls a face. "Come on. We're businessmen. We're not killers."

"Businessmen, huh?" I ask.

A cocky grin creases his lips. "Yep. We've got that entrepreneurial spirit."

"And what business are you in?" I ask.

"We're in the business of happiness," he replies. "We help people escape from their miserable lives and feel good for a little while."

"Tell me something, how is it that members of rival gangs are sitting at this table together?" Astra asks. "Correct me if I'm wrong, but you were a member of the West Side Kings, weren't you, Raymund? And Hector, you were one of the Disciples, yeah?"

"We saw the error of our ways," Bullet says. "We're reformed."

"Yeah, we left that life behind and went into business for ourselves," Razor adds.

"And your business model depends on people paying their debts, right?" I ask.

"Of course," Poke says.

"And if they don't pay, there are consequences, right?"

Poke spreads his hands out in front of him. "Look, I'm not gonna lie. Dustin was behind, and that was a problem for us. Yeah, we tuned him up pretty good to encourage him to pay his tab," he says. "But we didn't kill him. That's just bad business."

"Unless you were trying to send a message to anybody else who might be thinking about not paying their tab," Paige says.

Poke's face hardens, and his lips curl back over his teeth. "Look. We do a lot you law enforcement types might not be too thrilled with, but we didn't kill the dude. I don't know how many different ways I can tell you that before you get it through your heads."

I exchange glances with Astra and Paige. I'm having trouble with this one simply because I think he's telling me the truth. They're bad guys, to be sure. But they might actually be innocent of Dustin's murder. We'll have to dig into their alibis, of course, and drill down on their movements that night, but my gut is telling me we need to look elsewhere to find Dustin's killer.

"I've got one more question," I say.

"What else?" Poke snaps.

"I assume you fine, upstanding businessmen are carrying?"

"I can neither confirm, nor deny. And you don't have probable cause to search us."

"Easiest way to get us off your back is to show us your pieces," I say.

"What, so you can arrest us for havin' them on us?" Razor sneers. "You ain't nearly as slick as you think you are, *chica*."

"This is all off the record," Astra adds, seeming to catch on to where I'm going with this. "Let us see what you've got."

Bullet and Razor turn to Poke, who hasn't taken his cold, dead eyes off me. He purses his lips, then reaches behind him and pulls a handgun out of his waistband, then sets it down on the table with a hard thud.

"Ruger LCP," I say. "It's a .380."

"Lady knows her guns," he replies, then nods to his partners. "Whip 'em out."

Razor grins suggestively, his gold front teeth gleaming in the dim light as he turns to Astra, who holds a finger up.

"Don't even think it," she says.

"Show them your guns, you idiots. Having them hanging around here is bad for business," Poke grunts. "Let's go."

Bullet hesitantly pulls out a black Glock 21, a .45 caliber, while Razor reluctantly shows us his Rock Island 38 Super. None of them are carrying nine-millimeters.

"These your only weapons?" I ask.

"I've got a couple of shotguns at home," Poke says.

"I've got a .22 rifle," Razor tells us.

"I've got a MAC-10," Bullet says. "It don't work though."

"Thank God for small favors," Paige mutters.

"What was Dustin killed with?" Poke asks.

"Nine mil," I reply.

"As you can see, none of us has a nine," he says.

"All right, thank you for your time, gentlemen," I say.

"That's it?" Razor asks in disbelief.

"That's it."

"Wow," he replies. "I've never known a cop to keep their word."

"Must be all the estrogen making us soft," Astra says with a toothy smile.

"Have a nice day," I say and lead Astra and Paige out of the Wagon Wheel.

CHAPTER FIFTEEN

ATF Operational Center, Southwest Division; Phoenix, AZ

"STILL NO LUCK ON FINDING THE BREACH," NINA SAYS as we step into our makeshift war room.

"Keep looking. We need to know who and how," I say. "Rick, do me a favor and ping Razor, Poke, and Bullet's phones. I want to know where all three of those clowns were around the window of Dustin's murder. That was what, between eleven and three?"

"Correct," Nina affirms.

"Got it. On it," he says.

I drop into my chair at the table and give Rick a minute to work his magic. As he does, I think more about our conversation with Poke and his associates. The more I replay it in my head, the more convinced I become they aren't responsible for Dustin's death. While they could have dumped the actual murder weapon, which might account for their willingness to show us their personal weapons—an idea Paige suggested—something about them just doesn't feel right. They're all rough and have a few violent offenses on their records, but none of them have a murder—or attempted murder—to their credit.

Paige thinks one of them is our guy. Astra is on the fence. That tells me we need to find something quick that either puts them firmly in the suspect pool or firmly excludes them.

"All right, here we go," Rick says.

A map of the city comes up on the monitor, and a set of red dots appears.

"The red dots show Razor's movements the day of Dustin's shooting," he says. "The green dots will be Poke's, and the yellow are Bullet's."

"None of them are close to where the body was found," Astra says.

"But where the body was found isn't our crime scene," Paige reminds her. "Dustin's body was dumped there."

"Right, but none of them ping off any towers close to where it was dumped," Astra counters. "It looks like they spent just about the entire day at that crappy little lounge. They hardly moved all day. And that's on the other side of town."

"Maybe one of them left their phone there, went out, killed Dustin, and drove him to the dump site," Paige says.

"It's possible," she admits.

I sit back in my chair and frown as I study the map. The problem as I see it is that since my gut feeling isn't evidence, Paige could be right. It's entirely possible that they know we can track their phone data, so one of them left theirs at the Wagon Wheel, found Dustin, killed him, then transported the body to the dump site and ditched the gun somewhere. It's feasible. And with how vast the desert is, I stand better odds of being struck by lightning while being attacked by a shark at the same time I'm winning the Lotto jackpot, than finding the gun used to kill him.

"So, how are we going to rule them in or out?" Astra asks.

"It's a good question," I say.

Continuing to stare at the map on the monitor, I rack my brain, trying to figure out how we're going to get something that tells us definitively if these guys are involved or not. That's when I think about the weapons they showed us and sit forward as an idea pops into my brain.

"I've got it," I say. "It's underhanded and shady, but I have an idea."

"I like it already," Astra says.

"Their weapons."

"What about them?" Paige asks. "You said you didn't care about them."

"Here's where the underhanded and shady part comes into play," I reply. "I am certain none of those guns are registered—"

"Can confirm," Nina interrupts. "None of the three has a gun legally registered to them."

"Shocking," Mo says. "They struck me as such fine, upstanding, rule-following young men."

"They're just small business owners to hear them tell it," Paige replies.

"Anyway," I say with a grin. "We saw the guns. We know they have them, so that should give us probable cause to get a warrant to search their places and their vehicles. Mo, go get a warrant to search their homes and cars, then get a forensics team out there. If they had to move the body, there will likely be blood or trace evidence in one of their cars, if not their houses. If we get really lucky, we'll find the crime scene."

Astra whistles low. "Going back on your word like that is going to piss them off."

"The overabundance of estrogen gives me license to change my mind," I reply. "Besides, they're criminals. If they don't want cops screwing with them, they should find another vocation."

"Cold-blooded," Paige says.

I give her a half shrug. "A girl's got to do what a girl's got to do."

"Love the idea," Astra says.

Mo gets to her feet. "I'll go get the warrant."

"Paige, go with her since you can attest to and identify the weapons you saw," I say.

"Let's roll," she chirps excitedly as she jumps up.

Paige and Mo head out to get the warrant and execute the searches. We haven't yet had any movement on the cartel front, which is both good news and bad news. It's bad news because I'm not the most patient person in the world and this op is a lot like fishing. And I hate fishing. All we can do is bait our hooks, throw out the lines, then sit back and wait for something to bite. Things never move with the speed I'd like them to. But this is the job. Something is eventually going to pop off. It's a matter of time.

It's good news because my cover still seems intact. The more time that goes by, the safer I feel. The flip side of that is that it makes me even more curious about our mysterious helper. They'd tipped us off to a trap and the real shipment. Why? Who is this person? And why are they willing to give us sensitive intel and keep my secret but refuse to work with us directly? Worse, they refuse to tell me who they are or why they're doing what they're doing.

I have no doubt this person has some ulterior motive. It could be somebody from a rival cartel looking to weaken the Ariases, if not undermine and destroy them completely. It could be somebody within the organization itself looking to move up the ladder. Those are the only options that make sense to me. The trouble is, that suspect pool is simply too vast for us to be able to feasibly vet them all and figure out who was behind the tip. The mystery person has their own agenda, and not knowing what it is concerns me.

Nina slides a plastic bag down the table to me. "Sonny dropped this off for you earlier."

"What is it?"

"Dustin Kemper's personal effects," she replies. "He picked them up from Tempe PD today. He thought they might be useful."

I open the bag and start pulling everything out, laying it all on the table in front of me. At the time of his death, Dustin was carrying a lighter, keys, a cell phone, his wallet, a pack of cigarettes, and not much else. I slide the cell phone back to Nina.

"See about cracking this," I say. "I want to know what's on it and who he was talking to."

"Comin' right up."

Picking up the wallet, I flip through it. His driver's license expired about six months ago, there's no cash, he's got a debit card, a credit card, and a few slips of paper. Pulling them out, I give them a look and pause.

"What is it?" Astra asks.

"This is a receipt from a diner the afternoon he was killed," I say. "Looks like he went to lunch with somebody."

"Not his girlfriend," Astra says. "Daisy said she hadn't seen him in a couple of days."

"Right. And I don't get the impression he's a guy with a lot of friends."

"Yeah, I don't get that sense either."

"Might be nothing," I say, holding the receipt up. "But it's worth checking out."

"Indeed, it is."

"To quote Paige, let's roll."

CHAPTER SIXTEEN

Eggs & More Diner, Roosevelt Row District; Phoenix, AZ

DEEP IN THE HEART OF THE CITY'S ARTS DISTRICT SITS
Eggs & More, a small, unassuming diner whose sign
boasts that they've been proudly serving the city of
Phoenix since 1980. And the interior of the place looks like it's
true. It's a throwback to the eighties with an overabundance of
neon, pastel colors, and music of the era playing. It seems as if
instead of refurbishing to keep up with the times, the owners
leaned into the decade even harder. It's clean and tidy. It's just
very... retro.

"Wow," Astra says. "I feel like I just stepped back in time."

"It's kind of charming in a way."

"I'm not sure what way that is, but okay. If you say so."

"Afternoon, ladies," a short, petite blonde twenty-something greets us. "Table for two?"

"No, thank you," I say and discreetly flash her my badge. "We actually need to speak with somebody who was working the afternoon shift a few days ago."

"Well, I was here," she says. "I usually work most afternoons during the week on account of me taking classes at night."

"Great. Maybe you can help us then," I say.

"Sure. And you are?"

"Is there somewhere more private we can talk... Elsa?" I say, reading her name tag.

"Yeah, of course. Just... give me a minute? I need to get somebody to cover my tables," she says. "Just wait right here."

"Will do."

Elsa darts over to a brunette girl about her age standing behind the counter and shares a few words with her. The brunette nods, and Elsa turns and waves over to a side station just off the main dining room.

"You're really with the FBI?" she asks.

"We are," I respond, and we both show her our badges again. "I'm Blake, and this is Astra."

She takes a minute and scrutinizes our badges and credentials like she knows how to spot a counterfeit. She nods as if she approves.

"So, what is this about?" she asks.

I pull out my phone and call up the DMV photo of Dustin Kemper, then turn the phone to show her. She scrutinizes it just as hard as she had our IDs.

"You were working the day shift the other day you said?" I ask.

She nods. "I was. From nine am to five pm. It wasn't super busy."

"And do you remember seeing this man in here? Do you recognize him?"

She squints her eyes and stares at it closely. "Oh yeah, I remember him. Yeah, he was in here the other day," she says, and then her face blanches. "Did he do something? He must have done something to have the FBI in here asking after him—"

"Elsa, going by his receipt, he was here with somebody."

"Umm... yeah. He was. He was here with a woman. She was around his age."

"Can you describe the girl he was with?"

"I didn't really get a good look at her."

"But you remember him clearly?" Astra asks.

Her cheeks flush. "Well... he was cute."

"Think hard, Elsa. Please," I say. "Can you recall anything about her?"

"I mean, she had kind of white-blonde hair," she said. "She was curvy. Had a nice figure."

Great. That narrows it down to several thousand women in the Phoenix metro area alone.

"Oh, they were arguing," Elsa says. "She didn't look happy. Like, not at all."

"Did you happen to overhear what they were arguing about?" Astra asks.

She shakes her head. "No, they stopped talking whenever I walked over, and I wasn't gonna eavesdrop on them or anything. I just remember it seemed pretty intense."

"You didn't happen to catch a name?" I ask.

"No. I'm sorry. Like I said, I wasn't really listening in on them."

A frown creases my lips, and I glance at Astra. She seems to be at a loss too. This is our most promising lead so far, and it's a dead end. Elsa's description is basically nothing. It's so generic that it's completely unusable from an investigative standpoint. As I'm trying to figure out how to salvage something useful out of this interview, my eyes fall on something that gives me a spark of hope. I point to the fixture high up in the corner.

"Those cameras," I say. "Can we get a look at the footage?"

She winces. "Those cameras don't work. They're just for show. The owner says they're just a deterrent."

And just like that, the spark of hope in my chest is snuffed out. Elsa must see it on my face because an expression of tense sympathy crosses her features.

"I'm really sorry," she says.

"It's not your fault. Nothing for you to be sorry about."

I pull a card out of my pocket and hand it to her. "We appreciate your time, Elsa. And if you think about it and can remember anything, please give me a call."

"I will," she replies. "He must have done something pretty bad, huh? I mean, to bring the FBI here, it must be pretty bad?"

"I'm sorry. I'm afraid we can't talk about an ongoing investigation."

She nods. "I knew you were going to say that."

"Just give me a call if you think of anything."

Astra and I turn and walk out of the diner and climb back into the Suburban, both of us more than a little deflated.

"An angry woman with blonde hair," Astra says. "I hate to say it, but Daisy has blonde hair. And she admitted they were having a fight."

"I was already kind of thinking that too," I respond.

"I didn't get that sense from her though."

"Neither did I. But how often is it the significant other?"

"Often enough for it to be a cliché."

"Right. So, let's go dig into Daisy and see what pops up," I say as I drop the Suburban into gear and pull out of the parking lot.

CHAPTER SEVENTEEN

Hair Haven, Roosevelt Row District; Phoenix, AZ

BETH CANORA SITS IN ONE OF THE PLASTIC LAWN CHAIRS set up behind her salon. She leans back and takes a deep drag from her cigarette and turns her face up to the sky. The sun glints off the piercings in her ears, nose, and lips. She's got so many piercings in her face I would be surprised if she didn't set off metal detectors when she went through them. Her fire engine red hair is up and bound in a blue handkerchief, and she's got an alternative-goth, pinup-girl kind of style.

"Daisy's been working for me for a couple of years, yeah. She's good. She's got talent, and her clients love her," Beth says as she blows a thick plume of smoke toward the sky. "I gave her a few days off. I mean, after what happened to Dustin … it only seemed right."

"That's kind of you."

She shrugs. "She's in a bad place right now. The last thing she should have to be worrying about is somebody else's hair."

"Did you know Dustin?" Astra asks.

She grimaces like she just bit into something sour. "Yeah, I knew him."

"I take it you don't have a very high opinion of him," I say.

"Should I?"

"That's not for us to say," I respond. "But what was your issue with him?"

She draws on her cigarette, then blows it out again. "Other than he was a drugged-out deadbeat, he was great, I guess. But I always thought Daisy could do better. She deserved more than what he was giving her. I mean, she had his kid, and rather than help provide for them, he was still out there doing his thing."

"We were led to believe he'd been clean for at least six months," I say. "Daisy—"

"Daisy is a sweet girl, but she's naïve and sometimes only sees what she wants to see," Beth says. "Dustin told her he'd been clean for six months, so she didn't dig any deeper. She didn't really want to know."

"I take it you don't believe him."

"He's a junkie. And what do junkies do? They lie," she says.

Her tone is acidic, and there's a bitterness in her eyes that's impossible to miss. Beth's disdain for Dustin is more than obvious and hints at a more personal connection between the two than she's letting on. She's couching her concerns in her friendship with Daisy, but it just feels like there's more there. I could be wrong, but that's the feeling I'm getting. It seems like there's something there, just beneath the surface that she's not saying.

"Beth, I'm getting the sense there's more to your relationship with Dustin than you're saying," I tell her.

She pulls a face. "Trust me, there was nothing between me and Dustin. I wouldn't have dated the guy if he was the last man on the planet."

I study her for a moment and can't shake the feeling there is something more to the story that she's not telling us. The silence stretches out, and she shifts in her seat, seeming to be uncomfortable. Beth takes another drag of her smoke and blows it out noisily.

"Look, I don't think he was a bad guy. He was just bad for Daisy. They weren't good together. It was toxic, and he was taking advantage of her," Beth said.

"Taking advantage of her?"

"He contributed nothing to their child's life. To her life," she explains. "All he did was take her money to go get high. Oh, he talked a good game. Kept filling her ears with promises that he was going to do better—that he was going to turn his life around for her and Amelia. But he just kept using her and leeching off her."

Beth's view of Dustin mirrors Daisy's mother's. It makes me think the two women are right about him and that Daisy's vision is indeed clouded—that she was only capable of seeing him through the rose-colored glasses of a young woman's love.

"You said they were toxic," I say. "Did they ever fight?"

She scoffs. "Of course, they did. They had some real knockdown, drag-outs. Always about his drug use and his broken promises," she says. "But he always knew how to sweet-talk her—always knew how to pour honey in her ear with new promises, and she always took him back."

Astra glances at me, and as if catching some hint of the silent communication that passes between us, Beth sits up straighter, her eyes narrowed and her lips turned down.

"Look, I'm not an idiot. I see where this is going, and you're way off base here," she says.

"And where do you think this is going?" Astra asks.

"All these questions about Daisy? About her relationship with Dustin? I see that you're trying to build a case against her. You think she did it."

"Do you think she did it?" Astra asks.

"Hell no."

"Do you think she's capable of it?" I question. "I mean, you do acknowledge they had problems—that their relationship was rocky."

"Going from a rocky relationship to murder is a pretty big jump."

"Not in our business," I say. "You'd be surprised how quickly people make that turn."

"Yeah, well, that's not the case here. Daisy did not kill him."

"How can you be so sure?"

"Because she was here the night he was killed," Beth argues. "She had clients up until about eight and was here another hour cleaning up. I've got security cameras inside the shop. You're welcome to take a look at the footage, and you'll see she was here."

Given that he was killed between midnight and three, even if she was here until nine, Daisy very conceivably could have killed Dustin and dumped his body.

"Do you know what she did after that?" I ask.

"She went home to see her daughter," Beth responds hotly. "Like she does every night. She's a devoted mother."

All we have to corroborate Daisy's alibi is her mother's word—which is to say there is a gaping hole in her timeline… one we're going to have a hard time filling in.

"All right, thank you for your time, Beth."

"Sure."

She gets to her feet and drops her cigarette to the ground, crushing it beneath her Doc Marten boot. The woman gives us a tight smile, then walks back into her shop and closes the door.

"What do you think?" Astra asks.

"I think we've got a lot of work to do."

"Anything breaking with the op?" I ask.

"Not yet, Cap'n," Rick says.

I sigh dramatically and flop into my chair. The long periods of nothing with the few thrilling moments is getting exhausting. The comparison to fishing couldn't be more apt. I feel like we're in a boat, sitting on our hands, just waiting for something to happen. Which, of course, we are. At least we have something to occupy our time and minds. I suppose in that regard, I should be grateful Sonny leaned on me to take this case.

"I do have an interesting piece of information you've got to hear, Chief," Nina says.

"Talk to me."

The monitor lights up, and I find myself staring at the booking photo of a young woman with champagne-blonde hair. There are dark half-moons beneath her eyes, her skin is shallow and pock-marked, and her cheeks are sunken. She's got the hardened, almost desperate appearance of a habitual user. It's too bad. She was probably a very pretty, almost wholesome looking girl before she started chasing a high.

"And... *voila*," Nina chimes.

"Who am I looking at?" I ask.

"This is Chana Alexander," Nina trumpets.

"And who is Chana Alexander?"

"Chana Alexander, twenty-two years old, high school graduate, took a few courses at the local JuCo, and oh yeah, is Dustin Kemper's ex-squeeze," Nina says.

"Okay, and why is she important?"

"She's important because Dustin took out a TRO against her."

My mouth falls open as I stare at the booking photo, and the wheels in my head start spinning wildly. Astra glances at me, and I can see we're on the same wavelength. Knowing he took out a restraining order against this woman changes things and is compelling me to look at the whole situation differently.

"Blonde hair," she says. "Curvy build."

"She has a passing resemblance to Daisy," I add.

"Looks like Dustin has a type."

"Looks like he has a type," I agree. "And it's very possible this is the woman Elsa saw in the diner with him the day he was killed."

"What was the restraining order for?" Astra asks.

"Umm... stalking. Vandalism. Criminal threats," Nina tells us. "It's pretty vague—"

I stroke my chin. "But shows there was some animosity there."

111

"What else can you tell us about Chana?" Astra asks.

"She's got a pretty lengthy sheet. Drug charges mostly, but she also caught some charges for assault and battery. Looks like our girl is not afraid to throw down."

"So, a history of violence, was possibly with the victim the day he was killed, and has an active restraining order against her," Astra muses.

"If all that is true, why would Dustin be meeting with her?" Rick asks. "Why would she risk going to jail for violating the restraining order?"

"Restraining orders only work if the police are called," Astra says. "It's possible they met to talk things out or come to some sort of peace between them."

"Or maybe they met because they were hooking up," Nina offers. "I dug through Chana's socials, and it's very clear she has not let go of her feelings for Dustin. She's almost obsessed with him. It seems like she got even more obsessed after he took out the TRO."

"We always want those things we cannot have," Astra notes.

"Right," I say.

Chana Alexander and this TRO put a new spin on this whole situation that gives us an entirely different direction to investigate. I'm doing my best to temper my expectations, but this could be the break we've been searching for.

"This is outstanding work, Nina," I say. "Absolutely outstanding."

"Hey, I helped," Rick chimes in.

"Gold star for you too," Astra says.

"Thank you."

As laughter ripples around the table, my cell phone rings. I pull it out of my bag, and adrenaline surges through my veins as my stomach tightens. It's my cover phone.

"Quiet," I say and hold up the phone. "Somebody's calling Nadia. I need quiet."

Astra jumps up and runs to the door, quickly closing and locking it as the room goes completely silent. I clear my throat and close my eyes, taking a beat to ground and center myself as I slip into my role. When I'm ready, I connect the call and press the phone to my ear.

"Yes?" I say in my faux-accent.

"We need to talk," Rico Nagy says brusquely.

"Then talk."

"Not on the phone," he replies. "Face-to-face."

"And why would I agree to meet with you in person? I do not trust you."

His chuckle is low and gravelly. "Public place. One guard. No weapons."

I glance at my watch, knowing it's going to take at least an hour to get into costume and character then get to whatever meeting spot we choose.

"Very well. There is a coffee house at the Biltmore Fashion Mall," I tell him. "I will see you there in three hours."

"See you then."

I disconnect the call and drop the phone onto the table. The air in our war room crackles with tension, and everybody seems to be sitting on pins and needles. I can relate. My stomach is churning, and my pulse is racing. We're at the brief but frantic flurry of activity that's intense and exciting in our fishing trip. I blot my hands on my slacks and nod.

"Okay. We need to get set up. We've got our meeting with the Prophets," I say. "Time to put the rest of the balls in play."

CHAPTER EIGHTEEN

Desert Grounds, Biltmore Fashion Park; Phoenix, AZ

TUCKED AWAY AT THE FAR END OF THE OUTDOOR MALL IS Desert Grounds, which is just a bougier version of Starbucks. After talking to Rico on the phone, Sonny got the makeup team down to the ops center where they did a quick but thorough job, transforming me and Astra into our Ukrainian counterparts in record time. I will never not be in awe of their skills. I barely even recognize myself as I look at my reflection in my small compact mirror.

From the corner of my eye, I see Astra get to her feet. Closing the compact with a click, I drop it into my bag and raise my eyes as Rico emerges from the crowd. He's shed his kutte and is dressed in blue jeans and a simple red flannel with a black T-shirt underneath it. A chain runs from his belt loop to the wallet in his back pocket, clinking sharply as he makes his way over to the table and sits down across from me.

A tall, lean man with a jagged scar from the corner of his right eye to the corner of his mouth stands behind him, arms hanging loosely at his side. His bodyguard has long black hair, a thick mustache, and reminds me a lot of the actor Danny Trejo. The man opens his black leather jacket to show me he's not packing. Astra does the same.

"I almost did not recognize you without your uniform," I say.

"It's just a vest. Not a uniform. And I'm trying to keep things here low-key."

"And why is that? Are you afraid there are eyes on you?"

"Always eyes on me. Comes with the job."

The corner of my mouth twitches. "I can relate to this."

"Oh, good. We have some common ground after all," he says.

"That should not be surprising given that we are in the same line of work."

"True enough," he responds. "So, did you want to pat me down?"

"Do I need to?" I reply. "Are you not a man of your word?"

"I am a man of my word. You said no weapons, I have none," he says. "I just thought I'd offer to make you comfortable."

"I'm comfortable enough."

"Mind if I pat you down?" he asks suggestively.

"You must not enjoy having hands."

He chuckles. "You're funny."

"Glad I could amuse you," I reply. "Now, what is this about?"

"You know what this is about."

"Pretend I do not."

The corner of his mouth quirks upward. "I have to say, I underestimated you. Hitting our stash houses is one thing. But hitting an Arias truck? That's wild. Do you even know who these guys are?"

115

"I am aware."

"Then you know these guys do not play around."

"I would think by now, you realize that I do not either."

"I can see that," he says. "Your boldness earns my respect. But you're playing with fire by ripping off the Arias brothers. You're going to bring a lot of heat down on this city."

My shoulders go up, and I give him an unconcerned expression. "Men like these… I have dealt with them all my life. And yet, I am still here, and I am thriving. Ask me where they are."

He sits across the table staring at me closely for a long minute. The wheels in his head are turning, and there's a thoughtful expression on his face. Frankly, I'm surprised he didn't come in here dropping threats and ultimatums. I'm also surprised he abided by the terms I set for our meet. I didn't. I've got undercovers scattered throughout the crowd, ready to leap into action if needed as well as a pair of snipers concealed with orders to put him down if I give them the signal.

The fact that he didn't storm in here with blustering bravado, waving a gun around and threatening my life, tells me he feels the winds shifting. It tells me that he might be more open to switching teams than I expected.

"You took our product and our money. I should kill you for what you've done to me and my guys—for what you've taken from us," he says gruffly.

"And yet, you have not. Why is this?"

"My first instinct was to hit back, sure. You hitting our stash houses put us in a pretty bad spot with the Ariases. I don't appreciate that."

I remain silent, simply studying him from across the table, and wait for him to go on. Rico is uneasy. His shoulders are bunched, and his expression is tense. My gut is telling me he's seeing how the board is being laid out, knows he's in deep with the cartel, and thinks the only way he's going to save his skin is to ally with me. Not because he wants to. Because he thinks I can offer him protection from the Ariases' wrath. The enemy of my enemy and all that.

"Wars are expensive. They cost money and blood. A lot of it," he says. "I've done my homework on you, and think I understand the force you can bring to bear. I've studied up on some of your past exploits—"

"*Alleged* past exploits," I say, pleased to hear my cover is holding firm. "I have never been charged with a crime."

He chuckles. "Right. Of course. You're slick. You're smart. And I'm not into fighting unwinnable wars. I won't waste the lives of my men by throwing them into a meat grinder for a cause I'm not really married to in the first place."

"And what cause are you willing to fight for?"

"Money," he replies simply. "Me and mine, we got to eat. It's why I went into business with the Arias brothers in the first place. We made a lot of money."

"This is something I understand well. I came from nothing and had to build what I have," I tell him. "I understand what it is to be hungry. To have mouths to feed. And I know you have to be willing to do anything to stake your claim. That is how I live my life and run my businesses—by being willing to do whatever it takes."

"Right," he says, eyeing me closely. "Doing whatever it takes. Is that what Taras taught you when you were coming up in Kyiv?"

It's a test. Rico is a smart man, and he obviously does his homework. By throwing out the wrong hometown and my uncle's name, I know he's testing me. He's trying to trip me up. Rico has suspicions, so he's trying to see if he can get me to blow my cover. It's a pretty transparent tactic, but it's one that works more times than it should on trained, undercover operators who should know better—who should be looking for tests like this.

"Taras was my uncle. My father was Stepan, and he was the leader of a small offshoot of the Ukrainian Mafia. He taught me much as I grew up in Odessa, not Kyiv," I tell him. "He was killed by a rival when I was thirteen. That is when I was sent here to live with my aunt."

He nods. "Right. That's right. I do remember reading that."

I lean back in my chair and fold my hands together in my lap. "So, what are we doing here, Mr. Nagy?" I ask. "What is this about?"

He strokes his goatee and seems to be considering his next words carefully. I've obviously passed his test—at least this one—I'm sure there will be others.

"I'm like you, Nadia. I'm just a businessman with mouths to feed. And I have a good sense of which way the wind is blowing."

"And which way is it blowing?"

"You've set your sights on Phoenix. Probably on the entire southwest. Right?"

I allow a sly grin to tug the corner of my mouth. "My plans are my own."

"You play things close. I get it. And from what I understand, when you set your sights on something, you tend to achieve it."

"Now you are simply trying to flatter me."

"I'm just stating how things are. This is what I've learned about you," he replies. "When you take over an area, you take it over completely and drive out your competition fully and completely."

"If I do not, if I allow elements to remain, I am inviting resistance."

"You're ruthless but not punitive. That's something I respect. That is something my current partners are not," he says.

"So, you are looking to make a deal with me."

"It's crossed my mind."

"And you are considering it because the Arias brothers are not pleased with you for losing so much of their product," I point out. "It seems to me that you are running to me to escape their wrath. You are looking for protection for you and your men. Yes?"

He frowns, and his face tightens. He's not a man who enjoys having his failures thrown back in his face or being made to look a fool.

"Cards on the table? That has a little something to do with it. I'm not going to lie," he says. "But the other side of that coin is the money. I can make you a lot of money, Nadia."

"How is this?"

"I have connections all over Arizona, New Mexico, Colorado, Texas—everywhere. If you want the entire southwest, I can deliver it to you," he tells me.

"And why is it you have never delivered the entire southwest to the Ariases?"

"They think small. They move small. They talked about expanding outward, but they never had a plan for it. They never acted on it."

"Or perhaps they had plans but did not share them with you."

He shrugs. "Possible. But that's their mistake then," he says. "From what I understand of you, you think big and move big. If you want to make serious money and secure your foothold in the southwest, you'd be smart to ride with me."

"And what makes you think I need you?"

"Because you don't have the connections I do. The Prophets have chapters in almost every single state. You want secure pipelines and protection for them? I'm your guy," he presses.

I smirk. "Protection? You couldn't even protect your supply from me."

He grimaces like he has something sour in his mouth. "I'll be straight up. You caught us with our pants down. I didn't know what I was dealing with. I do now," he says. "And I know the Ariases better than you. I know how they operate. When you start expanding, you need protection from them, and that's something me and my boys can give you."

I blink slowly, making a show of studying him. This is all going exactly the way I wanted it to go. So far, we're avoiding war and are taking the Ariases' key ally off the board. And if we successfully flip him, if the Arias brothers have any hope of holding on to their territory, they're going to be forced to come here themselves to secure a new alliance... and to possibly deal with Rico for his betrayal. But I can't let on that I'm excited about that. I can't jump too quickly and need to let this all play out.

"It is an interesting proposition," I say.

"If we're going to team up, there's one thing I'm going to need from you. I need you to show me you're all in."

"And how am I supposed to do this?"

"I need you to wipe out the Arias brothers. As long as they have a foothold here, they'll keep coming. And I can't do my job for you if I'm constantly having to look over my shoulder and play defense. Know what I mean? If we're going to work together, the Ariases need to be gone. They need to be gone for good. It's like you said, if you leave elements of the former regime behind, you're just inviting resistance. Getting rid of them is a win for both of us."

"You make an interesting point," I say. "I will consider your proposal."

His face tightens. He'd clearly come here expecting to sweep me off my feet and get me to agree to what he wanted with little to no resistance. Rico seems to be a man used to asserting his will and getting his way. He's clearly not used to having somebody dictating terms to him. That may be how things work in his MC, but I'm not part of his club and I won't let him think he can dictate terms to me. Keeping him back on his heels works to my advantage.

"I will consider what was said here today and get back to you, Mr. Nagy."

He stares at me for a moment, then nods. "All right. Just don't take too long. You just never know what might happen."

"Noted."

I get to my feet, and with Astra at my back, we walk away, leaving him at the table.

"So? How do you think it went?" she asks once we're out of earshot.

I give her a grin. "Even better than we hoped it would. We are in business."

CHAPTER NINETEEN

Pierce Residence, Holdeman District; Tempe, AZ

"DO YOU KNOW WHO DID THIS YET, AGENTS?" DAISY asks.

"We're still investigating. We just have a few more questions for you."

Daisy's eyes are still red, and she looks like she hasn't slept in days. She's a wreck. She leads us into the kitchen and motions to the table we'd sat at with her before. We take a seat as Daisy grabs a bottle of water out of the refrigerator then turns to us.

"Did you guys want something?" she asks.

"No, we're fine. Thank you," I respond.

She shuffles over to the table and slumps into her chair. We give her a minute as she twists off the top her bottle and takes a long swallow.

"You don't have any idea who killed Dustin?" she asks.

"We're running down a few leads. I'm afraid I can't be more specific than that at the moment," I tell her. "How is your daughter doing?"

"She's fine. She doesn't understand what's happening, thank God. I just put her down for a nap," she says and rubs her eyes. "What did you want to ask me?"

"Do you know a woman named Chana Alexander?"

Her face immediately darkens, her lips pressed together in a tight line. Her jaw is clenched so tight, she could probably bite through a solid bar of steel.

"I take it you do know her," I say.

"Yeah. I know her."

"Can you explain your relationship with her?"

"We don't have a relationship," she seethes.

"All right, can you tell us how you know her?"

Daisy snatches up her bottle and takes another swallow of water. It seems like she's trying to tamp down a sudden flash of anger. I give her a second to compose herself.

"I know her because Dustin cheated on me with her," she says.

"He cheated on you?"

"Well, yeah—I mean—the first time we were on a break. So, I guess that technically doesn't count," she tells us. "But when we got back together, he stopped seeing her. Or so I thought."

The gleam in Astra's eyes tells me she's thinking the same thing I am—that this is getting a lot more complicated than we'd originally thought.

"I take it he didn't stop seeing her," Astra says.

"He did at first," she replies. "But I found out he started seeing her again about a month after we got back together."

"May I ask how you found out?" Astra asks.

Her expression is bitter. "Because I found her panties in his car."

"Oh. Sorry," Astra says.

"I know this is difficult for you, but it might be important—"

A stricken expression crossed her face. "You don't think she—"

"We're not saying anything. We just need some information. That's all," I tell her. "Now, can you tell me what happened when you found her panties?"

She sniffed loudly. "I confronted him. I was upset."

"Of course. That's understandable," Astra says. "And how did he react?"

"He said he was sorry. He said he messed up," she tells us and sniffs. "He promised that he would break things off and never see her again."

"And did he?" I ask.

She uses the sleeve of her hoodie to wipe away the tears that had spilled down her face. "He did. He told her it was over."

"And how did she take that?" Astra asks.

"Not well."

"Is that why he took out a restraining order?"

She sniffs. "Yeah. She just went crazy."

"How so?"

"She showed up at his place with a baseball bat and just started smashing up his place. Then she went after his car," Daisy explains. "And when he finally got the bat away from her, she pulled a gun on him. She threatened to shoot him."

Her voice trails off as she takes a few moments to gather herself. I get to my feet and walk to the bathroom to grab a box of tissues. After I set it down in front of her, she pulls out a tissue and wipes her eyes, then crumples it in her hand.

"Thank you," she says.

"Of course."

"So, anyway, Dustin managed to talk her down," she continues. "He was able to get her to put the gun down and calmed her down enough to get her to leave. After that is when he went down and got a restraining order."

"Why didn't he call the police?" Astra asks.

"He cared about her," she said with a weak shrug. "He didn't want to see her get into trouble. She already had plenty of problems with the cops, and he didn't want to add to that."

"That must have upset you," Astra says.

"I wasn't thrilled with it, no. She's freaking nuts, and I wish he would have had her locked up," she said. "But he finally saw how crazy she is, and it was finally over. I was satisfied with just getting her out of our life altogether."

"Daisy, do you know what kind of gun she had?" Astra asks.

She raises her shoulders. "It was black. I don't know anything about guns. I'm sorry."

"That's all right. You're doing great," Astra replies softly.

It seems to be a pretty damning picture that she's painting. And everything she's telling us lines up with the information we've been able to dig up on our own. Daisy's eyes shimmered, and her nose was as red as her cheeks.

"Do you think she did this, Agents?"

"We really can't say at this point. This is just one avenue we need to investigate," I tell her. "It's possible she had nothing to do with it."

Daisy studies me for a minute, her jaw set. "How did you get her name?"

"We found the TRO Dustin had filed against her."

She takes a quick drink of water, a myriad of emotions scrolling across her face as she processes what we've told her. Daisy sniffs and wipes her eyes again.

"There's more to it than that, isn't there?" she asks.

"Daisy, you told us you hadn't seen Dustin for a couple of days before he was killed," Astra says. "Were you telling us the truth about that?"

"What? Yes. Of course, I was telling the truth."

"And you're sure Dustin hadn't been seeing Chana since he broke things off?"

She shakes her head. "No. I mean... he promised me he'd never see her again. I believed him. Why are you asking me that?"

We don't answer her question, and in that silence, she seems to put two and two together on her own. Pain and grief fill her eyes as her face reddens. It's hard to not feel bad for her.

"He was seeing her again?" she asks, her voice cracking.

"We don't know for sure. But we do know he met somebody for breakfast on the day he was killed. A woman with blonde hair,"

Astra says. "And if you're telling us you didn't see him, then it's possible it was her."

"Possible, but it's not definitive," I interject. "We haven't spoken with her yet."

Daisy trembles wildly as she buries her face in her hands and begins to sob, making me feel like an absolute heel. Not only is she dealing with the death of the man she loved, now we're telling her he may have been seeing the woman he'd had an affair with again. It's got to be a lot to take in. Daisy shakes her head miserably as the tears keep falling.

"I always feared she'd do this," she says softly. "She always told him that if she couldn't have him, she was going to make sure nobody did."

"She actually said that?"

The girl nods. "Yeah. More than a few times. That's part of why Dustin got the restraining order in the first place. He was afraid of her. But… it's been months. *Months.* I didn't even think about her when you came before."

"This is ridiculous. What are you doing here?"

We turn to see Shirley standing in the doorway of the kitchen, arms folded over her chest, her face pinched and angry.

"We just had a couple of follow-up questions," I say.

"Do we need to get a lawyer?"

"A lawyer?" Daisy gasps.

"That's your right, Ms. Pierce," I say. "But we were just trying to get some context for some information we uncovered."

"And did you get it—this context you're looking for?"

"I believe so."

"Then it's time for you to go," she snaps. "And the next time you want to talk to my daughter without me, don't."

"Your daughter is an adult, Ms. Pierce," Astra says. "She doesn't need—"

"Let me clarify for you, Agents. The next time you wish to speak with my daughter, contact our lawyer first. Is that in any way unclear?"

"No ma'am," I respond.

"Good. Then please leave."

I turn to Daisy as I get to my feet. "Thank you, Daisy."

I give Shirley a tight smile that I hope seems polite as we make our way out of the house. Everything Daisy told us tracks with what we know. I wasn't sure what we were going to get from Daisy, if anything, but she's helping to fill in some of the blanks for us, so this was far from a wasted trip. Taken as a whole, what we know of Chana Alexander paints the picture of a possessive, jealous, and unstable woman. Sonny isn't going to like it, but this is looking more like a domestic thing that got way out of hand rather than a cartel hit.

While he won't like it, if this ends up panning out the way the evidence is pointing, he'll still have to accept it.

CHAPTER TWENTY

ATF Operational Center, Southwest Division; Phoenix, AZ

"How'd things go serving the warrants?" I ask as I take a seat at the table.

"Not exactly smoothly, but we got it done," Mo replies.

"They were pissed," Paige adds with a snicker.

"Told you they would be," Astra says.

"They made a fuss but ended up cooperating," Mo says. "Their cars are at the lab being processed as we speak. I told them to expedite it and get us the results as fast as possible."

"And other than the shotguns that were mentioned, we didn't find any other weapons," Paige adds. "But they still could have ditched the murder weapon."

"Good. Good work, both of you. Thank you," I say.

"How'd it go with Daisy?" Mo asks.

"Fine until her mom gave us the boot. Again," Astra says.

"Momma Bear is fierce," Paige says.

"Can't really blame her," I say as I take my seat. "Daisy has been through a lot."

"Most of which, was optional," Astra says. "She made a lot of bad choices. Not leaving Dustin in the rearview a long time ago was just one of them."

"It's not always that simple. Or easy. In a lot of ways, this was an abusive relationship, and she seems pretty co-dependent on Dustin. You've seen her. She doesn't exactly seem filled with confidence and self-esteem," I say. "You also know how difficult it is to break those cycles. It's probably why Shirley is so protective of her. It's understandable."

Astra nods, conceding the point. She's sometimes a black and white absolutist... especially when it comes to things like leaving a bad or abusive situation. What she fails to acknowledge is that not everybody has her strength. Very few people I've ever known have had the level of confidence and self-esteem Astra has. Not even me. It's something about her I have always admired.

That confidence and strong sense of self she has is a gift not all of us have. Many of us deal with insecurities that are sometimes crippling. Those insecurities often lead us to make bad decisions, like staying with somebody who's lied to, abused, and/or cheated on us. We find excuses for them. We make up all sorts of reasons and justifications for staying in relationships we should have gotten out of long ago. Many of us don't have the strength it takes to get out of those bad situations. That's what I see with Daisy.

"So, what's our next step?" Paige asks.

"Rick, ping Chana's phone. I want to know where she was around the time of Dustin's killing," I say. "And while you're at it, ping Daisy's phone as well."

"You got it, Boss."

Astra cocks her head. "Daisy's phone?"

"I'm not ready to rule her out just yet."

"Aren't you the one who said she's grieving?"

"I just want to make sure all our bases are covered. No stone unturned and all that," I reply. "You're also the one who reminded me that the significant other is always a viable suspect. I just want to cover all bases."

"That's fair," Astra says. "If she caught him with Chana again after promising they were done, that might have pushed her over the edge. I can see it."

"Exactly."

Everything we've dug up to this point is leading us to think that Chana Alexander is our most likely suspect. She certainly fits the profile. But there's a nagging suspicion in the back of my mind that won't let up. Something about the girl's response is bothering me. I've been around long enough to know that judging a person's reaction in the wake of a personal tragedy is about the most unreliable way to judge them. No two people will react the same. Their behavior and emotional response to whatever tragedy has befallen them will be very different.

That being said, while Daisy's emotional outbursts are understandable and are perhaps even relatable, something about it, to me, seems over the top. In a way, it feels performative. It's almost as if she's putting on a show for our benefit. And underneath all her words, I hear a quiver of fear. This very well could be my own personal biases and a case of my seeing what's not really there, which is why I want to look into her a little deeper before dismissing her possible involvement. Hard evidence proving her alibi will greatly put my mind at ease.

"Okay, here we go," Rick says.

The monitor flares to life with the map of the city, and a series of red dots is overlaid on it a moment later. The dots, though, make it clear Daisy hadn't moved around much at all.

"These are Daisy's movements the day Dustin was killed," Rick says. "It looks like she was at home that morning before going to work at the salon where she remained until around nine that night. After that, it appears she went home and stayed there the rest of the night."

"That tracks with what she told us," Astra says.

It does. It also tracks with what Shirley and Beth both told us. It seems as if Daisy's alibi has been confirmed by witness testimony backed up by actual data.

"Okay, let's see Chana's," I say.

A series of yellow dots appears on the map showing that Chana had been a busy girl the day Dustin was killed, her path crisscrossing all over town. But the trail abruptly stops.

"What is that big blank spot?" I ask.

"It appears that she turned off her phone around eleven that night, then turned it back on at nine the next morning," Rick tells us.

"So, she went dark for ten hours," Astra says.

"Because that's not suspicious or anything," I muse.

"She pinged off towers near the diner Dustin was at around the time Elsa told us he was in there with our mystery woman," Astra notes.

Pinging off the towers near the diner doesn't definitively put her inside the diner having an angry conversation with Dustin. Nor does going dark prove she killed Dustin. They're suggestive as hell, but we still need to prove it with actual evidence.

"I see that," I say. "Paige, Mo, head down to the diner and talk to Elsa. Show her a photo of Chana and see if she can confirm. Also, show her a photo of Daisy and ask the same."

Astra turns to me, her eyebrow raised. "No stone unturned, huh?"

"No stone unturned," I tell her. "Just because her phone pinged at home doesn't mean she was actually at home."

"Fair enough."

Paige and Mo get to their feet and head out to the diner. Sitting back in my seat, I tap my pen on the table, trying to figure out what's next. We're still in a holding pattern with the Prophets and the Arias brothers, and if this doesn't pan out with Chana and

Daisy, we'll be back to square one. We obviously need to develop a wider suspect pool.

"I don't suppose Chana has any weapons legally registered to her?" I ask.

Rick pulls a face. "You're funny."

The chair squeaks as I sit back and turn my face up to the ceiling. "Well, we know she has a gun. We just need to figure out how to get our hands on it."

"Get your hands on what?"

I turn to see Sonny step into the war room. Rick pulls down what's on the monitor, and Nina closes the open file in front of her, drawing a wry grin from the DEA man as he turns to me. I spread my hands out in front of me.

"I told you that you're not part of this investigation," I tell him.

"I'm not looking to horn in on things, darlin'. I'm letting you do your thing," he says. "But if there's something I can help with since I have contacts in this part of the world that you don't, you just give me a holler."

"Thanks. I'll let you know."

"I'm going to go out on a limb and say you haven't found anything connecting Dustin's murder to the cartel, huh?"

My lips form a tight line across my face, and I glance at Astra who raises her shoulders, the question I don't want her asking in her eyes.

"He's right. He's got access we don't," she says quietly. "Why not read him in?"

"Blake, I promised to let you run your investigation without interfering. I've done that," he says. "At the end of the day, I just want to bring Dustin's killer to justice regardless of who it is. Read me in. Let me help."

"We could use the help," Astra presses.

I hate to admit that she's not wrong. Nor is he. We don't have the sort of law enforcement contacts in the city that he has. And if we're going to get our hands on Chana's weapon, we're going to need their help… and the easiest way to facilitate that is to read Sonny in.

"Nothing changes," I say. "This is our case. No interference from you."

131

He raises his hand, giving me the Boy Scout salute. "No interference from me. You have my word. Again," he says lightly. "I just want to help."

I blow out a long breath as I weigh the pros and cons of letting Sonny get his fingers in the pie. He's a man used to giving orders and having them obeyed. He is definitely not a man used to taking a subordinate role. I suppose I'm the same way. And knowing that makes me think that including him in this investigation will lead to a lot of butting heads. The phrase "too many cooks in the kitchen" comes to mind.

"Please, Blake. Let me help," he says.

Everything in my brain is screaming at me to say no—to find another way to get what we need that doesn't involve Sonny simply because I'm afraid it's going to be a disaster. And if I'm being honest, there's a piece of me that's terrified if I let him in and give him access, that the disagreements sure to arise from our differing investigative styles is going to put one hell of a strain on our relationship.

I know it shouldn't factor into my thinking. The status of our relationship should be the furthest thing from my mind. It shouldn't matter. But it does. I can't keep it out of my thinking no matter how hard I try. And I hate that I can't.

"Blake?" Astra prompts.

I scrub my face with my hands and try to silence the cacophony of voices in my head as I focus my thoughts. I tell myself that Sonny and I do not matter right now. Our relationship is irrelevant. All that matters right now is getting justice for the victim of this crime. The only thing I need to be thinking about is doing right by Dustin and trying to bring in his killer. The case— the job—is the only thing that matters. It's the only thing I should be thinking about.

"All right," I say, my eyes fixed firmly on Sonny. "But this is *my* case. What *I* say goes."

"What you say goes, Boss," he replies with a crooked grin.

I give Astra a nod. "Read him in."

She fills him in on the investigation so far, which takes an appallingly short amount of time. He listens, the wheels in his head spinning. But he surprisingly takes the news that this is shaping up to be a domestic incident, rather than a cartel hit, a lot better than I thought he would. When Astra is done speaking, he nods.

"So, you need to get this Chana's weapon?" he asks.

"It would be nice."

He tips me a wink. "I've got an idea how to do that."

"Yeah?"

"Yes, ma'am," he says. "Just let me work my magic."

I groan but laugh. "Work your magic then."

"I'll get that in the works," he says. "Now that we have that out of the way, we all need to talk about our op. We've got some movement."

I stare at him, incredulously. "Way to bury the lede."

"I didn't want to interrupt what you had goin' on," he says lightly. "And now that we've taken care of that, let's move on to this."

Frustrated, I blow a lock of hair out of my face. "The floor is yours."

CHAPTER
TWENTY-ONE

ATF Operational Center, Southwest Division; Phoenix, AZ

"WE'VE GOTTEN WORD THROUGH THE PIPELINE that Santiago and Diego will be coming to the US in the very near future," Sonny says.

A surge of excitement, blended with irritation, rushes through me like a tsunami.

"And you didn't lead with that? Seriously?" I ask.

He gives me a toothy smirk. "It's not like they're here right now. We could afford to wait the five minutes to finish up with Dustin's case."

I roll my eyes but try to tamp down my annoyance with him. The Arias brothers are the only reason we came to Arizona in the first place. It's the case that should be at the top of the list. Dustin's case, as callous as it is to say, is our side project and the one we can afford to put off. I know it means a lot to Sonny, but it's a lower priority than our cartel op.

As much as I want to chastise him for putting Dustin's murder ahead of our op, I swallow it down. It won't do anybody any good to get into an argument about it. And ultimately, he's right. We have time to plan for the Arias op. I'm just upset because it seems like he's stepping on my toes. This is my op—and my case—and I don't like anybody else dictating the pace of events to me. Which is what he did.

As if picking up on my irritation, Sonny adopts a conciliatory expression. "You're right. I should have brought this up first. My bad. I apologize."

His apology takes the steam out of my annoyance, and I sit back in my chair as if deflated. Astra's lips quiver like she's holding in a laugh.

"Did you want to break out the rulers and measure them right here?" she asks.

"I'm game," Sonny says.

I want to be mad, but when everybody else starts laughing, I can't stop from joining in. A laugh bursts from my mouth despite my best efforts to hold on to my irritation.

"Shut it," I tell her.

"So, we're not measuring?" Sonny asks.

"You shut it too."

"Shutting it," he replies as he tries to keep the smirk off his face.

The laughter eventually tapers off, the heavy air in the room suddenly lighter. After having our little showdown, we probably needed a moment of levity.

"All right," Sonny starts. "Back to business."

"Please," I say.

"As I said, we got word from our CIs that Santiago and Diego will be traveling here," he says. "We don't have a firm date yet, but we're pressing our sources to get that. More than likely, we're not going to have more than twenty-four-hours' notice—if that. So, we need to get our plans firm and set so we can be ready to roll when we get word."

Things are starting to happen, and I have that sense of momentum building in my gut. To overuse the fishing analogy, it's like after waiting around with our thumbs up our backsides for far too long, we're finally starting to get a nibble on the line. We just need to sit back and let the fish swallow the hook and let them run with it a bit. That's when the real fight will happen. Now is the time we need to sit up and pay attention.

"We did what you asked, Blake, and started quietly putting out word on the streets that the Prophets are playing ball with Nadia," Sonny says. "With the Arias brothers scheduled to come to the States, it seems to be having the effect you figured it would."

"I figured they wouldn't be able to pass up the chance to put Rico and his boys down personally. I don't think the Ariases tolerate betrayal very well," I say.

"No, they do not," Sonny confirms.

"Dangerous game," Astra says.

"Calculated gamble," I correct.

"Semantics."

"Probably," I admit. "But it's getting the ball rolling."

"You said it."

Glory walks into the room pushing a whiteboard. Astra chuckles and nudges me.

"A woman after your own heart," she teases.

"Some of us are just old school like that," Glory says.

"I'm with you," I chime.

"Luddites. Both of you," Rick says.

"Quiet, nerd," Glory says, and he does with a smirk.

Photos of the cartel's organizational structure, as the DEA knows it, line the whiteboard. At the top, photos of the Arias brothers are side by side. Below them are their lieutenants, and below them are their soldiers. But it's the piece of paper just above the Arias brothers that catches my attention. It's the outline of a person that's grayed out with a black question mark.

"And who is that?" I ask.

"That is… well… we're not sure."

"Explain."

"We've heard rumors about the brothers having a boss," Sonny replies.

"Wait, they're not the head of the cartel?" Astra asks.

"As far as we know, yes, they are," he replies. "We've heard some people talking about there being a third person—somebody the brothers report to—a person who prefers to remain in the shadows. But it's just a rumor. It's nothing we've ever been able to corroborate. Our opinion is that the brothers themselves have been propagating that rumor."

"That doesn't make sense. Why would they claim to not be the bosses?" Astra says. "That world relies on machismo and swagger. By admitting they're not the top of the heap, they'd make themselves look weak."

"Actually, it's kind of genius," I say.

"How so?"

"By claiming they're not the bosses and spreading the rumor there's somebody above them, they've caused the alphabet agencies to chase their tails and waste time looking for this mythical person while they continue to run amok," I respond. "It's a way to make their enemies—be they US agencies or a rival cartel—waste time and resources looking for somebody who doesn't even exist."

Astra sits back in her chair and frowns. "That's devious."

"But kind of genius," I say and turn to Sonny. "How much time have you all spent looking for this mystery boss?"

He chuckles ruefully. "More than I care to admit."

I glance at Astra. "See?"

"In our defense, we're not saying there isn't another silent partner, but we haven't been able to dig anything up to substantiate it."

"Okay, well, all we can do is focus on the bird in hand," I say. "And that is the Arias brothers themselves. Tell us more about them."

"Weirdly, neither of them came up in the cartel. They actually grew up in an affluent family in Zapopan. Their parents were both computer engineers," he tells us. "Santiago is fifty-two—four years older than his brother—and is the brains of the outfit. He's ruthless and smart. He attended the Technological Institute in Monterey, and early on he seemed to be following in his parents' footsteps. But they died while he was in college, and he dropped out of school. His history is opaque after that, but the next time he pops up on our radar, he's heading this cartel."

"It would be nice to have some idea what happened in between him dropping out of college and becoming a drug kingpin," I say.

"It would be nice, but we haven't found a thing. And trust me, we've looked," he says. "But we believe he started with running guns during that time. That business helped him make the contacts to branch into the drug world, and from there it's assumed he simply took over an existing cartel. It's the only thing that seems to explain his meteoric rise to the top of one of the most powerful cartels south of the border."

"Well, perhaps we can ask him ourselves when we drag him in," Astra says.

"Good thinking."

"Let's move on to Diego," Sonny says. "Now, this guy is bad news. Santiago is the brains and Diego is the brawn. The sociopathic brawn. He kills people just because he likes it."

"Wonderful."

I look at the pictures of the two men side by side and think Sonny's description fits. Santiago has a head of thick, curly black hair, a neatly trimmed beard, wire-rimmed glasses, and an almost scholarly air about him. Diego is bald and has a bushy black goatee. He's got a silver tooth, a white, puffy scar across his forehead, and tattoos around his neck. His eyes are flat and reptilian, and the menacing curl of his lips gives him the look of a man who likes hurting people.

"All those pictures you've seen of people flayed, beheaded, or killed in the most horrific ways? This guy's handiwork," Sonny tells us. "He doesn't pass it off to one of his goons. He handles all the wet work himself."

"Sounds like a real gentleman," Astra says.

"Yeah, you're not going to want to bring this guy home to mom," he replies. "I tell you all of this because when they get here, you'll want to keep your eyes on Diego the most. Santiago isn't much for killing. He will if he has no choice, but he doesn't have the taste for it like his brother does, and he will usually delegate the wet work to his hired guns."

"How many do you estimate they'll be traveling with?" I ask.

"Unclear right now," he replies. "I'd prepare for half a dozen. Maybe more. And these aren't going to be their normal muscle. The Arias brothers have a personal guard that's a lot like the old Praetorians that surrounded Caesar. They're all highly trained, many of them ex-special forces soldiers. They're cold-blooded killers."

"This just gets better and better," I say. "Is there anything else?"

"We do have one more bit of intel. We've been told that while the Ariases are coming to deal with the Prophets, their main motivation is to meet with a new distributor to replace the MC," he says. "And before you jump on me for not leading with that, it is just a rumor at this point. We have no idea who they might be meeting with, or if it's even true. We're still working on getting the details. These guys have become masters of misinformation."

I gnaw on my bottom lip as I digest the information. There are still so many unknowns that I'm not very comfortable going into this. If they bring a small army of trained killers along for the ride, I'm not sure how we'll be able to take them down without suffering collateral damage since I doubt they'd be dumb enough to set up in some desolate, out-of-the-way place. No, if they're coming, they're going to be posting up in a place where civilians abound just to limit our ability to react.

"Just a question," Astra says. "Are we going to let them wipe out the Prophets? Or should we have somebody watching them who can step in if needed?"

"My instinct tells me they won't move on the Prophets until they've locked down a new distributor. If whoever this mystery person they're coming to see falls through for whatever reason, it's possible they mend fences with the MC," I say. "But you're right:

let's get somebody shadowing Rico to keep an eye on things, just in case I'm wrong. They might wipe out the MC just for kicks."

"Diego would," Sonny says dryly.

"All right. So, now we know the players. Is there any other intel you're sitting on?" I ask.

"Nope. That's it."

A wry half smirk tugs the corner of my mouth. "Better be."

"Promise."

"Okay, then let's start running through scenarios and come up with a plan."

CHAPTER TWENTY-TWO

Cactus Flower Apartments, South Mountain District; Phoenix, AZ

ALTHOUGH THEY LOOK LIKE NEWER BUILDINGS, THE Cactus Flower Apartments are still shabby and rundown. The paint on the stucco is faded and missing entirely in places. Some of the red tiles on the roof are missing, and more than a few windows are either cracked or have cardboard taped over panes that are completely missing. And as we walk into the courtyard, competing strains of rap and country music are playing as loud as the stench of pot in the air is thick.

A pair of men are sitting on plastic lawn chairs in front of an open door that's got a Kendrick Lamar song playing inside. The man on the right is heavyset and is wearing black jeans, a dark blue sweatshirt, and a Yankees ball cap. His partner is tall and lean and has a gray long-sleeved T-shirt, dark blue jeans, and a Bulls hat on. Yankees hat smirks but doesn't even flinch when he sees us. Instead, he takes a deep drag on the joint in his hand and gives me a nod.

"It's for my glaucoma," he says dryly.

I laugh. "Is that so?"

"Sure is. You want a hit?" he asks and offers the joint to me.

"Yeah, I'm not suffering from glaucoma. But I appreciate the offer," I say.

"You sure? It's good stuff."

"Smells like it," Astra says. "You don't buy the cheap stuff, do you?"

He scoffs. "Why would I do that? You pay twice as much to get half as high."

"That's an excellent point," I agree.

"Feds, huh?" Yankees hat asks.

"What makes you say that?"

"Y'all are wearin' some expensive suits. Locals don't dress half as sharp," Bulls hat replies. "Y'all must be pullin' government money to dress like that."

Astra and I laugh. These two are perceptive. Or they've had a lot of experience with both local and federal law enforcement. Or perhaps it's a combination of the two. I flash them my badge, and they both whistle low, then chuckle.

"Somebody's in deep to bring the FBI to their door," Yankees hat says.

"Nothing too heavy. Just looking for some information right now," I reply. "Listen, fellas, do you guys know Chana Alexander?"

They exchange a glance and snicker. Yankees hat turns to me and nods. "Yeah, man. And let me tell you, that chick is nuts."

"Chick is crazy as hell," Bulls hat agrees.

"How so?" Astra asks.

"Man, she's always screamin' at somebody about somethin'," Yankees hat says. "Always tryin' to fight somebody."

"She's got a temper," Bulls hat agrees. "We've offered to smoke her up just to mellow her out some, but she just threatened to kick our asses if we speak to her again."

"She's that unstable, huh?" Astra asks.

Yankees hat nods. "Yeah, that's part of it. The other part is she doesn't seem to like gentlemen of our... complexion."

"She said that?" I ask.

"More than once. And she's sure to drop the hard R on it," Yankees hat says.

"Wow," Astra replies.

"She ain't shy about usin' that hard R; that's for sure. It shouldn't, but every time she drops it, it makes me laugh," Bulls hat agrees.

"Same," Yankees hat says.

The two men laugh heartily. It's good they can find the humor in somebody else's racism, I guess. I tend to give people the benefit of the doubt, but I've got lines in the sand that when crossed, it's hard to come back from. And what the guys here are telling me is one of them.

"Like we said," Yankees hat says. "Chick is crazy."

"She sounds like a real peach," Astra says.

"Is she home?" I ask.

"Yeah, man," Yankees hat says and points to a second-floor unit in the far corner. "Heard her yellin' at somebody about half an hour ago. That chick needs to learn to mellow out, or I swear to God she's going to have an aneurysm."

"I'll be sure to pass on your concerns," I tell them dryly.

"I'd rather you not mention us at all, if it's all the same to you, Boss," Yankees hat says. "It's better if we fly below the radar... if you catch my meaning."

"Understood," Astra says.

"Hey, one more thing. Does she have a gun?" I ask.

Yankees hat shrugs. "I'm not sure, man. I ain't never seen one, but I wouldn't be surprised if she went strapped. That chick has some shady friends who are into some shady stuff."

"All right. Thanks for your time, fellas," I say.

ELLE GRAY

"Good luck," Bulls hat says wryly.

They chuckle as we turn and head up the flight of stairs and to the door they'd indicated. With my hand near the butt of my weapon, I approach cautiously, listening intently. As if expecting her to start firing through the door, Astra takes a position on the right side of the door, and I stand to the left, then reach out and knock hard.

"What?" a woman screams from inside the apartment.

"Chana Alexander," I call. "FBI. Please open the door."

I hear the two men downstairs snickering, having a good time with it all, and just shake my head. Astra grins wide.

"What the hell do you want?" Chana calls through the door.

"I want you to open the door so we can talk."

A moment passes, and nothing happens. I'm about to pound on the door again when it flies open and Chana Alexander stares at us with red, bleary eyes and her lips curled back over her teeth. Five-six with dirty blonde hair, blue eyes, slim but curvy—she very well could have been Daisy's sister. The biggest difference is that despite only being a year or so apart, Chana has a worn, rugged look to her that Daisy doesn't have. She looks like life has chewed her up a bit more.

She's wearing stained and faded pink shorts and a black tank top that's cut so low, it leaves little to the imagination. Her hair is mussed and sticking out in a thousand directions. She's got dark half-moons beneath her eyes, dried crust at the corners of her mouth, and the wired, harried look of somebody coming off a three-day bender.

"Chief Wilder, SSA Russo," I announce, as we flash her our badges.

"Yeah? And?"

"We need to speak with you, Chana."

"About what?" she sneers.

"May we come in?" Astra asks.

"No."

Astra arches an eyebrow. "Do you really want us airing your business out in public like this?"

She scoffs. "Like I give a damn what any of the dirtbags around here think."

"Look, if you're worried about us seeing any drugs or paraphernalia—"

"I'm not," she cuts Astra off. "I just don't want you in my place. And unless you got a warrant, you got no reason to come in."

She's right. If she'd been on probation, we could have entered her residence over her objections and rattled her cage about whatever we found. But she's not, so we can't.

"All right. Fair enough," I say evenly. "We're here about Dustin Kemper."

The words had barely cleared my lips when an expression of anguish crosses her face. Tears race down her cheeks, and she bows her head, her shoulders trembling as she fights to keep from breaking down. Chana wraps her arms around her midsection, hugging herself protectively. It's not hard to see her pain. Or possibly it's her sense of guilt pressing down on her. We give her a few moments to gather herself, and when she's ready, she finally raises her head again.

"Wh—what about it? I heard he's dead," she said, her voice quavering.

"Yes, he was unfortunately killed—"

"So, why are you at *my* door? You think I did it or something?"

"Did you?" Astra asks.

Her face darkens with anger as she glares at Astra with eyes narrowed to slits. "No. I didn't kill Dustin. What the hell kind of question is that?"

"A necessary one," I say.

"Well, whatever. But no, I didn't kill him," she stammers. Then in a slightly softer voice she adds, "I wouldn't. I'd never hurt him."

"Can you tell us the last time you saw him?" I ask.

She gives me a dejected half shrug. "It's been forever."

"So, if we were to tell you we have a witness that saw you having breakfast with him at the Eggs & More Diner, what would you say to that?" Astra asks.

"Then I'd say your witness is either mistaken or lying," she responds. "I haven't seen Dustin in months because of that b… *witch* of a girlfriend he's got."

"Yeah, imagine that. Not wanting your boyfriend to be shtupping somebody on the side," Astra says. "What a monster."

145

Not missing Astra's sarcasm, Chana glares hard as she clenches her fists at her sides. Her teeth are clenched, her body tenses, and I'm half-afraid she's going to take a swing at Astra. She really does have a temper. But she manages to reel it back in and unclenches her hands.

"Not that I need to explain myself to *you*, but Dustin and me, we had a connection that was spiritual," Chana hisses. "It was the kind of connection he didn't have with her. And for your information, he was going to *leave her*. We were going to be together. He promised me."

How she spits the word "her" like an epithet, unable to bring herself to use Daisy's name, isn't lost on me. I can also tell she really believes he was going to leave Daisy for her.

"So, you didn't have breakfast with him—"

She rounds on me. "Didn't I just say that? No, I didn't have breakfast with him, and like I've said a few times already, I haven't seen him in a long time," she spits. "Did I use words small enough for you to understand this time?"

"You did," I reply.

"Now, is there anything else? I've got things to do."

"One more question," I say. "Do you happen to own a gun?"

"No. I don't have a gun," she says quickly.

"No? Because we were told you shoved a gun in Dustin's face and that's what convinced him to finally take out a restraining order against you."

"That restraining order was *her* idea. Dustin would never have done that to me on his own," she said hotly. "And it was all crap to begin with. She lied. I don't have a gun, and I certainly didn't shove it in his face."

"A judge found it credible enough to grant the TRO," Astra pointed out.

"Yeah, well, I got no idea what to tell you. I don't have one," she responds. "Now, if that's it, like I said, I have things to do."

We have no grounds to enter her residence to search for the gun nor to detain her. She's being evasive and isn't telling us everything. Of that, I'm sure. But to prove it, we'll need to develop the necessary evidence another way.

"Okay, that's all we have for now then," I tell her. "We'll circle back to you if we have any further questions."

"So, do us a favor and stick around the city for a bit," Astra says.

"Not like I have anywhere else to go anyway," she grumbles, then slams the door.

With nothing else for us to do, we walk back down to the ground floor. As we head through the courtyard, the two guys we spoke to earlier are still sitting in front of their apartment, Snoop Dogg now playing inside.

"She's everything you guys said and then some," Astra says.

"Told you. Chick is crazy," Yankees hat says.

"Bat-crap crazy," Bulls hat agrees.

"Y'all get what you needed?" Yankees hat asks as we pass by.

"Not yet," I reply. "But we will."

He chuckles. "All right, G-women. You're all like Eliot Ness. You always get your man."

"You better believe it," Astra says.

"You two be good and stay out of trouble," I say.

That gets them laughing as we exit the complex to the street where we left the Suburban parked.

CHAPTER TWENTY-THREE

ATF Operational Center, Southwest Division; Phoenix, AZ

"PAIGE AND MO CHECKED IN," RICK SAYS AS WE WALK in. "All quiet on the western front."

"No news is good news," Astra says.

It is good news. At least, a form of it, anyway. The fact that neither the Prophets nor anybody representing the cartel have showed up to Frost is a good thing. It suggests to me that the Arias brothers are waiting to see how this deal with their mysterious new business partner shakes out before deciding what to do with Nadia. If they work out a deal with this new player, Nadia is expendable, and they'll likely move on her. If they can't work out a deal, they'll need to approach me as an ally and potential partner.

Our best chance to end this without a full-scale war breaking out in the streets of Phoenix is to identify this new business partner before they meet and find a way to put the kibosh on their alliance before they can even make the pitch. But the trick is that we need them to keep believing it's all still intact and get them here before springing our trap on them. It's a complicated and dangerous dance we're doing, and there are a million different ways it can go wrong. I'm just hoping we can find the one right path we need to travel to bring this to fruition.

So far, so good.

"Let's hope it stays that way. I need you two to dig up anything and everything you can on Chana Alexander," I say, then belatedly add, "please."

"She our bad guy?" Nina asks.

"She's not a good guy," Astra notes as she takes her seat.

"We're not sure where she fits into all this, but the woman has a temper, is known to have brandished a weapon, and had motive to kill," I say.

As Rick and Nina do their thing, I grab a bottle of water out of the small fridge in the corner, then return to the table and take my seat. Dropping heavily into my chair, I open the bottle and take a long swallow. Astra spins in her chair and stares at me, the expression on her face telling me she's got a thought to share.

"Let's hear it," I say.

"You'd agree that Chana is very hooked on Dustin, right?"

"I would."

"Wouldn't it make more sense for her to kill Daisy instead of Dustin?" she asks. "Bump off the romantic rival and he's all hers?"

"It does. And I've considered it."

"And?"

"I'm not ruling it out. But she's also got a track record of violence, seems unstable, impulsive, and very well could have issues with hearing the word no," I say evenly. "While her killing Daisy to get rid of her romantic rival makes sense, I think it's also just as possible that she got tired of Dustin putting her off or she figured out he was never going to leave her, got upset, and in a fit of rage, killed him."

Astra considers it for a moment. "It's possible, sure. But the fact that she couldn't use Daisy's name tells me she's already depersonalized her. She's not a person to Chana. She's a thing. Or more to the point, an obstacle that needs to be removed. The dehumanization tells me it's more likely she'd take Daisy out instead of Dustin."

"Yeah, I caught that too."

"And you still think it's her?"

"I think based on her track record, we at least need to do a more vigorous dive into her," I respond. "She lied about having a gun. And when you lie about one thing, we have to wonder what else she's lying about."

"That's fair."

"Do you have any other suspects you want to throw into the pot?"

"Daisy," she says, like it's obvious.

I frown. It's possible, of course. Under the right pressures and in the right circumstances, anybody can kill. I've considered Daisy as a suspect. But the woman doesn't seem to have the personality or the temperament of somebody who would pull the trigger. She's meek. Mild. She's let herself be a doormat and has taken Dustin back after he's cheated multiple times.

"Could be that she finally had enough of Dustin cheating on her," Astra offers. "And it doesn't seem to me like Dustin was as clean and sober as everybody seems to think he was. What if Daisy finally got tired of his lies, his infidelities, and decided to put an end to it once and for all?"

"All right, if we're digging deeper on Chana, it only seems fair to dig deeper on Daisy too," I say. "Let's see if we can poke holes in her alibi and if there's anything out there that puts a gun in her hand. She told us she doesn't like guns, so let's see if that holds up."

"I'll start scrubbing her socials and work a little more of my magic to see what I can find out," Nina says.

Rick scoffs. "Please. My bag of tricks is so much bigger. I'll work *my* magic—"

"Let's play a game," I cut him off. "The first one who puts a gun in Daisy's hands wins."

Rick and Nina exchange mischievous expressions, then turn back to their computers. After a couple of moments, Nina looks up.

"Oh, I forgot to mention that when Paige called in, she said they'd spoken with that waitress, Elsa, and she wasn't able to identify either Chana or Daisy," she says. "So, we still have no clue who had breakfast with Dustin the day he was killed."

"Yeah, I kind of figured that was going to be the case," I mutter. "Elsa was a bit too taken with Dustin to notice anything or anybody else."

"The restraining order doesn't mention a firearm. They documented the vandalism, but didn't mention a gun being used," Rick says. "And looking at the photos of the damage she did, all I can say is, wow. Chick is crazy."

"You're not alone in that opinion," Astra says with a chuckle.

"Sounds like your perfect woman to me," Nina says.

Rick flashes her the finger and laughs as he gets back to work. As they do, my cover phone rings, and I jump to my feet, adrenaline pumping through my veins. Astra dashes to the door, closing and locking it, then leans back against it. Rick and Nina both sit back in their chairs and fall silent. Seeing the unknown number ringing in, I figure it's either Rico or one of the Arias brothers; I take a moment to focus myself, let out a breath, then connect the call.

"Yes?" I answer in my faux-accent.

The line is silent for so long that I start to think whoever called had hung up. But then I hear a crackle and a soft hiss; a moment later, I hear that tinny, modulated, almost robotic-sounding voice.

"Congratulations on your successful mission," they say. "You have kicked up quite a hornet's nest down here."

By down here, I assume they mean in Mexico, and knowing it's my secret source who already knows my true identity, I don't see the need to continue speaking as Nadia. I motion to Rick and Nina to record the call and start a trace on the line to see if we can figure out who our secret friend is, or at least where they're calling from.

ELLE GRAY

"Your intel panned out," I say. "Thank you for that."

"It wasn't an altruistic gesture."

"Then what is your agenda here?" I ask. "What's the endgame?"

"All will be revealed in due time," they reply. "Also, tell your techs, Rick and Nina, that running a trace is useless. I won't be on the line long enough for them to get a fix."

Their eyes wide and faces blanching, Rick and Nina turn to me. I wave them off. Using their names is a transparent attempt to intimidate us. Whoever is on the other end of the line wants us to understand they've done their homework and create the impression that they can get to us.

"Who are you?" I ask.

"As I said before, that information is unnecessary. All you need to know is that for the moment, our agendas are aligned."

"And what is your agenda?"

"Same as yours," they reply. "To take Santiago and Diego out of play."

"And why would you do that? With your access to intel, I assume you're in the inner circle. Are you planning on taking over the cartel once we do your dirty work?"

The sound of the small laugh coming through the voice modulator is unsettling. It's creepy. It has the same disturbing effect on the others in the room.

"Yes, I suppose I am having you do my dirty work for me. But let us not pretend that you will not benefit from a successful operation," my new friend says. "The accolades you and your team will reap from dismantling one of the largest cartels in Mexico will be too numerous to count. You might even find that Agent Sonny Garland, fresh off a coup like this, will have a Golden Ticket to any job, anywhere in the country like say… Seattle?"

The amount and level of information this person has is well beyond disturbing. The depth of the homework they've done on us is partly meant to be a show of intimidation but suggests to me there's a deeper motive at work here. What that motive might be, however, I have no idea. But flaunting that knowledge the way they did somehow seems personal to me. It's like the person on

152

the other end of the phone wants me to understand they're three steps ahead of me.

"I want to know what your agenda is here," I say.

"I'm sure you would."

"You need to give me something here. I need a reason to trust you."

"My intel is good," they replied. "That should be reason enough for you to trust me."

"I need more than that."

"My information kept your team out of an ambush, allowed you to arrest a team of heavily armed men who were sent to kill you, and enabled you to seize a fortune in drugs. That should be reason enough for you to trust me," they replied curtly.

"It's not."

"It will have to be," their irritation clear even through the modulator.

"Listen, you're expecting us to do your dirty work for you. That requires a level of trust that we don't have right now. I need to know who you—"

"I have a gift for you."

"I want to know who you are and what you're about before I accept anything from you."

"Are you sure about that?" they ask. "What if I can tell you who the Arias brothers are coming to the States to meet?"

I grit my teeth. As of this moment, Sonny and his team haven't been able to dig up that specific piece of information. The clock is running, and the Arias brothers will be in the States soon. We need to have that name before they get here if we want any shot at figuring out where they'll be and putting a plan in place to take them down. We need that intel. But I'm just not sure we can trust this mysterious new friend. At the same time, I'm not sure I can afford not to. They've got me cornered.

"We're your only shot at getting what you want," I tell my new friend. "If you had some other way to get rid of the Ariases, you wouldn't be selectively feeding me intel."

"You're not my only shot. Simply my best shot," they counter. "I have studied your team well and believe you have the skills required for my purposes. But don't think for a moment that I don't have other methods of getting rid of them. You don't have the leverage here, Blake. I do. So, you can either take my intel, vet it, and figure out it's good... or you can be a fool and turn me down and try on your own to find out when the Ariases are coming and who they're meeting. But the clock is ticking, and if you don't act quickly, your window will close."

I grit my teeth and tamp down the anger that's flaring within me simply because they're right and it irritates me. Raking my fingers through my hair, I turn to Astra and shake my head.

"Fine. Who are they coming to meet?" I ask.

"Do you trust me?"

"Do I have a choice?"

"Not really," they reply. "I just wanted you to come to that understanding."

"The name?"

"Isaac Correa," they tell me. "I don't have the specifics of their travel plans just yet, but I'll get in touch with you after I find out. For now, though, you should be able to start digging into him and figure out what Correa is all about. That would be a good place for you to begin."

I quickly jot the name down on the pad in front of my chair, then drop the pen. I hate having to rely on intel from sources I don't know, let alone trust. But they're right—I don't have much of a choice but to take the name and vet it. I give a quick nod to Rick and Nina, silently telling them to start the due diligence.

"All right, I'll look into this Correa guy," I say.

"I assumed you would. I'll be in touch when I have more information for you."

"Great. But if I get the idea that you're playing us, I will come for you, and I will not stop."

"I would expect nothing less."

"Glad we're aligned on that," I say, acidic sarcasm dripping from my tongue.

"Oh, and one more thing, Blake," they say.

I roll my eyes. "What?"

"You're welcome."

The line goes dead in my hand, so I drop the phone onto the table in front of me. The tone of smug amusement in their voice, apparent even through the modulator, is like nails on a chalkboard and sets my teeth on edge. Closing my eyes, I hold my breath and count to five, then slowly release it, trying to settle my nerves. When I'm ready, I open them again and look at my team to find that Astra has an amused sparkle in her eye.

She grins. "Did you want to talk about—"

"Nope," I respond. "We've got work to do, so let's start by digging into Isaac Correa."

CHAPTER
TWENTY-FOUR

ATF Operational Center, Southwest Division; Phoenix, AZ

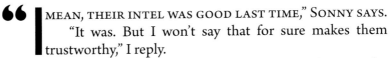MEAN, THEIR INTEL WAS GOOD LAST TIME," SONNY SAYS.
"It was. But I won't say that for sure makes them trustworthy," I reply.

"Why would they lie?" he asks. "If their goal is to have us take out the brothers for them, then why would they purposely feed us bad intel? It doesn't make any sense."

"And it makes sense that somebody would call us out of the blue and give us sensitive intel?" I ask incredulously. "Multiple times even?"

"Sure, it does. If they're trying to take over the cartel but don't want to get their own hands dirty doing it, why not pass on that information to those of us who will?" he points out.

"It's like we said before," Astra starts. "If they were looking to take us out, why would they have warned us about the ambush? Why not just let us walk into it?"

The chair squeaks softly as I lean back and tap my pen against my lips and think about it. They're not wrong. If this were about eliminating us, the easiest play would have been to let us walk into the buzzsaw that had been set up for us... not warn us then give us information that led us to a major bust. But that's not the only thing that's bothering me about all this.

"This person, whoever they are, has access," I say. "They're making sure I understand that they have intel on all of us. That they know my cover ID is more than troubling."

"Granted. It's very troubling," Sonny says. "But they seem content to wave that in your face without using the information to come after you. They've had more than a few opportunities."

"So far," I reply. "But we still need to figure out how they got it."

"Whoever it was didn't leave any fingerprints I can find," Rick says, sounding troubled. "We still have some other things we can do, but so far, the servers are clean."

"Whoever did this is freaky good," Nina agrees.

"The cartels are sophisticated these days," Sonny tells us. "They recruit black hats from all over the world... throw the kind of money at them not even the big tech firms can offer."

"In addition to the piles of cash, some of them just prefer living that outlaw life and can't fathom using their superpowers for good, no doubt," Astra muses.

"No doubt," I agree.

"Good thing we're not like that. I'm more than happy to use my superpowers for the greater good," Rick adds with a toothy grin.

"And the benefits and pension," Nina chimes in, earning a thumbs up from Rick.

"Well, keep looking. Our mystery friend might be good, but they're not infallible," I say. "We really need to find out who has access to our most sensitive information. It might not just be my cover ID that's been compromised."

"We'll keep at it, Chief," Nina says.

"Good. Thank you. Now, back to the topic at hand," I say as I turn to Sonny. "What can you tell me about Isaac Correa?"

On the monitor at the front of the room, a photo of Correa comes up. It's of him and a couple of other suits at what appears to be a groundbreaking ceremony. While the other two are still wearing jackets, Correa has his off and his sleeves rolled up. Tall and handsome, he's lean and trim with great bone structure and a warm, tawny complexion. He's got movie star good looks, salt and pepper colored hair cut short and neatly styled, a thin, trimmed beard along a strong jawline, and a dark, brooding gaze. He reminds me a lot of that actor, Danny Pino.

"Well, hello sailor," Astra says and whistles.

"Down girl," I reply with a laugh and turn to Sonny. "You were saying?"

"Honestly, not much. He's a high-end real estate developer in the area who's got a sterling reputation and from what I've seen; he's got respect from the movers and shakers in the city," he says. "He's never popped on our radar about anything."

"High-end real estate developer," Astra says. "Lots of fun and creative ways to launder the cartel's dirty blood money through his projects."

"Nothing we haven't seen before," I add. "In fact, it's a pretty old play."

"Can't blame the Arias brothers for sticking with the tried and true."

"If this guy is involved," I state, "we need to drill down on him and see if there are any connections with the Ariases."

"That's something I can help you with," Nina says. "Isaac Correa is forty-nine years old, holds dual US/Mexico citizenship, and graduated with a business degree from Arizona State and a Masters in real estate development from the same."

"A Sun Devil through and through," Astra says.

"Indeed," Nina replies. "He is also disgustingly wealthy and has taken a small commercial real estate business his father built and turned it into a billion-dollar empire. He develops high-end commercial spaces along with luxury high-rises."

"So, he builds safe spaces for the wealthy," Astra says.

"Pretty much, yeah."

"But what is his connection to the Arias brothers?" I ask.

"I'm not seeing any overt connections," Nina says. "He moved to the US with his parents, who also hold dual citizenship, when he was twelve years old—"

"Where in Mexico was he born?" I ask.

"Umm… in Jalisco. Zapopan, to be precise," she replies.

A hit of adrenaline bursts in my stomach as I sit up. Sonny and I lock eyes, and I see the same excitement in his eyes that's mirrored in my own.

"That's it. That's our nexus," Sonny says.

Astra snaps her fingers. "That's right. The Ariases were born and raised in Zapopan."

"It's an interesting data point but not definitive proof of anything," I point out. "Zapopan has a million and a half residents. Just because they were all born there doesn't mean they knew each other. It's possible they never even crossed paths."

"That would be one hell of a coincidence, darlin'."

"It would be," I agree. "So, let's find something that puts them in each other's orbits. Scrub their socials, look at phone records and school records, scan old photographs or yearbooks. Find me anything that will tie them all together."

Astra frowns. "That's a big ask. A guy like Correa, in the business he's in, is going to be very conscious of his image. He's not going to have any public ties to guys like the Arias brothers."

"Probably not. But he can't scrub everything," I say. "And he might not be able to control what the Arias brothers put up. There might be something they've posted that ties them together."

"It's worth looking at," Sonny relents. "But I tend to agree with Astra. I doubt you're going to find anything tying Correa to the Ariases."

"No stone unturned," Astra says. "That's our motto around here."

"It's a good motto to have."

"It's how we get things done," she replies.

"Noted."

"Okay, so right now, we've got a tenuous connection between Correa and the Arias brothers," I say. "But we have our mysterious friend telling us the brothers are definitely coming here to meet with him, which obviously implies a deeper connection."

"And let's not forget that Correa's businesses would also be a simple way for the cartel to wash their cash," Astra says.

"Haven't forgotten that. I was just trying to figure out how to best use that information."

"And what did you come up with?" Sonny asks.

"I'll have Mo look into Correa's business dealings, especially the cash flow," I answer. "Nina, send her a message and bring her in."

"Copy that, Chief."

"Why Mo?" he asks.

"Her background is in white-collar crimes," I tell him. "She's great at being able to pick up discrepancies in the accounting and seeing patterns that imply laundering or embezzlement."

"Makes sense," he says. "Wow. White collar, cyber, profiling—y'all really are a one-stop shop for all things criminal. It's no wonder you're able to do the things you do."

"No wonder at all," Astra replies.

Sonny tips her a wink. "So, what do you want to do? Go rattle Correa's cage a bit?"

"Definitely not," I reply. "The last thing we want to do is tip our hand and let Correa know we're looking at him. That'll spook the Ariases, and they'll for sure cancel their trip up here."

"Right. We don't want that," Sonny says.

"We don't have anything that will get us a warrant," Astra offers. "We won't be able to get up on his phones, computers, home, car… nada."

"I'm aware. So, we'll just have to be creative," I say.

"Why do I get a bad feeling when you say that?" Sonny asks.

"Because you know her so well," Astra replies.

"Whatever," I say, a smile curling my lips. "What I want is for you to detail a couple of your people to shadow Correa. Discreetly. Quietly. I don't want him knowing they're there. But I want to know who he meets with, who he's talking to… I want to know what he eats for breakfast."

"You got it," he replies. "I've got a good team for that."

"Excellent. Get them on that right away."

Before he can say anything more, his cell phone rings. He quickly pulls it out of his pocket and connects the call, then puts it to his ear.

"Garland."

He listens for a moment, and I watch as his expression goes from pensive to amused. A crooked grin touches his lips. He thanks the caller, then disconnects the call and turns to me as he tucks his phone away.

"We have a date," he says.

"Oh, do we?"

"That thing I was working with PD on about Chana Alexander?"

"Yeah?"

"It just paid dividends," he says. "Let's roll."

CHAPTER
TWENTY-FIVE

Phoenix Police Department, West Division Precinct House;
Phoenix, AZ

"THIS IS CRAP," SHE SHOUTS. "YOU HAD NO RIGHT TO arrest me!"

Sonny and I stand in the observation room watching Chana Alexander sit at the table in the interrogation room and scream at nobody. Her wrists are cuffed and attached to the bar in the center of the table, and she yanks so hard, I'm worried she's going to hurt herself.

"How'd she end up in the box?" I ask.

"You told me to work my magic, and I did just that," he says. "I do aim to please, after all."

"That is very true," I say and give him a wink.

"Why, Chief Wilder, are you flirting with me?"

"Maybe. If you play your cards right."

"Yeah? And how might I do that?"

"You can start by telling me how Chana ended up in that box."

"You are such a manipulator."

I shrug. "I'm just a girl who knows how to get what she wants."

"That you do. That you do," he says with a grin. "To answer your question, I've got some friends on the force here. They did me a solid by keeping tabs on Chana, and when she gave them cause to pull her over, they acted. And you're never going to guess what they found."

"Judging by how high she looks, I'm guessing they found drugs."

"Correct," he replies. "And what else?"

"There's more?"

"Oh yes. There's more."

"Tell me."

Sonny reaches into a large paper bag and pulls out a plastic evidence bag. And inside that is a black-handled Glock-17—a nine-millimeter. A bright white ball of adrenaline bursts in my belly and quickly flows through my veins, filling me with excitement.

"We need to get that down to ballistics for comparison," I say.

"We will. I just thought you might want to have a conversation with Chana about it first."

"Excellent thinking," I say.

Snatching the bag out of his hand, I head for the door. Sonny follows me out of the observation room and down the hall to the interview room where Chana is cooling her heels. Even out here in the hallway, we can hear her screaming. It's muffled by the door, but the string of obscenities flowing out of her mouth is clear enough.

"They Mirandized her, right?" I ask.

He nods. "They did."

I open the door and step inside. Sonny follows me in and closes the door behind us, then leans against it, folding his arms over his chest. Chana glares at me darkly as I take a seat across from her. I make a show of setting a file and the bag with her Glock down on the table between us.

"That's quite the vocabulary you've got, darlin'," Sonny says.

"That ain't mine," she grumbles.

The chain connecting her cuffs to the bar on the table rattles as she clumsily tries to motion toward the gun sitting between us.

"No?" I ask. "Then why did PD find this in your car when they pulled you over?"

"They planted it. This whole thing is a frame job," she responds. "They had no right to pull me over and search my car."

I casually flip open the file sitting in front of me and scan the report the arresting officers put together. I already know what's on it, but I want her to see me reading it.

"Looks to me like they had plenty of cause to pull you over, Chana," I tell her. "You were driving erratically and were pulled over on suspicion of DUI. The officers smelled the weed in your car, and you refused a field sobriety test. That's more than enough cause to arrest you and search your car. You've been in and out of the system enough times to know that. Hell, you've been in and out of the system enough that you can probably be an attorney by now."

"You think you're funny?"

I shrug. "Sometimes."

"She makes *me* laugh," Sonny says.

"Good for you," Chana sneers.

I rap on the table with my knuckle to pull her attention back to me. "Chana, we're going to send this gun to ballistics. Is there anything you want to tell us before we do?"

"About what?"

I arch my eyebrow. "Come on, Chana."

"What? What do you want from me?"

I tap on the gun. "You lied to me about having a gun."

"It's not mine," she replies quickly.

"Let's not do that."

"Do what?"

"Lie to me again," I respond. "The gun is going to be printed—and we both know your prints will be the only ones on it. And after that, it's going to be ballistically tested. What do you think we're going to find when it is?"

"I have no idea what you want me to say."

I blow out a loud breath and sit back in my seat. Chana sits across the table glaring daggers at me. But she's also fidgeting. Beads of sweat dot her brow, and I see a slight tremor in her hands as she bounces her leg wildly beneath the table.

"Jonesing pretty bad, aren't you?" I ask.

She mumbles something that doesn't even sound like words and turns away. Chana looks like she's starting to crawl out of her skin, and if she doesn't get a fix soon—which she isn't going to—she's going to be absolutely useless to us. Unless I press her now, she's going to shut down.

"Chana, you lied to me about having a gun," I say. "Did you lie to me about not having anything to do with Dustin's death?"

"I didn't lie to you."

"Did you kill Dustin, Chana?"

"I didn't kill him."

"Are you sure?"

"I didn't kill him," she repeats.

"Maybe you realized he was never going to leave Daisy and it upset you? I mean, he did have a kid with her after all—"

Her lips curl back over her teeth. "He was going to leave her."

"Was he though? I mean, why would he? He's got his family, he's got you on the side whenever he wants. Seems like he's got the best of both worlds. Why would he leave her for you?" I ask. "I mean, no offense, but you're kind of a mess, Chana. At least Daisy seems like she's got a good head on her shoulders and has something going for her."

"Screw you."

"Did you get upset that he wasn't going to leave Daisy and lash out?"

"I didn't kill him."

"Maybe you didn't mean to. Maybe you were just angry, and things got out of hand, and you acted without thinking about it," I say.

"I didn't do it. Why aren't you listening to me?"

"I'm listening… I just don't know if I can believe you," I respond. "I mean, you lied to me about having a gun. You see how that makes it harder for me to believe what you're telling me?"

She lowers her gaze and shakes her head miserably. Her tremors are starting to get worse, and she's bouncing her leg so hard, the whole table is shaking. The stress is obviously getting to her, and she probably needs something just to level her out.

"I didn't do it," she says quietly.

"I'd really like to believe you, Chana. I just don't."

"Then I don't know what to tell you," she hisses. "You seem to have made up your mind already, and I guess now you're just going to make the facts fit your predetermined conclusion. I mean, that's what you people do, right?"

"We're just trying to get to the truth."

"No, you're trying to pin this on me."

"That's not what's happening here."

As the beads of sweat roll down her cheeks, she scratches her arms like she's trying to dig something out of her skin, leaving long, bright-red furrows along her pale flesh. The woman's need for a fix is getting more intense. It's kind of sad.

She finally raises her head, her eyes burning with anger. "You know what? I'm done talking to you. Lawyer. I want a lawyer."

I sit back and look at her for a long, quiet moment. She just keeps scratching her arms and bouncing her leg beneath the table. Ballistics will give us what we need, but it would have been nice to put a big bow on it by getting a confession.

"Okay. That's certainly your right," I say as I get to my feet. "We'll get your lawyer."

She doesn't say anything. She just lowers her gaze and goes back to scratching herself again. The way she's twitching and digging at her skin, you'd think her arms were covered in ants. I gather my things, then head out of the interview room with Sonny in tow.

"What do you think?" he asks.

"I think it would have been good to get a confession."

"You really think she did it?" he asks, his voice colored with doubt.

For reasons that are beyond me, I know a part of him is still invested in the idea that the cartel was behind Dustin's death. But from where I stand, this is looking more and more like a domestic problem. Maybe that's just too common of an explanation for his liking. I just hope when we're able to confirm that, he'll be able to accept it.

"I guess we'll have to wait to see what the science has to say," I tell him.

CHAPTER TWENTY-SIX

ATF Operational Center, Southwest Division; Phoenix, AZ

W E WALK INTO THE WAR ROOM AND FIND MO GOING
through everything we've been able to dig up on
Correa's businesses. Rick and Nina have their heads
down and are banging away on their keyboards. All three look
up when I close the door behind us.

"All right, where are we at with Correa?" I ask.

"Everything I've found through public records paints the
picture of a squeaky-clean businessman. I haven't been able to

find anything shady," she says. "Now, if you were able to get me a warrant to dig into his not-so-public dealings, I'm sure we'd find all the dirt. In my experience, guys as successful as Correa always have skeletons in their closets. Some of them have entire graveyards. Most of them, if I'm being real."

"Believe me, I'd love to get you that warrant. But thanks to Correa's squeaky-clean image, we don't have anything that gets us close to being able to get us one. I doubt any judge would be willing to go out on a limb for us," I say.

"Can confirm," Sonny says. "Judges around here have to run for election, and not a one of them has the stones to go up against high-powered, rich-as-hell business types whose money is the lifeblood of their campaigns."

"Everything always comes down to money," Mo grumbles.

"Haven't you heard? It makes the world go 'round," Astra says.

"Yeah, great. We'll have to see if we can find a work-around that will make a judge more willing to lean our way," I say. "In the meantime, any word from Paige?"

"Just her regular check-ins," Rick reports. "All still quiet."

Sonny turns to me. "Oh, I forgot to mention that since you called Mo back here, I had Glory sit with the makeup team and sent her over to Frost to back Paige up. I hope that's all right."

"Yeah, that's great. I appreciate you having her back," I say.

The truth is at this point, I'm not expecting there to be any trouble. The Prophets seem to be hiding under a rock holding their collective breath, waiting to see how this power play all shakes out. And the Arias brothers can't act until they know if they have a new distribution partner in Isaac Correa. So, for now, I think we're safe. But it's still good to have Paige out there as the canary in our coal mine, and it's even better to have somebody as capable as Glory backing her up just in case something does happen to pop off.

"Okay, so what's next for us?" Astra asks.

Before I can respond, though, my cover phone rings. I hold a finger up to call for silence, and Sonny closes and locks the door. The call is coming from an unknown number, so I quickly slip into character before answering. When I'm ready, I put the phone on speaker.

"Yes," I answer as Nadia.

"It's me. No need for the theatrics," says the strangely robotic sounding voice.

"Fair enough," I respond. "Are you going to tell me your name this time?"

"No."

"Can't blame a girl for trying," I say. "So, I assume you're calling with more information?"

"You are a perceptive one, Chief Blake. Maybe this career as an investigator was the right choice for you after all," they reply.

Sonny hides his smirk behind his hand, then turns away. I frown at him and resist the urge to shoot him the finger. After all, he's got his back to me and wouldn't see it.

"What do you have for me?" I ask.

"The Arias brothers will be meeting with Isaac Correa three days from now, twelve noon, at the Desert Regency Hotel," my mystery friend says. "I do not have the reservation name or room number, but the brothers will be flying a private charter under assumed identities. I do not have access to those either."

"How is it you have access to all this other information but not their IDs?"

"There are limits to the information I can get, Chief Wilder," they reply. "The brothers are more than cautious. They're paranoid. They hold some information tighter than the US government holds onto the nuclear codes—like their secret IDs."

"Then how are you in a position to know their travel plans?"

"I just am."

I drum my fingers on the table. "Look, you're expecting me to take you at your word. And you're expecting me to do that because it benefits *you*… because you're going to reap some big reward from us taking the Ariases down. But you're asking me to do it on faith. I don't work that way. Trust is a two-way street. If you want us to do this, then I'm going to need something from you in return. We're not your own personal police force that you can send to do your bidding."

There's a long pause on the other end of the line, but I'm content to wait it out. The ball is now in their court. The silence stretches out so long, I glance down at the phone to make sure the line is still open. It is.

"Fine," they finally say curtly. "I know their travels plans because I made the arrangements for them myself."

The news is surprising and yet, at the same time, it's not. We figured whoever this person is had to either be part of the inner circle or close enough to see and hear what was coming out of it. But knowing they're making the travel arrangements for the Arias brothers suggests they're even closer than I expected, which makes it increasingly likely that this is a power play—that they're having us remove the Arias brothers so they can move into the top spot.

"Is that good enough?" they ask.

"For now."

The robotic sounding laugh is eerie. "Three days from now. Desert Regency Hotel. Twelve noon. Do not be late, Chief Wilder. Your team may not get another chance. And just remember, you stand to benefit just as much as I do."

They disconnect the call, and the line goes dead. I lean back in my chair and scrub my face with my hands, processing everything our mystery informant just said. I know we're being used. They certainly aren't hiding that fact, which should make me feel better about the intel. After all, if we don't get what we want in taking down the Ariases, they don't get what they want, which should mean they'd feed us good intel. But something about this whole situation is bothering me on a deep level, and I can't quite figure out why.

"Sounds like you were right," Sonny says, cutting into my musings. "Whoever this person is, they're trying to engineer the downfall of the brothers to move themselves up in the world."

"Gotta respect the ambition," Astra says dryly.

"I might if they weren't trying to claim the throne of a violent, bloodthirsty, murderous organization whose product kills thousands a year."

"Well, yeah, there's that," Astra teases.

"We need to figure out who this person is," I say. "Otherwise, taking the Ariases down won't matter. It'll just be a case of meet the new boss, same as the old boss."

"I mean, that's kind of the name of the game here, darlin'. Cut off the head of the snake, a new one will always grow back. There will never not be a new cartel head or a new cartel altogether," Sonny says. "It's job security, I guess."

It's a depressing but accurate statement. Taking on the cartels is just a big game of whack-a-mole with much higher stakes. Take one down, another one pops up an hour later. Because it's a multi-billion-dollar industry, there will always be another one lured by the prospect of getting a slice of that pie. Take them down, and there will be another. And another. And another. It's the sad reality of the world we live in.

"How do you plan on figuring out who this person is?" Sonny asks.

"I have no idea at the moment. But we need to find a way."

"I don't disagree. But until we find that way, I suggest we start planning for the takedown," Astra says. "We've got three days to get our game plan in order."

"Right," I say with a frustrated breath. "Let's do that."

CHAPTER
TWENTY-SEVEN

ATF Operational Center, Southwest Division; Phoenix, AZ

"WELL, IF THE ARIASES WERE LOOKING TO EXPAND all across the southwest, they picked the right guy," Mo says. "Correa has offices, properties, and construction sites across the entire southwest, and he's beginning to creep into the south and Midwest as well. I've managed to dig up some statements from Correa himself saying he plans to expand even farther, talking about having offices in all fifty states as well as abroad."

"He's ambitious," I say.

"And apparently capable of pulling it off," Mo tells me. "He's smart and savvy as hell. The man also knows how to cover his tracks. I haven't been able to find anything in the public records that even hints at anything untoward going on."

"But you don't buy that," I say.

"Oh, heck no," she replies with a chuckle. "I guarantee the man has more skeletons in his closet than Forest Lawn."

"So cynical," Rick chuckles.

"Experience doesn't allow me to be anything but," she replies. "I can't even tell you how many supposedly squeaky-clean people turn out to be dirtier than a pig in a mud pit."

Mo puts up a map on the monitor with red dots that show Correa's current office locations along with blue dots denoting his planned expansion points. He's got his fingers either currently in all the pies of all the major cities or is planning to soon.

"That's a lot of pies," I mutter.

"All fifty and abroad. That would be quite the distro network," Sonny says.

"Right?" Mo asks.

"So, how are we going to nail him?" Sonny asks.

"That's the million-dollar question," I groan as I lean back in my chair. "We don't have cause to raid his properties, tap his phones and his computers, or drag him down here for a chat. Hell, right now, we can't even look at him sideways."

"Sounds like our only bet is to catch him dirty sitting with the Arias boys," Astra says.

I turn to Sonny. "Anything from the people you've got shadowing him?"

"Nada. He's just out there living his life not doing anything shady that they've been able to observe," Sonny replies with a shrug. "Doesn't mean he's not up to doing some dirty deeds in places they can't see or hear him."

"I would be shocked if he wasn't," Mo says.

Sonny chuckles. "You are a cynic, aren't you, darlin'?"

Mo grins. "Like I said, experience has taught me a lot."

"Clearly," he says.

"Just to play Devil's Advocate here, but isn't it possible that our mystery friend is just full of crap and is putting us onto this guy as a distraction?" Astra asks. "Maybe the original intel was designed to get us to trust them, that way when they deliver this bit of intel about the Ariases coming to the States, it seems credible and has us looking in the wrong place while they slip in, do their thing, then get out again?"

I purse my lips and think about it. It's an angle I haven't really considered before now… but maybe I should have. As much as I'd like to say I couldn't get roped in and duped like that, I'm far from perfect; and if I'm being honest, I'd admit that it wouldn't be the first time it's happened. Sometimes I get so locked onto one theory, I give myself tunnel vision. And as much as I want to believe the intel is good, the truth is, I can't say for certain that it is.

"It's an interesting thought," I admit. "And yeah, it's certainly possible that this is all just one big rope-a-dope."

Sonny frowns and strokes his chin. "Huh. That's interesting. I don't know that I would have been able to come up with that."

"Don't feel bad. I didn't either," I tell him. "It's why we keep her around. She comes up with things like that sometimes."

"I'm not just a pretty face, my friend," Astra says with a wink.

"Indeed, you are not, darlin'," he says, winking back.

"Alas, it's as much of an uncertainty as everything else is," I say. "What we need is some hard, concrete information."

"I might be able to help with that," Nina says.

"Talk to me."

"I found a reservation at the Desert Regency that was booked by IC Industries."

"IC," I say. "Isaac Correa."

"That is correct, *jefe*," Nina says. "It's one of the shell companies we dug up that belongs to the intrepid Mr. Correa."

Mo grins. "What did I tell you? What legit, clean businessman has a need for shell corps? Those are usually used by people doing shady things."

"Sometimes," Sonny agrees. "But sometimes it's for charitable reasons, tax purposes, or any of a hundred other things. And Isaac Correa is a big-time philanthropist."

"Well, we don't know which side of the ledger he's on without a peek at his real books, not the ones he's cooking for the IRS," Mo responds.

"That's fair," he concedes.

"What matters most, though, is that we have a Correa-linked company making a reservation at the Desert Regency," I say. "That potentially puts him in the same room with the Ariases."

"If we believe your mystery friend. For all we know, he's hosting a fundraiser or something at the hotel," Astra points out.

She's not wrong. That's the worst part of this. We could go through all the careful prep and planning to hit the Ariases at the Desert Regency only to find that they're meeting not with Correa, but with somebody else in an entirely different location. Or maybe they are meeting with Correa, but not at the Regency. It's all guesswork and a matter of faith right now.

"We can keep vacillating and playing the what-if game, but unless we have direct and credible intel that points us in another direction, at some point we're going to have to roll the dice," I finally say. "Let's start prepping an op for the Regency. If we get any intel pointing us elsewhere, we'll pivot. But I'd rather we prep and come up empty than sit on our hands doing nothing."

"Fair enough," Astra says. "We going to do it like we did in Cleveland?"

"That was my thinking."

"What did you do in Cleveland?" Sonny asks.

"Sit back and watch us work," I say. "This is the reason you brought us here."

"It is. But I'd like to be looped in, darlin'."

"All in due time," I reply. "Astra, I want you to run point. Get in touch with folks at the hotel and get things in motion. But be delicate. We don't want them knowing who our target is—"

She pulls a face. "You think I'm a rookie or something? I know what to do."

I laugh. "Sorry, sorry. Do your thing."

"I will, thank you very much," Astra says with a crooked grin.

"I have something else you might want to hear," Rick says.

"Lay it on me."

"I was able to dig into Dustin's phone and found some text messages he'd deleted."

"And?"

"And they don't paint a very good picture of Chana Alexander."

"No?"

"Definitely not."

"Show me."

CHAPTER
TWENTY-EIGHT

Phoenix Police Department, West Division Precinct House;
Phoenix, AZ

SIT ACROSS THE TABLE FROM CHANA IN THE SAME windowless interview room as before. This time, her lawyer is seated at the table beside her glaring at me just as hard as she is. Chana is looking less fidgety and doesn't seem bent on peeling the skin off her arms, so I'm assuming they gave her a dose of methadone or something, which is a good thing. Watching her in the throes of a withdrawal was ugly to watch.

Her lawyer, a prissy public defender whose name I did not catch and looks fresh out of law school, purses his thin lips and taps on the table with his pen.

"You asked for this meeting, Agent Wilder," he says. "What is this about?"

"This is about giving your client one last chance to get out ahead of the train that's bearing down on her, Counselor," I say.

"And how is that?"

"In addition to the gun we found in her possession—"

"A weapon that has not been definitively linked to the murder of Mr. Kemper, is that correct?" he cuts me off.

"Not yet. Ballistics testing is not back yet, but—"

"Then the weapon is irrelevant. Until you are able to conclusively link it to Mr. Kemper's death, there is no reason to even bring it up."

A corner of my mouth quirks upward. He's a young and ambitious public defender who sounds like he believes himself to be the second coming of Clarence Darrow. That's okay. I'll play his game… at least for a little while. I glance at Chana who is pointedly staring at the table rather than at me. Her face is pinched, and her body is coiled and tense like she wants to come over the table and throttle me but has been warned by her lawyer to sit still and say nothing. He's obviously got her on a short leash, and she does not like it.

"All right, Counselor. That's fine. We don't have to talk about the gun right now," I say.

I reach into my messenger bag, pull out her file, and set it down on the table in front of me. He's eyeing me closely as I flip it open and pull out a few of the pages Rick printed for me, then place them on the table in front of Chana. She doesn't look up. Instead, she starts gnawing on her thumbnail, which already looks bloody and raw.

"And what are those?" the lawyer asks.

"These, my friend, are text messages from your client to Dustin Kemper," I say. "And if you read them, you can see a very disturbing pattern emerging."

"And what pattern is that?"

"These messages make it clear that Dustin was attempting to distance himself from your client. That he had asked her repeatedly to stop contacting him," I say. "Your client not only didn't stop contacting him, she started issuing threats when he would not give in to her pressure to get back together with her."

The lawyer picks up the pages and leafs through them, doing his best to keep his face neutral. I can see the corners of his eyes crinkling as he fights to stop the disapproving frown that's flickering across his lips. He knows how bad these texts make his client seem. He manages to keep his cool and throws the papers down like they're no more relevant than yesterday's newspaper.

"These prove nothing," he says.

I pull the page I'd intentionally kept behind from the file and set it down on the table in front of Chana. Her eyes flick to it briefly, and she draws inward, tauter than a bowstring. The lawyer picks up the page and scans the text. He can't hide the worry in his eyes, and this time, he doesn't even bother trying to hide the frown on his lips. He cuts a glance at Chana who is drawn so far in on herself, she's practically disappearing.

"Again, this proves nothing," he says. "This is irrelevant."

I reach across the table and snatch the page from him. "I'm not playing, Dustin," I read from the text message. "Drop the skank. I'm tired of telling you that we belong together. You know it's true. Drop her, or you will regret it."

I pause and glance at the two of them over the page in my hand. Chana is still staring at the top of the table, and her lawyer is staring at me with dead, expressionless eyes.

"Chana, it's over. I'm with Daisy and my baby girl. You and me aren't a thing anymore. You need to stop coming around, and you need to stop texting me," I say. "That text is from Dustin Kemper, just in case it wasn't obvious."

"Yeah, I got that," the lawyer snaps.

"Okay, good. Just making sure," I reply. "To which Chana responded, 'Don't do this Dustin. You're mine. And if you don't come back to me, I will shoot you dead. You get it? I will kill you.'"

I set the page down on the table and turn first to Chana, then her lawyer, giving them a moment to soak in what I just read to them. Her lawyer's expression is that of a man who just bit into something either incredibly sour or incredibly rotten.

"These texts paint a very vivid picture, don't they?" I ask, breaking the silence.

The lawyer clears his throat. "Words mean nothing."

"They tend to mean a lot with a jury. I mean, follow along with me here," I say. "Your client violated a restraining order in order to threaten to shoot Dustin Kemper dead. And guess what? Dustin Kemper turned up shot to death. Now, you're the lawyer, so you tell me … how do you think that will play out with a jury?"

He sniffs indignantly. "Words mean nothing without something to back them up," he says. "And again, if the ballistics on the weapon seized from Ms. Alexander do not match—"

"Wait—so you want to talk about the gun *now*?" I say, cutting him off. I turn to Chana. "This is your life, Chana. Your lawyer gets paid and gets to go home to his own bed at night regardless of what happens to you," I say. "This is your chance to get in front of this."

She's quiet for a long moment, but I can see her face darkening as she begins to shake. As if sensing a Chernobyl-esque meltdown coming, the lawyer puts a hand on her arm and starts to lean close to whisper something to her. She jerks her arm back and waves him away. Chana glares at him for a moment, then turns eyes filled with hate to me.

"How many times do I got to tell you that I didn't do this?" she sneers.

"Chana, these texts kind of make it look like you did."

She slams her fists down on the table, her face twisted with rage. "I didn't do it. I didn't kill him. I loved Dustin! How many times do you need to hear me say that?"

"Chana, calm down," her lawyer says. "Getting upset helps nothing."

"Shut up. Don't tell me what to do!"

"Chana, this is your last chance to help yourself," I say. "You're going to be charged with murder. These text messages show premeditation which bumps it up to first-degree murder. You're going to spend the rest of your life in prison unless they give you the needle. This is Arizona, after all. They still put people down here."

"Enough of the theatrics, Agent Wilder," the lawyer said.

I turn to him. "You're a lawyer. You know Arizona executes by lethal injection. The moratorium was lifted back in twenty-two. How am I being theatrical? I'm just stating facts."

"Your implication that Ms. Alexander—"

"Unless she tries to mitigate the situation, I'm telling you, she will be charged with first-degree murder," I cut him off. "And you well know that capital murder gets the offender capital punishment. Again, these are just facts."

"Trying to scare Ms. Alexander is unnecessary."

"I'm sorry if facts scare you. But that's really not my problem," I say. "Chana, if you have something you want to say, anything that mitigates the situation, now is the time."

"I didn't do it."

"Did he come at you? Were you forced to defend yourself?"

"I didn't do it!" she shrieks.

A frown flickers across my lips. Clearly, I'm not going to get a confession out of her. She's going to stick to her story.

"Last chance, Chana," I say. "When I walk out that door—"

"Go. Then go," she says. "I. Did. Not. Kill. Dustin."

"It sounds like you have your answer, Agent Wilder," the lawyer says.

"All right. I guess that's it then."

I gather up my things, taking a little extra time to give Chana another chance to change her mind. She doesn't. Slipping all the pages back into my file, I stuff everything into my messenger bag, then get to my feet. The lawyer's face is ashen, as if he knows the size of the hammer that's about to drop on his client but doesn't know what to do about it. Chana simply glares at me like she wishes she was holding her Glock right now.

"Good luck, Chana," I say.

"Screw you."

Shaking my head, I turn and head out of the interview room. Some people just can't be helped. Nor will they help themselves.

CHAPTER TWENTY-NINE

ATF Operational Center, Southwest Division; Phoenix, AZ

"OKAY, SO I SPOKE TO THE MANAGER AT THE DESERT Regency," Astra says. "She was cooperative but understandably concerned."

"What did you tell her?" I ask.

"As little as possible. Just that we are running an investigation. She agreed to book Correa in a suite on the top level and to close off the rest of the floor," she tells me. "Sonny is sending one of his tech teams in late tonight to wire the suite to give us eyes and ears inside."

"And you told the manager to keep this under her hat?"

Astra pulls a face. "What do you think I am, a rookie?"

I laugh. "You know the old saying, there are no stupid questions."

"Whoever coined that phrase obviously didn't talk to very many people."

"That's probably fair."

"She agreed to let us do our thing and to keep a lid on it," Astra says.

"Good. That's really good."

"Do we have a plan?" Mo asks. "And don't say, we'll do it like Cleveland because I wasn't part of your team when you were in Cleveland."

Astra and I share a grin. It's sometimes hard to remember a time before this team. It's become such a large part of who I am and of my career that everything that came before seems to have faded into the background—everything but the lessons learned, both the good and the bad, anyway. There have been some hard lessons learned. I like to think those tough times have made me a better person and a better agent. Experience is always the best teacher after all.

"We're going to isolate the targets, observe, and when we get what we need, we'll move in and arrest everybody," I say. "Easy peasy."

"Nothing is ever easy peasy," Mo says.

"Well, that's why we had the manager close off the entire floor," Astra responds. "Just in case things go sideways."

"As they usually tend to do," Rick chimes in dryly.

"We'll fine-tune our plan when we get Paige and Glory back here," I say. "We'll need all hands on deck to make this work. Nina, send them a message and call them back, please."

"On it," she says.

I stare at the pictures of the Arias brothers and Correa that are on the monitor at the head of the room and frown as I tap my pen on the table.

"What's bothering you?" Astra asks.

"I can't get what you said earlier out of my head."

"I've said a lot. Can you be more specific?"

I give her a wry grin. "About this all being one big rope-a-dope. That we're setting up on the Desert Regency when the meeting is actually going to be somewhere else. I mean, I hate to say it, but it's a very real possibility."

"What can we do about that?" Mo asks.

I shake my head. "Nothing."

"Then it's like you said, we can either sit here and vacillate, or we can do something," she says with a casual shrug. "Looks like we're going to have to roll the dice and hope we win."

"Yeah," I grumble.

I study the pictures again, my mind spinning as I try to think through all the different angles. But I quickly realize there are too many I can't see. There are just too many blind spots for me to feel comfortable that I'm making the right decision to press forward with this op. But not going forward with it and possibly missing our one and only chance to put bracelets on the Arias brothers would be an unforgiveable dereliction of duty. I'd fire me for that.

"What's your hesitation?" Astra asks.

"The horrible feeling that we're either walking into a big nothingburger or straight into a buzz saw," I say.

"As skeptical as I am, I doubt we're walking into an ambush. If your source had wanted to cut us down, they wouldn't have tipped us to the sicarios in the truck and would have let us walk into that face-first."

It's a fair point and one I made before. This is a lot of trouble to go through just to do what they could have done earlier. Despite my current misgivings and hesitations, I feel as if my initial instincts about this whole thing still hold up. This isn't about us. This is about something else, and we're simply the instrument our mysterious friend is using to get what they want. We're doing the dirty work for them. I hate knowing that once we take the Ariases down, this person will rise up like—as Sonny said—another head of the hydra.

But that's the job. We can't worry about what comes next; we have to deal with what's on the plate right in front of us. And right now, the Arias brothers are on our plate. What comes after that is anybody's guess, but we'll deal with it when it happens.

"What's bothering you?" Astra asks.

I shake my head. "I'm not really sure."

Something about this whole thing isn't sitting right with me. A lot of things aren't, but more than anything, it's this mysterious informant. They have information they shouldn't have. How they got it is still a mystery, but they seem content to simply lord it over me—to let me know they're a step ahead, which makes me more than a little uneasy. But somehow, it feels personal. I can't explain it—hell, I don't even understand it myself—but it feels like this person knows me. And that, more than anything else, scares me. Their personal, intimate knowledge makes me feel like I'm holding a hand grenade and am just waiting for it to explode.

"You okay?"

"Yeah," I answer. "I'm fine."

"Any chance of this mysterious informant sending cleaners in behind and trying to take us out after we knock off the Ariases for them?" Astra asks. "Get themselves a twofer?"

Leaning back in my chair, I give it a minute's thought, then shake my head. "I don't think so. If they had the pull to take the brothers out themselves, they wouldn't need us. It'd be a lot of risk and exposure for them. No, I think they're content to let us do our thing and give them a clear playing field to make a run up the ladder when we do."

Again, I've given it a lot of thought, and although I can't explain it, I don't think our mysterious new friend has an ill intent. As has been pointed out, if they wanted to take us—take *me*—out, they've had more than enough opportunity. The fact that they know who I really am and—presumably—have a plethora of personal information, as they've intimated, they could have used it to send assassins to put us down already. That they haven't suggests their intention isn't to wipe us out but to do a job.

"I think the biggest thing we have to worry about is that we're being misdirected," I say. "Whoever this is doesn't have the reach to do what they need done, so they need us."

"But when this job is done, they won't have much of a need for us anymore," Mo points out. "What then?"

"We'll cross that bridge when we come to it," I respond. "But I honestly don't think this will come down to a shoot-out with whomever this person is."

"How can you be so sure?" Rick asks.

"I can't. I just don't feel like this person, whoever they are, is a threat to us," I answer. "I know it's weak, but I don't know how else to put it. Believe me, I've thought a lot about it and replayed those conversations in my head over and over again, and I don't think this person is gunning for us."

"They just want us to deal with their problem," Astra says.

I nod. "Exactly. And once they get what they want, we very likely won't hear from them again. Not unless—and until—we have to come back here and deal with *them* the way we're handling the Arias brothers."

I sound more confident than I feel. The truth is, if we have to come back to take this person down, I'm not sure how we'll go about it. They know who I am. They presumably know everything about my team. If we have to game-plan against them, that gives them a distinct advantage and puts them a dozen steps ahead of us. Not ideal circumstances, obviously.

But like I said, that's a bridge we'll jump off when we come to it. Who knows how this will all play out in the end? While I'm assuming the worst, there is still the slim possibility that this person just wants to dismantle the cartel entirely and be done with them. Is it likely? Probably not. But it's possible. And that's what I have to cling to right now.

"Okay, who's ready for some bad news?" Sonny asks as he steps into the war room.

"Do you ever come in with *good* news?" Astra shoots back. "It would be a really nice change of pace, dude."

"Sorry, darlin'. If I ever come across any of that, I'll be sure to bring it to you straight away."

"So kind."

"What do you have?" I ask.

He tosses the folder in his hand down on the table in front of me. I stare at it for a moment like it's a rabid badger ready to eat my face.

I gesture to the folder. "What's this?"

"You're going to want to read that," he replies.

"Why is that?"

"Because you're going to want to."

With a sigh and a growing sense of dread, I flip the folder open. It doesn't explode, bite, or otherwise maim me, but after pulling the single sheet of paper out and scanning the text on the page, I kind of wish it had.

"Dammit," I mutter.

"What is it?" Astra asks.

I put the paper back into the folder and slide it over to her. She stares at it as uneasily as I had and, unsurprisingly, doesn't move to open it.

"Ballistics on Chana Alexander's gun," I say.

"Let me guess, no match?" she asks.

"No match."

"Which means no suspect," Sonny says.

Kinda wish he had thrown me a rabid badger instead.

CHAPTER THIRTY

Desert Regency Hotel Security Office Subfloor A, Downtown District; Phoenix, AZ

"YOU LOOK TENSE," SONNY SAYS. "ARE YOU TENSE?"

"I'm fine."

"You sure? Because you look tense."

He tips me a wink, which makes me roll my eyes. "You're not as charming as you think."

"I know. I'm even *more* charming than I think. I really don't give myself enough credit. My humility is one of my greatest attributes."

"Yeah, I can see that."

He chuckles. I know he's just trying to settle my nerves. Although I appreciate the effort, it won't work. I'm always like this before a big op when lives are on the line. I subtly reach out and give his arm an affectionate but quick squeeze and offer him a smile I hope doesn't look too sickly.

"Seriously though. How are you feeling about things, darlin'?"

"Good. I'm good."

"You don't look so good."

"Thanks for that."

He grins. "Don't sound so gloomy. You got to think positive."

"I'm positive I'm going to punch you in the face if you tell me about the power of positive thinking again," I say dryly.

He chuckles and holds his hands chest high, palms facing me. "Easy, tiger. Don't forget we're on the same team. Boy, you weren't kiddin' when you said you got tight before a big game."

"I really wasn't."

I turn and scan the room. My team and Sonny's team are getting set up in the security office we commandeered. Rick, Nina, and the techs Sonny brought along are jacking into the hotel's security system while Mo and Paige, who are posing as employees, are finishing getting into their uniforms. Glory and her tac team are against the back wall. All of them are heavily armed and armored, and judging by the looks on their faces, are spoiling for a fight.

My shoulders are bunched and tight, and I'm fighting hard to keep the churning in my belly to a low quiver. I'm either sending my team into a fight with a bunch of heavily armed cartel fighters, or we're walking into nothing. Given the potential political fallout if we get this wrong, I think I'd rather face the bullets. Sicarios have nothing on politicians when it comes to flat-out viciousness.

"You ready?" Sonny asks.

"Yep. Let's do it."

"All right then," he says. "Okay, everybody, listen up."

The room goes silent, and everybody turns to us, eyes expectant, the air crackling with tension. Most everybody in the room seems to be feeling it right now. That's good. I want everybody a bit on edge. It helps keep us sharp. For Sonny and his people, they see the end of a case they've been working for a very long time in sight. For us, we have a chance to put a couple of guys on the Bureau's wish list away for the rest of their lives and put a couple of very big feathers in our caps. We just need things to break right.

"Most of you know Unit Chief Blake Wilder and her team," Sonny says. "They've got operational control on this job—"

Almost immediately, the grumbling and muttering begins; the DEA boys and girls obviously aren't thrilled with the idea of us running point on this op. Having us in to run the Nadia sting and assist with the main investigation is one thing. Having us run the big Arias op is something else entirely. Sonny's team has been on this case from the start, and they're obviously not happy with the idea of somebody else coming in to run the show. I can't say I blame them. In their spot I'd be just as angry. In fact, I've been right where they are, and it sucks.

"Shut it down. Everybody," Sonny calls out, his tone harsh.

The room falls silent again, and I survey the crowd of dark, angry faces. None of them want to feel like they're getting pulled for a reliever in the bottom of the ninth. But this is a delicate situation, and one wrong move can lead to their death or the death of innocents. And I won't have that. Pride and ego have no place here, and I'm determined to see we all come out of this without a scratch and with the bad guys in bracelets.

"Now, we called them in here for an assist primarily because we've been working these animals so long, we have to assume Santiago and Diego have files on all of us. We have to assume they know who we are, and if they see us, they'll open up on us," Sonny says. "Blake and her team here are an unknown quantity. They won't get picked out of a crowd by the Arias boys or any of their cronies. That gives us the tactical advantage. So, check the egos at the door, boys and girls. And if you can't do that, then go ahead and clock out right now."

There are a few additional mutters as everybody shifts on their feet, but the room is otherwise silent. Sonny's team stays put, nobody seeming to want to miss out on the op. He gives them another moment as he eyes them all, one by one, giving them every opportunity to opt out rather than let me command them. When he's satisfied, Sonny turns to me and nods.

"Very good," he says. "The floor is yours, Chief Wilder."

I return his nod and step forward. "All right, I have two undercovers from the local Bureau field office positioned in the lobby already. They'll give us the heads-up when the targets arrive," I begin. "The meeting is supposed to be at noon, which is a little more than an hour from now, so it's time to get our game faces on."

The mood in the room begins to shift as the nerves and tension start to ebb, replaced with an undercurrent of excitement. This has been a long time coming for a lot of these folks. Hopefully, we can bring it home without anybody getting hurt. Or worse.

"Our goal is to isolate the Arias brothers and their new distributor, Isaac Correa. The suite they'll be meeting in is wired for sight and sound," I say. "Once money changes hands or we have something tangible on tape, we'll move in."

"We want to make sure we keep them contained on the floor they're on," Sonny adds. "Glory, I want you to put half your team in the north stairwell, the other half in the south stairwell. Your task is to not let anybody by you. Containment is essential."

"Copy that," Glory confirms.

One of Sonny's men, Robbins, raises his hand. "If we're trying to keep civilians out of harm's way, why don't we just tail them after they leave the hotel and hit them on the street?"

"Because the name of this game is control," I answer. "We control the environment here which means we control the engagement. The best way to keep innocents from getting hurt is to keep them away from the action. A thousand things can go wrong on the street. We've had the hotel clear the entire floor of civilians, giving us total control of the environment. Therefore, we have the home field advantage."

"Also, you all know just how slippery these sons of guns can be," Sonny says. "You let them out on the streets, and it can all go sideways in a hurry. We give up containment, and those guys have a habit of disappearin' like smoke. We'll have them in the box on our terms, so we're going to keep them there. We good?"

Robbins nods and leans back against the wall, seemingly satisfied with the answer. "Yes, sir. We're good."

"Good," Sonny says. "Chief?"

"Okay, based on intel we've received, we expect the Ariases to arrive with six heavily armed men," I continue. "The guards will more than likely take up positions in the hallway. Once we have what we need, my team will move in, subdue the guards, then take the targets."

"You make it sound so easy. But you don't know these guys. They're animals. They'll shoot you without thinking twice about it," Robbins grumbles. "We've been working this case for a long time, so you can't seriously think you can waltz on in here—"

"Enough, Robbins," Sonny says.

"Sir, we can't—"

Sonny glowers at him darkly. "I said stow it. Now."

Robbins falls silent, but it's clear he doesn't like having to take a back seat. Not to us. Sonny continues glaring at him, giving the man another chance to speak. I get the feeling if he does, Sonny will scrub him from the mission entirely and send him home. He seems to sense it, too, because he frowns but says nothing more.

"Okay," Sonny finally says. "The rest of us will be providing operational support and watching everything from this office. Our eyes will be glued to those security monitors and alerting Chief Wilder and her team to anything and everything we see. We want zero surprises. Am I clear?"

"Yes sir," his team responds in unison.

"Target three is in the building," the hushed voice comes through my earpiece.

A frown touches my lips. "Correa is here."

"He's early," Sonny says, sounding alarmed.

"Better than being late," I say. "Okay folks, game faces on. It's showtime."

CHAPTER THIRTY-ONE

Desert Regency Hotel, Downtown District; Phoenix, AZ

"TARGET THREE IS IN HIS SUITE AND JUST ORDERED room service," Rick says. "A bottle of champagne and some fancy-sounding finger foods."

"Copy you," I say. "Station one, any sign of targets one and two?"

"Negative," comes the reply from our undercovers. "Lobby is still clear."

I glance at my watch and frown, a frustrated sigh bursting from my mouth. It's three minutes to noon, and we haven't had any sign of the Arias brothers yet. Astra and I are posted up in a room on the same floor but around the corner from Correa's suite while Mo and Paige are tucked away in a room on the opposite corner. Beads of sweat roll down my body, my vest making me uncomfortably hot. The seconds ticking by are only making me stickier. As Tom Petty said, the waiting is indeed the hardest part.

I key open my mic. "Overwatch, any sign of targets one and two in the parking lot?"

"Negative," Sonny's voice comes through my earpiece. "Parking lot remains all clear. Will advise when targets are on site."

"Copy you," I say.

I pace the room, agitated. Astra is sitting on the couch seeming to be far more relaxed than she has any right to be in the situation. But then, she's always been a lot more Zen about the calm before the storm than I have. I don't know how she does it, but I'd like to learn. Might save me from getting ulcers down the road. I check my watch again and mutter under my breath seeing it's only been a minute since the last time I checked. Astra laughs.

"You keep working yourself up like this, you're not going to have the energy for the fight that's coming," she teases.

"I will never understand how you can be so calm before we get into a gunfight."

"Hopefully, there won't be a gunfight."

"Yeah, but given who were facing off with, I'm not optimistic we can avoid it."

She shrugs. "Freaking myself out about things isn't going to change what's coming. If anything, getting all worked up about it will only distract me from what needs to be done and make it less likely I'll come home."

Pulling the curtain aside, I stare down into the parking lot below us as if I can somehow will the Arias brothers to appear. When they don't, I turn from the window with a growl and begin stalking back and forth across the room again. Astra shakes her head and snickers softly, knowing that trying to get me to calm down is a lost cause.

"This is station one, be advised, targets one and two are in the lobby," the hushed voice of my agent comes through my earpiece. "Repeat, targets one and two are inbound."

Astra and I share a glance, both of us wearing matching expressions of alarm. My stomach and shoulders both tighten as a steady rush of adrenaline begins flooding my veins.

"Overwatch," I say. "Can you confirm?"

"Stand by," Sonny replies.

The seconds crawl by like minutes, and with each tick of the clock, the knot in my belly gets that much tighter.

"We got 'em. They're at the elevators with six bodyguards," Sonny says.

"How did they get by you in the parking lot?" I almost shout.

"I have no idea," he replies. "But the doors are closed, and they're heading to you now."

Annoyed by the fact that our overwatch missed our targets entering the hotel, I grimace but swallow down my anger. There will be time enough for that later.

"Bravo, you listening?" I say into my mic.

"Copy that. Targets are inbound," Paige answers. "We're ready to move on your go."

"Targets are exiting the elevator and moving to the suite," Sonny says.

Dashing to the door, I press my eye to the peephole in time to see the entourage pass by. The Arias brothers are surrounded by their men—two in front, four trailing. If they're trying to keep things low-key, they're failing miserably. Behind me, Astra gets to her feet and stretches herself out as if she's about to do nothing more strenuous than some yoga.

I key open my mic. "Targets are inbound. Approaching the room now."

"Copy you. We have them on camera," Sonny replies. "Targets entering room now. Four on the door, two inside with the principals. Will advise when we have what we need."

"Copy that. Alpha team, standing by," I say.

"Bravo copy, standing by," Mo says.

"And we're back to playing the waiting game," I complain as I fold my arms over my chest and lean against the wall behind me.

Astra is doing torso twists, an amused smirk on her face. "Well, at least you've stopped pacing. I guess that's something."

"I might just start again if we're cooped up in here much longer."

"Good God, woman. I've seen five-year-olds on Christmas morning with more patience than you," she teases.

"I'm just anxious to get this done."

"We all are," she replies. "But you know better than anybody that if we go in there all keyed up, we're gonna have a bad time. So, take a little of your own advice, take a step back, take a deep breath, and relax before you do anything."

"Have I told you lately how much I hate it when you throw my words back in my face?"

"Only every day. That's why I do it."

I laugh. "You suck."

"Got you to laugh."

"Yeah, I guess you're good for something after all."

"I am. You should keep me around."

"I'll give it some thought."

I lean my head back against the wall and blow out a frustrated breath as I tap my foot on the floor. Okay, I guess perhaps five-year-olds on Christmas morning do have more patience than I do.

"How long is it going to take to put this deal together?" I ask.

"It's like any business deal," Astra says. "There's got to be a little wine, a little chit-chat, a few laughs, and a little foreplay before they officially climb into bed together."

I groan. "That's a visual I didn't need in my head, thanks."

"You're welcome."

My earpiece crackles. "Stairwells are secure, and we have what we need," Sonny says, his voice thick with excitement. "You are clear to move in."

Twin threads of eager anticipation and cold nervousness twine themselves around my heart and pull tight as Astra bounces on her heels.

"Let's get this going," she says.

"Let's do it," I reply, then key my mic. "Bravo team, you're clear to make contact."

"Copy you," Mo says. "Moving in."

Astra and I slip out of the room and move quietly down the hall, stopping at the corner. Not wanting to give our position away, I fight the urge to lean out and look around. Paige and Mo are disguised as housekeeping and their role is to draw the attention of the guards on the door. Once they're distracted, we'll come up from behind and, in theory, get the drop on them.

It's not the most elegant or sophisticated plan. But it's miles better than Sonny's idea of sending multiple tac teams from both sides to engage the men on the doors. In a space as confined and narrow as the hallway we're in, having superior numbers isn't an advantage. Instead of overwhelming the men on the door, it would likely be an utter bloodbath. And we're trying to avoid a massive shootout that would undoubtedly claim a lot of lives.

"Overwatch," I whisper into my mic. "What's the situation?"

"Bravo team is rounding the corner now. The Arias men are . . . looking their way," Sonny replies. "Go. Now."

Our weapons drawn, we come around the corner and move low and quickly down the hall toward the four large men. Our luck just needs to hold for another minute. It doesn't, of course. My heart drops into my stomach when I see one of the men turn. His eyes widen when he spots us, and I hear a groan drift from my mouth. Standing up straight, I raise my Glock.

"FBI!" I call. "Drop your weapons."

The four men all pull their weapons as they turn, their movements so graceful and fluid, it's like a choreographed dance.

"FBI!" Mo calls from the other side. "Do not move!"

Their weapons drawn, the men pause, looking at me, then turning to Mo, before they share glances amongst each other, indecision etched upon their faces. At least they're not shooting yet. That's a good thing.

"Nobody needs to get hurt today," I call out. "Just lay down your weapons and put your hands up. Do it now."

Nobody speaks and nobody moves for a long, drawn-out moment. I'm not sure any of us are even breathing right now. My body is taut, and my stomach is churning. It feels like the stare down before a gunfight on a dusty street at high noon. I can practically see a tumbleweed rolling. Part of me is still hopeful this can come to a nonviolent resolution, but that hope is dashed when I see one of the men's faces darken. He's come to his decision, and he's chosen to die on his feet rather than end up cuffed and on his knees.

"Oh, God," I groan.

The scene in the hallway descends into chaos in the blink of an eye as gunshots ring out. In a space that confined, it sounds like we're firing cannons at each other as chunks of plaster and wood are ripped from the walls around us. There is no cover for us, and if we can't end this quickly, the likelihood of taking a bullet increases with every passing second. Dropping to a knee, I open up, squeezing off shot after shot.

A chunk of plaster from the wall slices my cheek, and I feel a trickle of blood running down my face as one of my rounds punches through the man's chest. He drops, dead before he hits the ground. My stomach clenches, and a gasp bursts from my mouth when, from the corner of my eye, I see Paige go down. Although it's only a matter of seconds, the gunfire feels like it's gone on for days. But the silence that follows the brief battle is as jarring as the sound of the first shot.

As I get to my feet, my ears are ringing with the sounds of the shots, and my nose is filled with the thick stench of gunpowder. Smoke as thick as San Francisco fog hangs in the air around us, and once I confirm all four goons are dead on the ground and kick their weapons down the hall, I dash over to where Paige had fallen. Astra and Mo are already there, helping her into a sitting position, as I drop to a knee.

"Are you all right?" I ask.

Paige grimaces as she pulls her uniform jacket open and touches the bullet that had mushroomed against the Kevlar, and I breathe a sigh of relief.

"Yeah. I'm fine. My vest caught it," she says.

"Okay, good," I say. "Mo, get her downstairs, and have Sonny call a bus—"

"I'm good," Paige argues with a wince. "Let's finish this."

"You're going to get checked out."

"*After* we finish this," Paige argues firmly.

With Mo's help, she gets to her feet. Paige is gritting her teeth and moving gingerly, but she gives me a nod, telling me she's good to go. Astra gives me a smirk and a half shrug.

"All right," I say. "Let's finish it."

The four of us have to step around the bodies as we take up positions on either side of the door. My body is still tight, and adrenaline surges through me as I wait for bullets to punch through the door after I knock loudly.

"FBI," I call through the door. "We're coming in."

No bullets come through the door, but I can hear loud arguing from inside the room. Using the key card the hotel manager had given me, I unlock the door and push it open. Weapons raised, we move into the room and pause just inside the door. The two remaining henchmen are standing in the living room of the suite facing us, guns raised. Behind them are Santiago and Diego Arias who are speaking heatedly to Correa and another man in a suit beside him in rapid fire Spanish.

"Lower your weapons," I say coldly. "Now."

Correa straightens his jacket and puts a stern expression on his face as he steps in front of the two guards, gesturing to them to lower their weapons. The two men look to Santiago, and he nods, so they do. They hold their weapons down by their sides but don't drop them. Correa clears his throat, and it's like I can see him shifting into salesman mode. Tall and good-looking with a Hollywood smile, it's clear the man gets by on his charm.

The Arias brothers are coiled and tense. They know they're at a disadvantage but seem to be waiting for an opening to make a move. As if sensing what I am about to do, Mo and Astra walk farther into the room, taking opposite sides to flank them. If things do pop off, they aren't getting out of it unscathed. Diego, the more unstable of the two, bristles as his lips curl back over his teeth. The fourth man in the room, dressed impeccably in a stylish suit, pales and seems absolutely shaken. I don't know who he is yet, but if the sight of guns makes him wet himself, I'd say he doesn't have the constitution to be doing business with the cartels. My guess is he's Correa's lawyer.

"What is this about, Agents?" Correa asks.

"You're under arrest, Mr. Correa."

"This is absurd. Why would I be under arrest?"

My eyes flick to the pair of black duffel bags sitting on the coffee table. "Let's start with drug distribution, since I'm guessing we're going to find a lot of drugs in those two bags."

He chuckles. "I don't know what you're talking about—"

"Santiago and Diego Arias, you are both also under arrest for… a lot of things. Now, tell your men to drop their guns," I order.

"Heads up. We are entering the room behind you," Sonny's voice comes through my earpiece a moment before he and four of his agents step into the suite, fanning out in front of the doorway.

His four agents have their weapons raised and take firing positions, their faces hard. They are clearly thinking about their teammates the Arias brothers murdered and seem to be praying for the two men to give them a reason to open fire.

Correa puffs up his chest. "I am a respected businessman in this city and have many friends in very high places. I would advise you to turn around—"

"Your friends in high places won't be able to help you, amigo," Sonny says. "In fact, once they find out what we're taking you in for, I'd reckon they'll do everything they can to put as much distance between y'all as they can."

He turns to the man in the suit and hisses. "Do something."

Obviously recognizing the man in the suit as Correa's lawyer, Sonny walks over and slaps some papers into his hand. The papers rustle as he unfolds them, and his face blanches as he reads. He looks up at Correa, then cuts a glance at the Arias brothers, his eyes alight with fear.

The man shrugs. "There's nothing I can do. These are valid arrest warrants," he replies, his voice trembling.

Sonny casually strolls over to the coffee table, and I watch Correa's face fall as the bags are unzipped. Sonny whistles as he pulls out a white brick and hefts it in his hand.

"My, my, my," he says with a laugh in his voice.

"I—I don't know what those are," Correa says weakly.

"Really, genius?" Astra asks and points to where one of our cameras has been hidden. "Smile, you're on candid camera."

"That's right," Sonny says. "We've got your whole conversation on tape. There's no way for you to wiggle off the hook, Chief. It's in you every bit as deep as it's in these two clowns."

Correa closes his eyes and lowers his head. With a snarl and a maniacal expression on his face that makes him look as unstable as his reputation makes him out to be, Diego reaches for his weapon. He's obviously determined to go out in a blaze of glory rather than spend his life in a cage. Before his gun clears its holster, though, a booming shot rings out.

His body jerks, and he stumbles backward, a fount of blood bursting from his chest. Time seems to slow to a crawl as Diego frantically windmills his arms, sending his gold-plated .45 flying. The backs of his knees hit the couch, and he drops, falling into a sitting position, his breath heaving and ragged as blood flows from the center-mass wound pooling onto the couch cushions beneath him. After a moment, his head slumps forward, and he is gone.

An agonized shriek bursts from Santiago's mouth, and Correa falls to his knees, his face pale, eyes wide, horror etched into his features. The lawyer's legs seem to give out beneath him, and he drops onto the sofa behind him and trembles wildly. Santiago turns to Sonny who is standing still like a statue, eyes narrowed and jaw set, looking for all the world like an old west gunfighter. His weapon is trained directly on Santiago's face.

"Put your damn hands in the air, or you're going to end up like your brother," he says.

Santiago, the more rational of the brothers, puts his hands up, glaring at Sonny with pure rage and hatred gleaming in his eyes. Sonny moves in and puts cuffs on him. It's a moment I know means a lot to him. He turns to me with a shaky smile upon his lips, and having finally gotten justice for all the tragedies these men have incurred on him, his eyes shimmer with emotions he's fighting to control. I give him a smile in return, acknowledging his moment.

"Okay," I say. "Bracelets for everybody. Let's wrap this up."

The room buzzes with activity as evidence is tagged and collected and suspects are put in cuffs. We did it. Diego and Santiago Arias have been high on the Bureau's most wanted list for a long time, and we finally knocked them off. I know for Santiago, at least, the fight is just beginning. His case is likely going to be mired in the courts for years, and we can only hope he doesn't find a way to wiggle off the hook and escape justice one more time.

As I watch the suspects being marched out of the room, I'm left to wonder if we even did any good here. We got justice for Sonny's murdered people... at least, some part of it. But with my mysterious friend now poised to take control of the sudden vacancy at the top of the cartel's organizational chart, they'll likely be back to business as usual before I even get back to Seattle. We took out two bad guys only to turn things over to somebody who might be worse. So, what good did we actually do here?

"Come on," Astra says, as if intuiting my thoughts. "Let's go get a drink and get you out of your head before you go to that dark place you live in. Let's at least enjoy this for one day."

A weak smile flickers across my lips. "Yeah. I think I can do that."

CHAPTER THIRTY-TWO

ATF Operational Center, Southwest Division; Phoenix, AZ

MUSIC IS PLAYING, COOLERS OF BEER HAVE BEEN brought in, and out in the parking lot, a couple of Sonny's people are working a grill. Cheers and laughter ring out, the mood in the ops center celebratory. Ecstatic, really. The weight of this case that has been dogging Sonny and his team for a long time now has finally been lifted, and they're all feeling good. I can't be mad about that. I know what that feels like, and they've done such hard work and endured such catastrophic losses, they deserve to blow off some steam after notching a big W.

I'm sitting alone in the war room watching the teams celebrate together wishing I could feel the sense of relief and accomplishment that's painted on all their faces. The only bit of relief I feel is that aside from a deep bruise that's going to bother her for a while, Paige is all right. Watching her go down during the firefight was one of the scariest moments of my career. If anything had happened to her, I don't know that I could have forgiven myself.

Truthfully, guilt over what happened to Lucas Okamura still stains my heart. That was ages ago now, but I still feel it. Seeing Lucas in the hospital after such a savage beating, then having to see him after, as he struggled to recover, only compounded that guilt. My team is like family, and what happens to them hits me hard. It's probably not the healthiest thing, and most bosses keep their team at an arm's distance, but that's never been something I've been able to do.

"You're missin' the party," Sonny says as he steps into the room.

He brings a plate heaped with food over and sets it down in front of me. The aroma of barbecued ribs and sweet baked beans hits my nose and makes my stomach rumble, reminding me that I haven't eaten today. He sits down, then pulls a napkin and utensils out of his bag and slides them over to me.

"Thank you," I say. "I didn't realize how hungry I was until this moment."

He gives me that trademark wink. "I aim to please, darlin'."

The meat is so tender it falls off the bone, and as I sample the ribs, flavor explodes in my mouth, making an indecent groan float from my mouth.

"My God, that's good," I say.

"Denny is a wizard on the grill."

"Clearly."

Sonny reaches into his bag and pulls out a bottle of the Macallan Twelve and two glasses, quickly pouring each of us a couple fingers' worth.

"Wow," I say. "The Macallan. That's fancy."

"We're celebratin', darlin'," he says. "We closed a big one today. Got justice for my people. And honestly, a bottle of scotch isn't nearly enough to thank you."

I raise my glass. "It's a start."

"Damn straight it is," he says with a nod as he raises his glass. "To justice."

I tap my glass against his, then take a sip of the scotch, relishing the notes of vanilla, citrus, caramel, and ginger, among others, that sit on my tongue. It burns pleasantly as it slides down my throat, then ignites a ball of warmth in my belly.

"My God, that's good," I say.

"Right?"

We make small talk as I devour the plate he brought me in between sips of the scotch. It doesn't chase the darkness away completely, but this little feast vastly improves my mood.

"So, what has you sittin' in here all alone?" he asks. "We got a win. Why are you brooding?"

"I'm not brooding."

"You're broodin', darlin'. Broodin' and gloomy as hell."

He's not the first person to tell me I brood. Maybe there's something to it.

"I wouldn't say I'm brooding. Nor am I gloomy," I say. "I'm just… contemplating."

"All right, what are you contemplating?"

"Whether we're actually doing any good."

Sonny sits forward, hands wrapped around his glass, his eyes curious but concerned as he stares at me. "What do you mean?"

"We cut the head off the snake today, but we did it knowing another head is about to grow back," I tell him. "The Arias cartel didn't die today. For all we know, we made it worse. We don't know who this person is who's about to take over. They could be more vicious and brutal—"

"Or they could just let it die," he replies. "We don't know this person, you're right. And it's possible we were only carrying out a vendetta for them. It's possible they had some bad blood with the brothers and—for whatever reason they couldn't do it themselves—tasked us with taking them out."

I pull a face. "Do you really believe that?"

"I'm going to choose to believe that. At least for today," he replies. "Today I am going to celebrate a big win and enjoy the day."

"And tomorrow?"

"I'll worry about tomorrow... tomorrow," he tells me. "Honestly, that's something you need to learn to do, darlin'. You need to celebrate the wins because God knows, we don't always get them in this line of work. You know that. So, why not celebrate it when you do? We took down two of the most notorious and vicious drug lords in the world. Guys responsible for flooding our streets with their poison and dropping more bodies than we can count. More than we probably even know, if we're bein' honest. That's something to celebrate."

He stares at me over the rim of his glass as he takes a swallow, seeming to be savoring the flavor. His eyes sparkle with amusement, and the corners of his mouth are turned up softly.

"We don't have many good days in this business. This is one of 'em," he says. "I really think you need to learn to appreciate them when they come because you just don't know when you'll get another one."

I know he's right. And the whole stop-and-smell-the-roses thing is something I've talked with about Dr. Azar. She believes I'm so task-focused that when I finish one, I immediately pivot to the next one. She says I let myself be consumed with getting to the top of the hill, and when I finally do reach the summit, instead of stopping to appreciate the view, all I can see is the next hill to climb. It's not an unfair assessment. It's how I've always been, and frankly, I think it's what makes me good at my job. It's why I've had the successes I've had. Besides, I don't know how to change that at this stage of my life even if I wanted to.

"I'm just having a hard time shaking the idea we took out two monsters just to place a bigger monster on the throne," I tell him.

"And if that turns out to be the case, we'll deal with him then."

The chair squeaks as I sit back. "It's just this never-ending cycle. We take down bad guys, new ones pop up in their place. Drug lords, murderers, rapists... I'm tired."

"Humanity never runs out of ways to disappoint. Never runs out of new depravities and atrocities," he says. "It's why what we do is so important, darlin'. We're the ones who hold the line between the monsters and the good people. Can you imagine what this world would be like without people like us holding that line?"

"I shudder to think."

"Me too," he says softly. "I know you're tired. I am too. But what we do is necessary. People need us. You told me that's why you started doin' this job in the first place. To protect the people who can't protect themselves."

I nod. "It's true."

"Well, take solace in the fact that by taking out Diego and Santiago, you protected a lot of people. And got justice for even more," he says.

"But somebody else will rise and pick up the baton."

"As you always say: that's the job, darlin'. That's the job."

I take a sip of my scotch and let it roll around my tongue for a moment, savoring the rich and complex flavors, before swallowing it down.

"Yes, it is," I agree. "But our job is only half done. The guys who actually pulled the trigger on your agents are still out there."

"That they are."

"I expect Rico to call me, or rather, call Nadia, once news of the Arias brothers going down breaks," I tell him. "And once he does, we'll finish the job."

"Amen, darlin'. Amen," he says and taps his glass against mine again.

"Speaking of finishing the job…"

We look up to see Nina stepping into the conference room with her laptop in her hands and a sheepish expression on her face.

"Sorry to interrupt," she said. "But I just got some information and thought you might want it right away, Chief."

"You're good. You're not interrupting," I say. "What do you have?"

She sits down in the chair to my left, across from Sonny, and sets her laptop down. "I finally got the footage from the street cams near the diner where Dustin Kemper had breakfast with the mystery lady the morning he was killed."

He doesn't move, but I can feel Sonny tense up beside me. His jaw is clenched, and his expression is tight. I think in some ways, getting a suspect and closing out this case means just as much to him as closing out the Arias case.

"Did you get her face?"

She shakes her head. "No, but I did see something else you'll be interested in."

"Let's see it."

She hits a button and turns the screen toward me as the grainy, black and white footage begins to play. The view isn't perfect, but it's enough to show us the front of the diner. I watch for a couple of moments and am about to ask if anything actually happens when the door of the diner opens and Dustin steps out with a woman in a thick coat. She's wearing a hat and has her head tilted down, obscuring our view of her as if she's conscious of the cameras all around and is taking measures to hide her face. Clever girl.

But then Dustin walks the woman to a car parked on the curb in front of the diner and says something to her. Their conversation is animated. It looks heated. That would seem to corroborate Elsa's account of the chat Dustin and his guest were having inside the diner. The woman jabs her finger into his chest and seems to be screaming at him.

Dustin puts his hands on her shoulders and pushes her back, seeming to be trying to keep some space between them. She advances on him again, but Dustin pushes her away, then turns and storms away, leaving her to scream after him.

"Do we ever get a clean look at her face?" I ask.

"Negative. But look at the car, Chief," Nina says. "Recognize it?"

My gaze shifts to the car she's getting into, and when I see it, it feels like the final piece of the puzzle in my head snaps into place. I stare at it in shock for a moment, watching it pull away from the curb, then drive away.

"Did you get a license plate?" I ask.

"I did. And it matches."

"Son of a—"

Sonny's gaze flits from Nina to the footage on the laptop, to me, and back again, his face painted with confusion. He finally leans forward.

"Would you fill me in on what's goin' on here, darlin'?"

"Great work, Nina."

"It's what I do, Chief. It's what I do."

"Somebody goin' to fill me in?" Sonny asks.

I turn to him. "I think we know who killed your CI."

"Yeah?"

"Yeah. I think so," I tell him with a firm nod. "Looks like we're going to get true justice for at least one person today."

CHAPTER
THIRTY-THREE

Pierce Residence, Holdeman District; Tempe, AZ

“WHAT IS THIS ALL ABOUT?” SHIRLEY SCREECHES. I thrust a copy of our search warrant into her hands. “You can read it all here.”

After getting an evidence collection team from the local field office, Astra and I show up at the Pierce home. Both Shirley and Daisy are here, which is a lucky break.

“Ms. Pierce, please go sit in the kitchen with your daughter and stay out of our way,” I tell her. “We have a job to do.”

"Why are you harassing us?" she whines.

"Ma'am, please. You need to stay out of our way."

"This is *my house!*" she shrieks.

I direct one of my agents to escort her into the kitchen where Daisy is already sitting. The girl is sitting limply, her face blank, almost like she's shell-shocked. Shirley fusses and slaps the agent's hand away as he tries to guide her into the kitchen, but she goes, grumbling and cursing the whole way. One of the evidence techs, a twenty-something woman with black hair and an eager light in her eyes, walks over to me.

"Ma'am, where do you want us to start?" she asks as she snaps on a pair of black gloves.

"What is your name?"

"Rebecca, ma'am."

"Okay good. Rebecca, I want you to take one of the other techs and start with the cars," I tell her. "Strip them down to the frame if you have to, but search everywhere. Be very detailed and very thorough."

"Yes, ma'am," she replies and bounds away.

The rest of the team is searching the house. I directed them to be respectful and to avoid making a mess or breaking anything, but the sounds of the search deeper in the house are loud as they move furniture and search all the nooks and crannies. While that is going on, Astra and I walk into the kitchen. Shirley is sitting at the table, legs crossed, her arms folded over her chest. If this was a cartoon, she'd have steam coming out of her ears.

Daisy, on the other hand, is sitting slumped in her seat, eyes downcast, hands folded in her lap. She's pale, listless, trembling, and her cheeks are wet with tears.

"Are you all right, Daisy?" I ask.

"Don't you dare speak to my daughter," Shirley hisses. "Aren't you people doing enough to my daughter as it is? Why are you continuing to harass her?"

"We're following the evidence, Ms. Pierce," I say.

"Evidence? What evidence?"

"The evidence that led us here," Astra says.

"Are you trying to frame my daughter?" Shirley asks. "Is that what this is? You're trying to pin Dustin's murder on her because you don't have anything else?"

"I can assure you that's not what's happening here," I say.

"Then what is happening? What is this about?"

"Daisy," I say. "Can you look at me?"

She reluctantly turns her eyes up to me, and I can see the mélange of emotions cycling across her face. The girl is haunted by something. Tormented. Fresh tears spill from the corners of her eyes and race down her pale, trembling cheeks. I squat down and take her hands in mine and look her in the eyes. Shirley reaches across and yanks Daisy's hands out of my own and sneers at me.

"Don't you dare touch my daughter," she growls.

The corner of my mouth quirks upward, and I turn back to Daisy. "It seems like you're carrying something heavy. It seems like it's really weighing on you—"

Shirley jumps to her feet and stabs a finger at me. "Stop talking to my daughter. I will not stand by and let you railroad her. She will not be talking to you without a lawyer."

"Your daughter is an adult and can ask for a lawyer herself," Astra says. "Is that what you want, Daisy? Do you want a lawyer?"

"If you have nothing to hide, why would you need a lawyer?" I ask.

Daisy claps her hands to her ears and rocks back and forth, her body shaking wildly and groaning as the tears flow down her face in buckets. She's got a secret, and it's tearing her apart.

"Are you really going to do this to your daughter?" Astra asks Daisy.

"What I'm *not* going to do is let you do this to *my* daughter," Shirley snaps back.

"We're not doing anything to Daisy," I say. "We're just trying to get to the truth."

"You don't give a damn about the truth! You can't find who killed Dustin, so you're trying to pin it on my daughter. I'm not going to let you do that."

"Chief Wilder?"

I turn to see Rebecca standing in the doorway waving me over. From the corner of my eye, I see Shirley stiffen. Daisy keeps rocking in her seat, her hands clamped over her ears and still groaning miserably. She seems like she's about to spin out completely.

"Stay with them," I tell Astra.

"Copy you."

After casting a pointed glance at Shirley and Daisy, I walk over to the tech. Before she can say a word, though, I hold up a finger, then motion to take it outside. I'm hoping for good news, but I have no idea what she's about to say and I'd rather not have the Pierces overhear whatever it might be. Rebecca leads me out to the cars. Her partner is leaning over the open trunk taking photographs and documenting the evidence.

"What do you have?" I ask.

The tech steps back as Rebecca gestures to the open trunk and grins. I can't help but like her enthusiasm. She seems to genuinely enjoy her work, and I respect that a lot.

"Feast your eyes on this, Chief Wilder," she says, beaming. "We found it hidden in the compartment beneath the spare tire where the jack should go."

"That seems careless."

"Which is good for us."

"Which is *very* good for us," I respond.

Sitting on a black plastic bag is a black Glock 17 nine-millimeter. I stare at it for a moment, taking it in. It needs to be sent for printing and ballistics, of course, but my gut is telling me this is the weapon used to kill Dustin Kemper.

"Bag this for me, please," I say.

"You got it," Rebecca chirps.

She picks up the gun and ejects the magazine, clears the chamber, then drops both items into a plastic evidence bag. She seals it up, logs it, then hands it to me.

"Thanks, Rebecca. I'll get it back to you for processing in just a minute."

"You got it."

"Keep shaking this tree and see if you can get anything else to fall out."

She snaps me a salute. "Will do. We'll let you know if we find anything."

"Thanks, guys. Really good work."

"Thanks, Chief."

Carrying the bag, I walk back into the house then into the kitchen. The gun hits the table with a hard thud, and when it does, both Shirley and Daisy pale visibly. Astra cuts me a glance as a sly grin splits her lips.

"Look what we found," I say.

Shirley turns away as Daisy begins to shake again, her face turning a sickly shade of green.

"Do you know what this is?" I ask.

"It looks like a gun," Shirley growls as she turns to me.

Her face is tight, anger burning in her eyes and a snarl upon her lips. She seems to think she's going to bluster and bully her way through this.

"Is this your gun, Ms. Pierce?" I ask.

"I've never owned a gun in my life."

"How about you, Daisy? This yours?"

Daisy shakes her head. "No. I told you I don't like guns."

"Then why was this in the trunk of your car?"

She quickly lowers her head, refusing to meet my eyes. Shirley's lips are a tight slash across her face, and her gaze is hard as she sits back, folding her arms over her chest again, striking a defensive posture.

"And you said you didn't have breakfast with Dustin the day he was killed," I say. "Is that right, Daisy? That's what you told us?"

"I told you. I hadn't seen him for a while before... before..."

Her voice trails off, and she buries her face in her hands. Daisy's shoulders shake, and her breath bursts from her mouth in heaving sobs.

"Why are you doing this to my daughter?" Shirley cried. "She told you she didn't see Dustin. She told you she doesn't own a gun. Somebody is obviously setting her up to take the fall for this. Why don't you go out there and do your job and find that person?"

"That's a good thought," I say. "Ms. Pierce, can you tell me where you were the morning Dustin was killed?"

"I—I was at work. I had a morning shift that day," she says quickly.

"Huh," I say. "That's weird, because we checked, and you didn't work that morning."

Shirley's face grows white as a sheet, her mouth opening and closing like a fish that's been yanked out of water and thrown onto a dock. Daisy curls in on herself, covering her head with her arms like she's warding off blows, trembling so hard, I'm half-afraid she's going to shake herself right out of her chair. Shirley quickly recovers and stiffens, her face hardening.

"So, where were you that morning, Ms. Pierce?" I ask.

"That is none of your business."

"Actually, it is."

"Did you have breakfast with Dustin that morning?" Astra asks.

"No. Of course not."

"So, you're telling us you weren't at Eggs and More in Roosevelt Row with Dustin that morning?" Astra presses.

"I just told you I wasn't."

"Huh. That's weird," Astra says and pulls a still photo from the footage Nina had found and holds it up for Shirley to see. "Because that looks a lot like your car… and that looks a lot like you right there. Doesn't it?"

"Before you lie, we ran the plates, and that is, in fact, your black Audi. The one right out there in the driveway," I say. "We will, of course, be doing ballistics testing on the weapon, but I think we already know it's going to turn out to be the gun used to kill Dustin."

"We're also going to get gun and ammunition in the magazine printed. Is there any doubt about whose prints we'll find, Shirley?" Astra presses.

Shirley's face falls, and she seems to deflate. She runs a hand over her face and lets out a long, loud sigh, sounding utterly defeated. She seems to understand that we have her boxed in and there is no getting out of it. She turns to Daisy, her glare acidic.

"Why didn't you get rid of that gun like I told you to?" she hissed.

"I—I'm sorry, Mama," she whispered.

"Idiot," she hissed. "I did this for you. I did this all for you."

"Did you though?" Astra asks.

"You don't know anything, so you should just shut your mouth," she spits. "That boy was a drag on my daughter's life. No matter how bad he screwed her over, no matter how many times he lied, or got high, or cheated on her, she kept taking him back. He was like her drug, and she couldn't quit. I had to do something. It's my responsibility as a mother."

I pull a face. "I don't think murder is a mother's responsibility."

"You're not a mother, are you?"

"No."

"Then you'll never know."

I give her a half shrug. "Perhaps not."

"I'm sorry, Mama," Daisy says again, her eyes red and spilling tears.

"Just shut up. This is your fault."

Astra cuffs Shirley and begins reading her Miranda rights. Beneath her mother's withering, hateful glare, Daisy breaks down in sobs and runs from the room. It's hard not to feel sorry for her. One thing Shirley was right about, though, is that Dustin was absolutely her drug, and she couldn't kick him any more than he could kick the dope he was on. Addiction is a powerful and destructive thing.

"I want my lawyer," Shirley growls as Astra walks her toward the door.

"Yeah, you're going to need one," I say as I turn and follow them out.

CHAPTER
THIRTY-FOUR

ATF Operational Center, Southwest Division; Phoenix, AZ

"WOW. I DID NOT SEE THAT COMING," SONNY SAYS. "I thought for sure the cartel had something to do with Dustin's death."

"I know you did," I reply with a soft smile.

We sit across from each other at the table in the war room. Astra and Paige have taken Shirley down to Phoenix PD to have her booked and processed for the murder of Dustin Kemper while Mo, Rick, and Nina are putting together the package we'll be sending to the DA for her eventual prosecution. That leaves me and Sonny sitting in the war room waiting for Rico Nagy to call so we can put a bow on this whole thing once and for all.

"See? This is why I was right to ask you to look into it. You got to the truth of it when I would have been running around with blinders on."

"It's like you said, you DEA folk aren't built to handle murder investigations," I say with a mischievous grin.

"No. No, we're not. That's why it was important to me that you run the investigation. I knew you'd do it right. And I knew you'd do right by Dustin," he says.

"We did our best."

"Why do you think Daisy kept the gun? If she'd ditched it like her mom told her, we'd have had nothing. That street cam footage wouldn't have been worth spit."

I shrug. "Not sure. Part of me thinks she was on the fence about turning her mom in for it. I mean, whether he was good for her or not, her mom killed the man she loved. That's not an easy thing to forgive and let go."

"I suppose not," he says. "You don't think she was part of it?"

"Definitely not. Dustin was a drug to her, and no addict willingly gets rid of their fix. Not until they're ready," I tell him. "And she was not ready. No, I think her mom dragged her into it after the fact by telling her to get rid of the gun."

"Why would she do that to her own daughter?"

"Could be that she wanted Daisy to have some skin in the game. Could be that she just wanted to show Daisy what she was willing to risk and sacrifice for her. Who knows?" I muse. "I think in some dark, twisted way, Shirley was trying to show Daisy how much she loved her."

"Funny way to show your kid that you love them."

"I won't pretend to understand a mother's love. But I know that when you love somebody, you sometimes find yourself doing things you never expected you would."

Sonny's gaze lingers on mine, and the air around us is suddenly crackling with tension and the weight of so many unspoken words. I turn away, popping that bubble, and a small smile crinkles the soft lines around his eyes.

"Well, all that matters is that you got the right result. You got the right person and some bit of justice for Dustin. I'm grateful, and I owe you one."

"Boy, you owe me more than one."

"Probably so," he replies.

We share a laugh. The ease I feel around Sonny is unusual. Romantic entanglements have never been the most comfortable aspects of my life. I'm self-aware enough to recognize the problem is mostly me. I'm neurotic, don't trust easily, and I'm about as open with people as an Egyptian Pharoah's tomb. That's a me problem. I am very aware of that. It's something that's ruined more than one burgeoning relationship in my life.

It's something I've been working on with Dr. Azar, and perhaps that's why things seem to be coming a bit easier with Sonny. Or maybe it's just something about him. I don't know. But either way, things between us are good. We get along, and I feel more comfortable with Sonny than I've felt with anybody in a very, very long time. Honestly, it's a little disconcerting. But Dr. Azar says that if I want to progress as a person and build healthy relationships, I have to get used to being comfortable with being uncomfortable.

It's good advice, I know. It's just not easy to implement. Having been closed up tight all my life, it's not easy to switch gears and throw open the gates. It's not a switch inside of me I can flip. To his credit, however, Sonny knows my baggage, knows I'm not easy to deal with, and has been patient. He's never pushed me to give him more than I'm able to and never judges me for being a walking, talking bundle of neuroses. He just goes with the flow and takes what I'm willing to give.

Sonny is a good man. He's got a good heart, and honestly, his patience with me is one of the things I appreciate most about him. It's probably one of the biggest reasons I'm willing to try to be comfortable with being uncomfortable.

"Have you caught any blowback on the Diego shooting?" I ask.

"Nah. I have to sit down with the review board, but that's SOP," he says. "Everything that went down in the suite is on video. He went for his gun, so I'm covered."

"Good."

"They'll probably want a statement from you and everybody else in the room," he says. "They've got to cover their backsides."

"Of course. I wouldn't expect any less," I respond. "Are you okay with it? I know taking somebody's life takes a toll."

"I'm all right with it. For what they did to my team—to Sara—I'm honestly not going to lose a wink of sleep over it."

I study him closely as he speaks. Given what he's been through and the people he's lost, it's not surprising he'd feel this way. I've been where he is and have felt what he's feeling. And I know that in his line of work, as the head of an elite DEA unit, he has to carry himself with a certain swagger and bravado. But taking a person's life is no small thing, and there will come a time when it will hit him full force. I just hope he has the strength to reach out when that moment comes… because it's inevitable that it will.

"Just know I'm here to talk when and if you need to," I tell him.

"I appreciate that, darlin'."

Before I can say anything more, my Nadia phone rings. He jumps to his feet, closes the door to the war room, and leans back against it to keep anybody from bursting in. I take a moment to get into character, then connect the call and press the phone to my ear.

"Yes," I say in my Nadia voice.

"Looks like you did it. You cleared the board," Rico says.

"I told you that I would. And so, I did."

"I'm real glad to hear that."

"I am sure you are," I respond. "Now I suppose you will not have to be looking over your shoulder every day."

His chuckle is low. "No. I suppose I won't. So how about we meet face-to-face and talk about the path forward?"

"The same place we met before. Same rules apply," I tell him.

"Still has to be in public, huh?"

"I do not know you well enough yet to trust you," I tell him.

"Fair enough," he says, sounding amused. "All right, good enough. We'll meet—"

"I must wrap up a few things here, so meet me in three hours."

"Three hours. I'll see you then."

I disconnect the call and set the phone down. "Call the makeup team. They need to make me look pretty."

"Aw, darlin', you don't need a makeup team for that."

"Smooth," I say with a laugh. "Very smooth."

He tips me a wink, then heads out to get the team in.

We meet outside the same coffee house we met at last time. I've got snipers positioned on the roof and undercovers from the Bureau field office mixed in with the crowd. Rico is sitting across the table from me, and the mammoth man he'd brought last time stands behind him. Man Mountain blows a kiss to Astra, who's standing behind me, and even with her dark shades on, I can feel her glaring at the man like she wants him to start something.

"So, how'd you do it?" Rico asks. "How'd you put the DEA onto the Arias boys?"

We'd put the story out in the media that it was a DEA op that took the Ariases down. We put Sonny out in front of it to give them a recognizable face—a known enemy who'd been gunning for them for a long time—to sell it.

I chuff. "Do you believe I got to where I am without knowing a few people who can be useful to me when I need something done?"

He smirks. "Got some DEA bigwigs on the payroll, huh?"

"The structure of my organization is not your business," I say coldly.

"All right, all right. Don't get your panties in a twist, sweetie. I was—"

I lean forward. "You are going to need to learn to have some respect. You are not the only person I could be doing a deal with. Do not forget that you need me more than I need you and your club, Mr. Nagy. I have options. You do not. You should also not forget the force I can bring to bear against you should you… step out of line."

The smirk on his face falls away. He's an alpha—a man used to being the one who gives the orders. Taking them from somebody else, a woman no less, has got to be burning his butt. I loathe guys like him, so I take a special bit of glee in putting him in his place. He sits back in his chair and glowers darkly at me.

"The last time we spoke, you said you had the infrastructure to expand across the entire southwest, yes?" I ask.

He nods curtly. "Yeah. We've got chapters all over the southwest. We're making inroads into the Midwest and the south. We'll have a network across the entire country before long… as long as you can supply the product, we can sell it."

"This is good."

"Let's talk money," he says. "The way I see it, my boys are taking all the risk that comes with distro, so seventy-thirty with the seventy coming back our way sounds about right."

I laugh softly. "Do you think I am a fool, Mr. Nagy? Is this what you believe?"

He purses his lips but says nothing. He didn't really expect me to agree to those terms but figured he'd throw it out there just to see if I'm naïve enough to buckle. Rico is testing me to see how stiff my backbone really is.

"It is my product. I take all the risk associated with bringing it into the country. And as I told you before, I have options other than you—"

"Then why are you sitting here talking to me?"

"Perhaps I enjoy your company."

He scoffs. "There's risk on both sides. What do you propose as a fair split?"

"It will be seventy-thirty. However, the seventy percent will be mine," I say. "You will take the thirty and make far more money than you were making working for your former employers. Especially if we expand as you believe we can."

A frown flickers across his face as he glares at me, clearly unhappy with the proposed terms. He sits forward and looks ready to argue, so I hold up a hand to cut him off before he begins.

"Let me be clear, Mr. Nagy, this is not a negotiation. These are the terms. You can choose to accept them or not. I would remind you, however, that thirty percent of a fortune is far better than zero percent of nothing," I tell him.

I already know he's going to take the deal. This little dance we're doing is simply his way of feeling me out to see who he'll be dealing with, while also hoping to cut a bigger slice of the pie for himself. I don't blame him for trying, but I can't let myself be seen as soft or pliable since that might tip him off that something is up—that I am not who I claim to be. Drug queenpins aren't known for their generosity or yielding manner. As in most areas of life, women often need to be twice as ruthless to garner half the respect of their male counterparts.

"All right," Rico says. "But I want to reserve the right to renegotiate in a year. If we come through for you and expand your business, we'll deserve a raise."

"Fine. After one year we can talk about that," I tell him.

"All right. Deal," he says, satisfied with the terms. At least for now.

"Good," I say. "Then we will begin tomorrow. I will bring a smaller quantity—"

"Why not just lay it on us thick and heavy?"

"I want to see how you perform first."

"Still going to make me audition, huh?"

"As I said, I do not know you well enough yet to trust that you can do as you say. I want to ensure I am satisfied with your performance," I tell him. "We will start small and build up from there."

"Okay. Fine. Whatever you say. You're the boss."

"Yes," I say coldly. "I am."

He bristles, definitely not a man who enjoys being reminded of his place in the pecking order or that he's not at the top of the ladder.

"Text me an address where I can bring your first shipment," I say.

"Done. I'll text you."

"Good," I respond. "I am giving you an opportunity of the likes you could have never dreamed of, Mr. Nagy... please do not disappoint me."

"I'll do my best," he says, a cocky, lopsided grin on his face.

I get to my feet and glare down at him. "Do better than that."

CHAPTER THIRTY-FIVE

Road Prophets Clubhouse, South Mountain District; Phoenix, AZ

ASTRA PULLS THE YUKON THROUGH THE OPEN GATES and into the Prophets' compound. She gets out and opens the door for me, and I climb out, the dirt and gravel crunching beneath my boots. Piles of debris, mostly scrap metal, sit off to our left, and although the buildings in the compound themselves look old and worn, all have a fresh coat of paint. An American flag, a black flag for POWs, and a third flag bearing the Prophets' sigil fly out front.

The club's insignia etched in steel hangs beside the front door of the clubhouse, which I think was a ranch-style home once upon a time. It's hard to tell what the base structure was since there have been a lot of additions built onto it. Some of those additions seem so shaky I'm afraid a hard wind will huff and puff and blow their entire house down. It looks like a house straight out of Dr. Frankenstein's laboratory.

"Nice place," Astra mutters.

"There's your buddy," I say quietly.

Astra turns as Man Mountain, Rico's bodyguard at our meeting, steps out of the garage and into the sunlight. She bristles, and the muscles in her jaw flex as she grits her teeth. I laugh softly.

"What is it with you and that guy?" I ask.

"I didn't like the way he looked at me. The man was practically undressing me with his eyes," she hisses.

"Honey, I hate to break this to you, but most guys undress you with their eyes."

"This was creepier. It was gross."

"I just think you want to fight somebody and need a challenge."

"Maybe that too."

My lips flicker as I fight to keep the grin off my face. This is supposed to be a serious business, and we are supposed to be serious people.

"Let's get this done," I say.

Sunlight gleams off the chrome of the dozen motorcycles parked nearby, and a pair of large, rough-looking men clad in jeans and leather—every available inch of their skin covered in ink—standing by the open garage to our right stare at us. I glare back at them coldly, and they quickly turn away. I wait as Astra goes to the back of the SUV and pulls out the black duffel bags, then together, we cross the dirt patch that serves as their parking lot. We walk up the three steps onto the covered porch then through the open front door.

"Welcome, welcome," Rico says.

To our left is a bar, the wood battered, scarred, and covered in so many layers of shellac, it might just withstand a nuclear blast.

The Prophets' logo is etched into the mirror behind the bar, and all the racks that flank the glass hold bottom-shelf, rotgut liquor. I don't like to think of myself as a snob, but there's not a bottle I see that I'd drink. But hey, if your goal is to get hammered, I suppose any of that trash would do.

Aside from Rico, there are half a dozen men there. One is behind the bar, two seated at it, and three are sitting at a table in the corner smoking and playing cards. Rico is leaning casually against the bar, a bottle of beer in one hand, a cigarette pinched between the fingers of the other. He takes a drag and blows it toward the ceiling.

"Can I offer you ladies a drink?" he asks.

"No. Thank you," I reply.

"Suit yourself."

We cross to the bar, and Astra sets the duffel bags on top of it, then takes a step back. Rico opens the bags and whistles when he sees the load of bricks, courtesy of the DEA's controlled buy group, inside. He turns and flashes me that cocksure grin that irritates me. It's all I can do to keep from smacking it off his face. To ensure I don't actually do it, I clasp my hands together at my waist.

"I thought you said we were starting small," he says.

"This is small," I respond. "If you do not think you can handle this weight, perhaps I must consider some of my other options—"

He holds a hand up to cut me off. "Slow down now, sweetheart. I didn't say we couldn't handle it. We can. Easily."

I take a step forward, my eyes narrowed to slits and my jaw clenched. "Call me sweetheart one more time, Mr. Nagy. See what happens."

His men all turn to me, bodies tensing, hands drifting toward their weapons. Astra opens her jacket and puts her hand on the butt of her Glock. The air in the room is heavy with tension and the threat of violence. It's like a fuse just looking for a spark. My insides churn, and my heart races as I wait for somebody to make a move.

This is my fault. I shouldn't have let Nagy get under my skin like that. But being called demeaning pet names is one of my triggers. It's a sign of disrespect and never fails to set me flying off the handle. But in an undercover op, I need to learn to leave all that crap at the door. That is definitely something I need to work on with Dr. Azar… *if* we get out of this. Another long, painful moment ticks by before Rico holds his hands up to his chest, palms facing me.

"I didn't mean anything by it. It's just a saying. No offense, Nadia," he says. "Everybody relax. Get your hands away from your guns. We're here to do business. Jesus."

When his guys sit back down and relax, I let the tension in my shoulders drain. Nagy frowns and looks around the room, as if to make sure his guys are following his orders, before he turns back to me, a glint of mischievousness in his eyes. It was as if he knew he'd scored a hit by getting under my skin and found a chink in my armor. And worst of all, he'd enjoyed it.

Jerk.

"All right, anyway," he starts again. "As I was saying, we can carry this kind of weight. I was just surprised by the size of the initial shipment. That's all."

"Good. Because this is, as you said, your audition."

"Don't worry; we'll nail it, *Boss*," he says.

He spits the word "boss" like an epithet. That's fine. He wants to show his men his disdain for authority and that even though he works for me—they all work for me now—he's still independent. It's part of his image. He needs to project strength and can't be seen being subordinate to anybody, least of all a woman. Not feeling the need to emasculate him, I don't call him on it and let him have his moment since it's all about to come to an end anyway.

"There is one more thing," I say.

"What is that?"

"I understand you are the ones who took out those DEA agents," I say.

I can feel Astra and everybody else on the other end of the wire I'm wearing bristle. This isn't part of our plan. We were supposed to get in, drop off the dope, and get out again before the tac teams outside storm in and take the place. But with his casual sexism, Rico pissed me off, so I'm calling an audible.

I want to nail him and his men not just for the drugs and the guns I'm sure are somewhere in this patchwork Frankenstein of a clubhouse, but also for the murders of the agents too, since I'm sure they're the ones who dropped Sonny's men on the orders of the Arias brothers. I think it'll put a nice, big bow on this whole thing and help ease Sonny's conscience a bit. Rather than let his people go unavenged, I want justice for them.

"Where'd you hear that?" he asks.

"As I've told you before, you do not get and stay in my position without access to information and friends in places who are willing to share it," I say.

The smirk on his face tells me all I need to know. But that's not enough. I need him to admit to it on tape. It's the only way we're going to get justice for Sonny's people.

"I should not need to tell you this, but discretion is paramount in my business. I do not wish to have the scrutiny that murdering federal agents brings," I tell him.

He remains silent, but the arrogant smirk remains. He doesn't seem inclined to give me what I need, so I need to push him a little harder.

"Mr. Nagy, I need your assurance that you will not bring attention to my organization because you enjoy killing law enforcement officers. If you cannot assure me that you will not do this, then we will not be able to do business after all," I press.

He sighs and runs a hand through his hair. "Look, Nadia, Santiago asked me to deal with a problem for him. We handled it."

"Murdering federal officers is part of what got your former employers caught. It focused their attention. I need your assurance—"

"Look, those cops were getting too close. Santiago said we had no choice but to do them," he snaps. "Killing cops isn't usually our thing. We don't want the heat either. But if it means protecting what's ours, I'd do it again. And I'll do it for you too."

Bingo. It's a struggle to keep the smile of satisfaction off my face, but I somehow manage and keep my face stony and unreadable.

"I do not wish you to do this. Ever. I do not want the attention it brings; therefore I will never ask you to do such a thing," I tell him.

"Cool. Whatever," he replies. "I'm just a soldier who follows orders. That's all. If you say hands off, then it's hands off."

"Good. Then I believe we can do business," I reply. "Be in touch when you are ready for the next shipment of product."

"Count on it," he said. "Let the good times roll."

Astra and I turn and walk back to the SUV, climb in, and drive out, as per the plan. Once we get to the staging area, which is in the parking lot of an old motel about a mile down the road, the tac teams will move in and take them down.

"Nice audible," Astra says as she gives me her eyes in the rearview mirror. "You got them on the hook for killing those agents."

I smile to myself. "I wasn't going to let them get away with it."

"That'll make Sonny happy."

We pull into the parking lot where the teams are already armed and armored up. Astra parks, and we jump out as the trucks loaded up with their troops begin to roll out. Sonny is with his team and turns to me, his eyes bright, his smile wide, and tips me a wink before climbing onto the sideboard of his transport. As much as we wanted to be part of the takedown, Sonny didn't want us to burn our cover IDs given the likelihood we'll need to use them again … especially if our mystery friend does turn out to be worse than Santiago and Diego.

Astra turns the radio on so we can at least listen to the comms as we start stripping out of our characters. I peel off my facial appliances and pull the wig off my head, throwing them all into a bag. Astra hands me a wet wipe to wash off the makeup as we listen to contact being made out at the clubhouse. It sounds like there is a brief firefight, but the resistance melted fairly quickly. Astra and I exchange high fives.

"Nine in custody, two DOA," a voice comes over the radio.

A shot of adrenaline immediately hits my veins, and I turn to Astra. The wide-eyed expression on her face tells me she heard exactly the same thing I did.

"Eleven," I say. "There were twelve bikes out there."

"Who and where is the twelfth?"

As if in answer to her question, the rumble of an engine fills our ears a moment before a bike shoots past the motel parking lot.

"That was Rico," I say. "Get Sonny on the radio and get him here. Then track the SUV and get to me as soon as you can."

"Blake, you can't—"

I snatch the keys from her and jump into the Yukon, fire up the engine, then peel out of the parking lot with my tires squealing. Rico has a decent lead on me, but I can see him up ahead, so I hit the gas and race after him. He must have spotted the SUV because he makes a quick left and onto a street that has more traffic on it.

Because this is an undercover, I don't have flashers, so I can't warn other drivers to get out of my way. But there is no way in hell I'm going to let him out of my sight, so I increase my speed and keep weaving through the cars to keep pace with him. At least the traffic has the advantage of slowing him down as much as it's hindering me.

Up ahead, I see traffic has come to a grinding halt. He must see it, too, because he takes a quick left—cutting across traffic in a hail of horns and middle fingers from the drivers—into a parking structure. I jerk my wheel and cut in front of the cars who are still stopped because of Rico, earning more horns, curses, and middle fingers from the same drivers.

Rico is ascending the ramp to the second floor but seems to realize there's no way out because his taillight flares and he screeches to a stop. I hit the brakes and throw the Yukon into park, then leap out, pulling my gun. Before I can do anything more, though, Rico jumps off his bike, pulls his own weapon, and opens fire. The rounds from his .45 punch into the windshield and rattle the door I'm sheltering behind.

When he stops firing, I stand up. "FBI!" I call. "Stop!"

He turns to me, and I duck behind the door again as he fires the last few bullets in his clip, the shots booming as loud as cannon fire as it echoes through the parking structure. He dry fires, his magazine spent, so I stand again and squeeze off several shots. Sparks fly from my bullets hitting the concrete near the back of his bike, and the side window of the car he's standing beside explodes as a round tears through it.

Cursing, he turns and runs up the ramp and rounds the corner, disappearing from sight. Gritting my teeth with the barrel of my weapon leading the way, I take off after him. I can hear the hard slaps of his boots on the concrete ramp as I round the corner. A gasp bursts from my mouth, and I throw myself to the ground when I see Rico standing up ahead, his gun raised. The shots ring like thunder in my ears and hit the car beside me with hard thuds that make it shudder.

Getting to my knee, I peek over the trunk of the now bullet-riddled car and squeeze off a few more shots. None of my rounds find their mark as Rico dives behind the truck beside him.

"You've got nowhere to go, Rico!" I call. "It's over. Throw out your weapon and come out of there with your hands up!"

"You want my gun? You can come take it from me."

I hear the sound of sirens in the distance and can only hope it's my people and not city cops coming to see to the accident that snarled traffic down on the street.

"You hear those sirens? That's all for you," I call, hoping I'm right. "This building is about to be surrounded, Rico. Give it up."

"Screw you."

"There are only two ways out of here. You can either go in bracelets or in a body bag," I respond. "It's your choice."

The soft scuff of a boot on the concrete is close and sends a flood of ice through my veins. Leaning out from behind the trunk of the car, I see Rico moving toward me, weapon raised, malice in his eyes. Before he can react, I squeeze off a shot that sends a jet of blood onto the ground as it rips through his thigh. Rico lets out a hard grunt as he grimaces, and I have to pull back again as he empties his clip into the car I'm hiding behind.

When I hear him dry fire, I jump to my feet and rush forward, not wanting to give him the chance to reload. Blood is pouring down his leg, and his face is contorted with pain, but he's ready for me. And as I close in, Rico feints to the right. Like a damn rookie, I bite on the feint, then overcorrect and throw myself off balance. Before I can recover, his fist crashes into the side of my face hard enough that I see stars and my gun goes flying, hitting the ground with a clatter. I stagger to the side and almost go down, but somehow manage to keep my feet and turn to find, despite a halting limp, that he's already advancing on me.

The coppery taste of blood fills my mouth, and my ears are ringing. My gun is out of reach. Rico's lips are pulled back over his teeth, and his eyes are alight with rage as he pulls a long knife from the sheath on his belt. Scrabbling backward as fast as I can, I'm able to get far enough away that I can get back to my feet, but it puts me farther away from my gun. But like the Terminator, Rico keeps coming.

He closes in and draws his arm back, then uncorks a wild slash with his knife. The blade whistles by my midsection with scant inches to spare. The moment it passes me without connecting, I wade in and throw a left-right combination that snaps his head backward. I grab the wrist holding the blade and bend it backward. Rico cries out but manages to throw a punch with his off-hand that catches me across the chin with serious force.

The blow drops me to my hands and knees, but knowing if I don't move, I'm dead, I throw myself to the side. Rico's blade slices through the air I'd just occupied and throws up a few sparks as it strikes the pavement. He raises his head just as I piston my leg, the heel of my boot catching him square in the nose. Rico stumbles backward and falls on his backside with a loud grunt. Blood flows from his nose and mouth, spilling onto his shirt.

He's moving slowly and stiffly but is trying to get back to his feet. I rise first and deliver a fist to the side of his head with all the strength I can muster. The blow rocks him, and he topples to the side with a groan. A moment later, though, a searing pain tears through my leg, and I cry out. The handle of Rico's blade is sticking out of my thigh and sending waves of pain that feel like liquid fire flowing through my veins.

Gritting my teeth, I rear back, and with every ounce of strength I can muster, use my right leg to kick Rico in the face. His head snaps back, and a thick font of blood fills the air as he goes down, flat on his back. Holding onto the handle of the blade, trying to keep it from moving, I lower myself to the ground and find a position that's something less than agonizing, then crawl over to Rico's prone body and try to stave off the tsunami of pain washing over me as I roll him over.

The wail of sirens and the squeal of tires fills the air as my team races toward me. As Rico groans, a small crimson pool spills from his mouth. As DEA cars round the corner, I lean close to Rico's ear, and unable to resist, I slip into my Nadia voice.

"You are under arrest, you piece of garbage," I say.

His eye flutters, then opens wide. "You bit—"

I cut him off with a hard thump to the back of the head. "Watch your mouth."

As Astra jumps out of the SUV and races toward me, I flop onto my back and stare up at the ceiling of the parking structure. A laugh bursts from my mouth, a thread of happiness twining around the cord of pain that's gripping me tight.

"We did it," I say. "We did it."

CHAPTER
THIRTY-SIX

ATF Operational Center, Southwest Division; Phoenix, AZ

"WHAT ARE YOU DOING HERE?" ASTRA ASKS WITH a frown as I limp into the war room. "You're still supposed to be in the hospital."

"I shouldn't have been in the hospital in the first place."

"You were injured."

"I got stabbed. In the leg, not somewhere critical," I respond. "It's not like I had a heart attack or some other condition that required overnight observation."

"It's better to be safe than sorry."

"Thanks, Mom."

She sighs and shakes her head. "You're impossible."

"It's part of my charm."

"Is that what we're calling it?" she asks with a laugh.

"It's what I'm calling it."

"Why didn't you call for me to come pick you up?"

"If I had, I'm sure you would have talked them into keeping me another couple of days," I tell her. "I was ready to go, so I thought it safer to call a cab."

Still grinning, she shakes her head as she packs some things into a box. Other than Astra, the ops center is empty and eerily quiet.

"Where is everybody?" I ask.

"Sonny gave his team the day off to celebrate the big win," she says. "I told our people to go get a little R&R since I thought you'd be in the hospital a bit longer."

"They deserve a little downtime."

"They do."

"Why aren't you out there soaking up some sun and a few drinks poolside at the hotel?"

"I just wanted to get things here packed up and ready to go."

"Anxious to get home?"

"I am," she says. "I'm looking forward to an evening with my fiancé."

I laugh softly. "You know, I remember a time when you were the first one out the door to go party after a big win. Now look at you. You're all domesticated."

"I wouldn't say I'm domesticated," she replies. "My priorities have just changed over time. I'm not that girl I was back at the Academy."

"You most definitely are not."

She puts the lid on a box and turns to me. "Neither are you, you know."

"No?"

"Nah. Especially not these last few months you've been working with Dr. Azar," she says. "I see you being more open.

Especially with Sonny. There was a time when you wouldn't have given him the time of day. Now look at you."

"Yeah, look at me."

"You seem a lot closer to happiness than I've ever seen you before, Blake," she says. "That's a good thing. A really good thing."

"Honestly, it's the most uncomfortable I've ever been in my life."

She smirks. "For now. If you sit in that for a while and get used to the feeling, it won't be as uncomfortable in time."

"So say you and Dr. Azar."

"Because we are both incredibly wise women."

"That you are."

"He's good for you," she says.

"I think Dr. Azar is actually better for me."

"Probably," she says with a snicker. "But he's pretty good for you too."

I nod slowly. "Yeah. I think so too."

The sound of a knock on the door draws our attention. Sonny is standing in the doorway with a crooked smile on his face.

"Am I interrupting?" he asks.

"Nope. Not at all," Astra says brightly. "I was just leaving, actually. I've got a mojito by the pool waiting for me."

She squeezes my hand, then flounces out of the room, leaving me alone with Sonny. And almost immediately, the air in the room feels like it's been sucked out and refilled with an agonizing sense of anticipation. He walks over and perches on the edge of the table.

"I went by the hospital. They said you checked yourself out."

"I did. I stayed overnight, like you all wanted, but woke up this morning and didn't feel the need to be there anymore."

"I should have known you would," he says. "You're a stubborn one."

"You like that about me."

"I do. Very much, actually."

He takes my hands, his gaze lingering on mine, making that sense of anticipation grow even thicker than it already is. I think we both know this might be the last we see of each other for a bit. I'm heading back to Seattle, and from there—who knows?—

while Sonny remains based here. Not often being in the same time zone is one of the drawbacks to this thing between us. Or maybe that's why it works… familiarity breeding contempt, absence making the heart grow fonder, and all that.

"How are you feeling?" he asks.

"Been better, been worse," I respond. "It's a little sore, but nothing I can't deal with."

"That knife was buried pretty deep."

"But it's not anymore," I respond. "And they've got me on the good drugs."

"At least there's a benefit to all this."

I laugh. "Indeed."

Another long moment passes as we stare into each other's eyes. My heart picks up the pace, and my stomach churns, though not unpleasantly. I'm not used to feeling things like this, but Sonny just has a way of putting butterflies in my belly without even seeming to try. It's hardly how I expected to feel when he first swaggered into the Chapel to ask for our help. But it's how I feel now. It's uncomfortable but not unpleasant, which I know isn't the most romantic thing to say to a person, but it's where I'm at. And he seems to be okay with it… with waiting for me to turn that corner and learn to be an actual emotionally-functional human being. It's work I probably should have done a long time ago, but until now, I didn't think I needed a reason to.

"Thank you, Blake. You and your team are amazing," he says. "Y'all did a lot of good for a lot of people down here."

"You're welcome. I'm just glad we could help."

"What's next for you?"

"Well, we go home and see what Opal has waiting for us."

"I think you should take some time off and let that leg heal up before you get back to kicking in doors."

"I promise I won't kick in any doors until this is fully healed. How's that?"

"Not great."

"Best I can do."

He raises my hands and gently kisses my knuckles. "I guess I'll have to take it then."

"What's next for you?" I ask.

"Not sure just yet. But I'm sure something will pop off sooner rather than later."

"Always does."

"It's job security, I suppose."

I smile softly. "That it is," I say. "Any chance you'll be up my way any time soon?"

"I hope so. I need to review the active case load and see what we have in the Pacific Northwest. But I've also got some time off on the books I need to take, so maybe I'll take a few days and come up."

"I'd like that."

"Yeah, me too," he replies. "But, since I've got you free for a whole night tonight, how about I take you out for a nice and well-earned dinner?"

"That sounds really good to me."

"Dancing afterward?"

I laugh and slap him on the arm playfully. "Don't make me hurt you."

"You'd have to catch me first, gimpy."

"You're such a jerk."

He laughs. "Sometimes. Good thing you like it."

"Yeah. I guess I do."

He puts his arm around my shoulders, and we head for the door. Sonny plants a gentle kiss on the top of my head, and I lean into him. Astra was right. I do feel something close to happiness. It's a really odd, uncomfortable feeling, but for the first time in my life, I feel ready to just sit in it until it stops feeling that way. And I hope when it does, I can stop the feeling of dread that's gathering in my heart like thunderheads.

I hope I can learn to stop waiting for the other shoe to drop.

CHAPTER THIRTY-SEVEN

The Chapel, Industrial District; Seattle, WA

"WELCOME BACK, EVERYBODY. I HOPE YOU'RE ALL rested up and ready to get back to work," Opal says.

After returning to Seattle, I gave the team a day off to recoup. Honestly, my leg still feels like it's on fire, and I needed a day off. I guess Astra was right about needing to slow it down for a minute. Not that I'll ever tell her that. If I conceded the point to her, I'd never hear the end of it.

"Chief, how is the leg?" Opal asks.

"Good enough to get back to work," I reply. "Thanks for asking."

"She should really be off it for at least a week," Astra says.

I turn to her. "And where did you get your medical degree from?"

"The University of You're a Stubborn Ass," she says with a grin as she shoots me the finger.

The only person who doesn't laugh is Opal, of course. She's still trying to adjust to the dynamics of our team. She may not be as loose and freewheeling as the rest of us just yet, but we'll get her there. It'll just take some time. What's impressed me the most about her is that she's working hard to learn the team—our strengths and weaknesses, as well as studying the types of cases we're best at to better deploy our resources to do the most good.

It's what I was hoping she would become when I hired her. I wanted to have somebody whose judgment I could trust to take the administrative burden off my shoulders and let me focus on the investigative side of things. If she doesn't share our sense of humor or camaraderie, so be it. At least I've got a competent case officer running the Chapel while we're in the field chasing down the bad guys. I'm good with that.

"What do you have for us, Opal?" I ask.

"Quite a bit," she starts. "First, we have a case in Michigan I think is perfect for Mo's skill set. It's a white-collar financial case that came to us from the Michigan State Police who say they don't have the expertise to handle something like this."

Mo's face lights up like she was just given the greatest gift in the world. Opal passes her the case file, and she immediately digs into it.

"It's not likely to be a case that will involve any significant amount of danger, so I thought Mo and Rick could head out there to assist the Staties with their investigation," Opal said.

"Mo?" I ask. "Any objection?"

"Definitely not. We'll be on the first plane out."

Rick raises his hand. "Do you not think I can handle myself in a dangerous situation, Opal? Is that why you're sending me out there?"

"Precisely," she says simply.

There's a moment's pause around the table, and we all exchange glances before exploding in laughter. Even Rick gets a chuckle out of it. A sly smile touches the corners of Opal's mouth. Maybe she's catching on to the vibe of the team after all.

"Opal," Astra says. "You savage."

She says nothing and tries to maintain her prim, proper disposition, but I can see the crinkles at the corners of her eyes as she suppresses her smile. The laughter around the table slowly fades, and we all turn back to her. Before she can continue, though, my cell phone chirps. I pull it out of my pocket and frown when I see that it's Sonny calling. We're not supposed to talk until tonight.

"Give me a second," I say and get to my feet.

I dash to my office as quickly as my limp allows me to and close the door. I lean against my desk, grimacing as a white-hot flare of pain shoots through me, then connect the call and press the phone to my ear.

"Hey," I say. "Everything okay?"

"Looks like we were right," Sonny says. "You were right."

"I usually am. Can you be more specific?" I reply lightly.

He doesn't laugh, and his voice is tight, telling me he's dealing with something heavy on his end. I straighten up and feel my pulse race. I've got a feeling this is related to the Arias case, and I've got a stronger feeling I already know what he's going to say. But I close my eyes, swallow the lump in my throat, and pray I'm wrong.

"What is it, Sonny?"

"The Arias brothers have a sister we never knew about. They say her name is Inez, but I can't tell if that's true or not. We know nothing about this woman. We'd never heard of her until today," he says. "If the chatter we're hearing is correct, she's the one who put all the events that got Santiago arrested and Diego killed in motion. They say she was pulling the strings behind the scenes and may be your mysterious friend."

"Okay, but we accepted that might be the case—not that there's an unknown sister popping up, but that somebody might have been pulling the levers to rise to power," I say. "What has you so rattled?"

He's silent for a long moment, but I can practically feel his tension over the line. When he doesn't say anything for a minute, I find myself growing concerned for him but also curious. He's not a man who rattles easily.

"What is it? What's shaken you so bad?" I ask.

"We found thirty-seven bodies this morning. All of them beheaded. The heads were left in the mass grave with the corpses," he tells me. "But the bodies... they'd obviously been tortured, and they were torn up. It's like whoever did this enjoyed doing it to them. I've never seen anything like it before, which is saying something given how long I've been working cartel cases."

I whistle low and run a hand over my face. This is exactly what I was afraid would happen. I had a sick feeling somebody worse was going to take control. But what else could we have done? We had a chance to take out the Arias brothers, two men on the Bureau's most wanted list. We couldn't pass up that opportunity. Right?

"The bodies were all people known to us. Higher ups in the Arias cartel," Sonny says.

"So, this sister is cleaning house to install her own loyalists. Makes sense. That's the way these things are done."

"Yeah, I know. I just... I have a feeling this is going to get bad down here, Blake. Real bad. She's just getting started... and she's already dropped a lot of bodies."

A wan smile touches my lips. "Guess you're not going to be able to take that time off, huh?"

"Not for a while, I'm afraid," he says. "I'm sorry."

"Don't be. It's the job. I understand it better than most."

"Yeah, it still sucks though."

"It does. But we'll figure it out," I tell him. "Together."

"I like the sound of that, darlin'."

"Me too."

"Oh hey, before I forget," he says, "I have one more thing. I don't know if you can do anything with it, but I was hoping you could maybe work some sort of magic and get me an ID."

"An ID on who?"

"An informant sent me a picture of Inez's top lieutenant. Her enforcer," he says. "They say this person is Inez's attack dog and the one most likely to have put those bodies in the ground we found this morning. I found nothing in our databases, so I was hoping you could—"

"Say no more. I got you," I tell him. "Send me the picture, and I'll see if we can't figure out who this attack dog is."

"You're the best."

"I know."

Sonny laughs. "Talk to you tonight?"

"Looking forward to it."

I disconnect the call, and a moment later, my phone chirps with the incoming email. I walk around my desk and drop into my chair. After waking my computer up, I open my email program and quickly scroll by the nearly two hundred emails waiting to be read and open Sonny's. The picture comes up on my screen, and as it does, my heart falls into my stomach.

"No," I say softly. "No way."

My hands are shaking, and my throat is as dry as the desert as I stare at the photo of Inez's attack dog. The one they say put thirty-seven headless, mutilated, and tortured corpses into the ground. Waves of nausea batter me, and I taste bile, hot and acidic, in the back of my throat.

"It can't be."

No matter how hard I try to deny it to myself, the picture doesn't change, and the truth cannot be denied. I stare at the all-too-familiar strawberry blonde hair, the green eyes that sparkle when she smiles, and the lithe, lean dancer's body... and one of the deadliest and most dangerous women on the planet. A woman I know very, very well.

"What in the hell are you doing, Kit?" I whisper.

AUTHOR'S NOTE

Thank you so much for joining me on Blake Wilder's latest adventure in DOUBLE CROSS! From the sun-scorched Arizona desert to the shadowy dealings of cartels and outlaw MCs, Blake and her team faced a storm of danger, betrayal, and chaos. This series never lets up when it comes to action and surprises, and I hope this book was no exception!

And I'm sure that cliffhanger has you wondering what's next for Blake and her team. The good news? You won't have to wait long to find out. In THE SILENT HUNT, Blake is called to San Diego to investigate a chilling case involving multiple female victims murdered in their own homes—each attack more brutal than the last. As she digs deeper, unsettling questions arise. Could there be two killers working in tandem? While tracing the victims' lives, a farmer's market connection leads her down an unexpected path. And just as she begins to unravel the case, new intel about the Arias Cartel pulls her back into their dangerous web. With hidden truths, murderous secrets, and twists lurking at every turn, this next chapter promises to take Blake on her most perilous journey yet.

Your support is invaluable to indie writers like myself, helping to spread the word and keep these adventures alive. If you enjoyed DOUBLE CROSS, I'd be so grateful if you could take a moment to leave a review or recommend it to a fellow reader who loves action-packed mysteries. Every review, recommendation, and kind word helps Blake's journey reach new readers, and I can't thank you enough for being part of this adventure.

If you enjoyed the suspense and twists in this story, you might also love my Sweetwater Falls series. While Blake faces chaos on the front lines, Sheriff Spenser Song tackles crime in a quieter, but no less dangerous, corner of the world. In SINS OF THE FALLS, Spenser is drawn into a puzzling case after the murder of a renowned author she recently protected. What starts as a tragic homicide in the idyllic woods of Sweetwater Falls soon unravels into a web of passion, deceit, and deadly secrets. Like Blake, Spenser has a knack for uncovering hidden truths—but in Sweetwater Falls, the sins of the past can haunt you in ways you'd never expect. If you're looking for another thrilling mystery to dive into, I hope you'll check it out!

Thank you again for joining me on this exciting journey. Whether you're rooting for Blake, Spenser, or both, I can't wait for you to dive into their next adventures!

By the way, if you find any typos or want to reach out to me, feel free to email me at egray@ellegraybooks.com

Your writer friend,
Elle Gray

CONNECT WITH ELLE GRAY

Loved the book? Don't miss out on future reads! Join my newsletter and receive updates on my latest releases, insider content, and exclusive promos. Plus, as a thank you for joining, you'll get a FREE copy of my book Deadly Pursuit!

Deadly Pursuit follows the story of Paxton Arrington, a police officer in Seattle who uncovers corruption within his own precinct. With his career and reputation on the line, he enlists the help of his FBI friend Blake Wilder to bring down the corrupt Strike Team. But the stakes are high, and Paxton must decide whether he's willing to risk everything to do the right thing.

Claiming your freebie is easy! Visit
https://dl.bookfunnel.com/513mluk159
and sign up with your email!

Want more ways to stay connected? Follow me on Facebook and Instagram or sign up for text notifications by texting "blake" to 844-552-1368. Thanks for your support and happy reading!

ALSO BY
ELLE GRAY

Blake Wilder FBI Mystery Thrillers

Book One - The 7 She Saw
Book Two - A Perfect Wife
Book Three - Her Perfect Crime
Book Four - The Chosen Girls
Book Five - The Secret She Kept
Book Six - The Lost Girls
Book Seven - The Lost Sister
Book Eight - The Missing Woman
Book Nine - Night at the Asylum
Book Ten - A Time to Die
Book Eleven - The House on the Hill
Book Twelve - The Missing Girls
Book Thirteen - No More Lies
Book Fourteen - The Unlucky Girl
Book Fifteen - The Heist
Book Sixteen - The Hit List
Book Seventeen - The Missing Daughter
Book Eighteen - The Silent Threat
Book Nineteen - A Code to Kill
Book Twenty - Watching Her
Book Twenty-One - The Inmate's Secret
Book Twenty-Two - A Motive to Kill
Book Twenty-Three - The Kept Girls
Book Twenty-Four - Prison Break
Book Twenty - Five - The Perfect Crime
Book Twenty - Six - A Shot to Kill
Book Twenty - Seven - Double Cross

A Pax Arrington Mystery

Free Prequel - Deadly Pursuit
Book One - I See You
Book Two - Her Last Call
Book Three - Woman In The Water
Book Four- A Wife's Secret

Storyville FBI Mystery Thrillers

Book One - The Chosen Girl
Book Two - The Murder in the Mist
Book Three - Whispers of the Dead
Book Four - Secrets of the Unseen
Book Five - The Way Back Home

A Sweetwater Falls Mystery

Book One - New Girl in the Falls
Book Two - Missing in the Falls
Book Three - The Girls in the Falls
Book Four - Memories of the Falls
Book Five - Shadows of the Falls
Book Six - The Lies in the Falls
Book Seven - Forbidden in the Falls
Book Eight - Silenced in the Falls
Book Nine - Summer in the Falls
Book Ten - The Legend of the Falls
Book Eleven - Whispers in the Falls
Book Twelve- Sins of the Falls

A Chesapeake Valley Mystery Series

Book One - The Girl in Town
Book Two - The Lost Children
Book Three - The Secrets We Bury

ALSO BY
ELLE GRAY | K.S. GRAY

Olivia Knight FBI Mystery Thrillers

Book One - *New Girl in Town*

Book Two - *The Murders on Beacon Hill*

Book Three - *The Woman Behind the Door*

Book Four - *Love, Lies, and Suicide*

Book Five - *Murder on the Astoria*

Book Six - *The Locked Box*

Book Seven - *The Good Daughter*

Book Eight - *The Perfect Getaway*

Book Nine - *Behind Closed Doors*

Book Ten - *Fatal Games*

Book Eleven - *Into the Night*

Book Twelve - *The Housewife*

Book Thirteen - *Whispers at the Reunion*

Book Fourteen - *Fatal Lies*

Book Fifteen - *The Runaway Girls*

A Serenity Springs Mystery Series

Book One - *The Girl in the Springs*

Book Two - *The Maid of Honor*

Book Three - *The Girl in the Cabin*

Book Four- *Fatal Obsession*

ALSO BY
ELLE GRAY | JAMES HOLT

The Florida Girl FBI Mystery Thrillers

Book One - The Florida Girl
Book Two - Resort to Kill
Book Three - The Runaway
Book Four - The Ransom
Book Five - The Unknown Woman

Made in United States
Cleveland, OH
04 February 2025

14015787R20140